Chris Nickson, author of th  d
raised in Leeds, England. A w s
written many celebrity biogra
to numerous music magazine:

Praise For Chris Nickson

'Fascinating tale of murder and deception set against the political tensions
between Mosley's Blackshirts and working-class Communists in 1930s
Leeds. Perfectly captures the atmosphere of a city struggling to shake off
the effects of the Great Depression.'
– A.J. Wright, bestselling author of *Sitting Murder*

'Nickson paints precise pictures with words'
– Booklist USA

'The author has a real art for making you care about these people that
you've just met'
– classicmystery.wordpress.com

Also by Chris Nickson:

Richard Nottingham Mysteries
Laura Benton Mysteries
Medieval Mysteries
Tom Harper Mysteries
Dan Markham Mysteries
Solid Air: The Life of John Martyn

THE DEAD ON LEAVE

CHRIS NICKSON

ENDEAVOURQUILL

AN ENDEAVOUR QUILL PAPERBACK

First published in 2018 by Endeavour Quill
This paperback edition published in 2018
by Endeavour Quill

Endeavour Quill is an imprint of Endeavour Media Ltd.
Endeavour Quill, 85-87 Borough High Street,
London, SE1 1NH

ISBN 978-1-911445-61-6

Printed and bound in Great Britain by
Clays Ltd, Elcograf S.p.A.

www.endeavourmedia.co.uk

Contents

One

Leeds, September 25, 1936

He saw the cardboard signs in the shop windows as they strode past. All so familiar. *Bisto. Mazawattee Tea. Uncle Joe's Mint Balls.* The names rattled through his mind as the hobnails on his boots struck up tiny sparks from the pavement, a fast rhythm on the flagstones.

He'd set off from City Square, right at the heart of Leeds, just a few minutes before, wearing an old suit that was shiny at the elbows and seat, a cap on his head, shirt without a collar, and a glum expression on his face. He looked like hundreds of other men out searching for work. God knew there were still plenty of them in 1936. Things might be improving down south; up here the Depression still had its hands round the North's throat. Hard times for decent men.

But Urban Raven did have a job, a very steady one. He was a detective sergeant with Leeds City Police, fifteen years on the force, working his way up the ranks. Now he was surveying the route Oswald Mosley and his Blackshirts would take for their march and rally on Holbeck Moor this Sunday. Two more days until it happened. Already shopkeepers were starting to nail boards over their windows and people were ready for the worst. That would come. It would definitely come. The pressure was building all over the city. You could cut the atmosphere with a knife.

'It's going to be a bloody disaster.'

'Sarge?' The young man beside him jerked his head around. Detective Constable Daniel Noble, not long out of uniform and into plain clothes. Clever, when he put his mind to it. All too often, though, the lad was a dreamer. Never mind, Raven thought; he'd grow out of that sharpish. A year or two in CID would put a spine in him.

'Too many places to attack the fascists.' He gestured with an arm. 'Look at it. All they need to do is wait at the end of every street. It's going to be a massacre. They might as well hang signs round their necks saying, *Please attack me.*'

'I thought you didn't like them,' Noble said.

'Can't stand them,' Raven snapped. He'd no time for anyone who liked Hitler and thought they had all the answers. Not that the communists were any better. 'But we'll be the ones who'll have to clean up the mess. The coppers.'

They were close enough to the moor to hear the carpenters building a stage. The sound of hammers, shouting, laughter. Paid work. No one was going to turn that down. Didn't matter if you liked Mosley or loathed him.

'Do you really think it'll be that bad on Sunday, Sarge?'

He looked at the lad. Noble hadn't been on the force during the General Strike nine years before. There'd been plenty of violence back then, wading in with truncheons and boots to get the job done. And the lad had been far too young for the Great War. Just as well, maybe; he wouldn't wish that experience on anyone. Still, with Germany growing more powerful every month, the lad might have his chance of service in a few years.

'Bad?' He shook his head. 'For God's sake, they've been out painting swastikas on the Jewish businesses along North Street. Then the Watch Committee dithered about whether they'll allow the march. Meanwhile, we've got the communists chalking notices on every street corner about where to meet and what weapons to bring.' Raven was close to shouting; he stopped himself before heads started to turn. 'That's worse than bad. I tell you what, Danny boy; you'd better get ready for a pitched battle.'

'My missus says they won't be that stupid.'

His missus was in for a shock, then. By Sunday night they'd be mopping the blood off the cobbles. A pair of motor cars went by, a Morris and a Jowett, a lorry close behind them. All bloody speed these days, he thought. They crossed the road and stood at the bottom of Holbeck Moor. A broad, empty space of hard earth and scrubby grass. Nowhere to hide when things turned ugly. The force was going to need plenty of coppers along the route and many more here. A fair few in plain clothes among the crowd. And even then they didn't have a cat in hell's chance of stopping things.

'They'll all be spoiling for a fight,' Raven said with a sigh. 'Come on, we might as well go back. Before you know it we'll be seeing more of this than we want.'

It was a grey day, late September on the slow glide into autumn. But there were precious few trees in Holbeck to shed their leaves. Just street after street of back-to-back houses, bricks dulled black from generations of smoke in the air. Around here, life was dour shades of brown and grey, everything quilted in grime. Here and there, small groups of unemployed men, the future leached from their faces, stood and talked on the corners. Even they seemed muted, pushed down. But what could you expect after no job for years and none on the horizon? The only colour came from the posters; they filled every empty space. Advertising sales at the shops, shows at theatres, the latest and the best. Coming attractions at the City Varieties and the Empire. Everything and anything that was here today and old news tomorrow.

Back in town they crossed Duncan Street. Around them, people moved quickly on the pavement or waited in the tram shelters. The light bulbs in the Bovril sign across from the Corn Exchange constantly flickered on and off. Once it had been an attraction, a sophisticated novelty; these days hardly anyone noticed it. Since 1929 and the Crash, Leeds had become a grey, colourless city, all its heart vanished.

A motorcycle roared by, the rider's head hidden by goggles and a leather helmet. Sometimes Raven wished he could cover himself the same way; it might make life easier. He noticed how men and women glanced away quickly as he passed. Raven didn't pay them much mind anymore; after the better part of two decades, he was used to it. The people who looked didn't even see the worst of it.

Born with the century, he'd joined the Leeds Pals on his eighteenth birthday. Training, then a posting to the trenches of the Western Front at the start of October 1918. He'd scarcely been there for two weeks, not even fired a shot, when a Hun shell exploded in a fuel dump as he was walking by.

He was lucky to be alive; that was what they told him later. There were plenty of times he doubted that, when the pain felt like a punishment, a torture for something he'd done. Months of surgery and skin grafts. Days and weeks when he disappeared into the agony.

The burns covered half his body: his chest, his arm, neck, his left cheek. He knew the surgeons had performed a miracle. He *knew* it; everyone told him so it had to be true. But whenever he stared in the mirror, all he saw was the ugly, charmless reality of the surgery. It was impossible to feel grateful. To feel anything at all. He only saw the scars and the shiny new skin and wondered where the person he'd once been had gone.

Here and there he saw men like himself. For a moment they'd glance at each other with that sense of recognition. Not brotherhood, but understanding. Then they'd always turn their heads, full of shame and self-loathing.

Urban Raven had a face that people remembered. It was a face that scared people; maybe that wasn't such a bad thing when you were a policeman.

*

Raven sat in the CID office at headquarters with Inspector Mortimer and Superintendent Kennedy. The sergeant was pointing out the most dangerous spots on a large map, spread out on the desk, of the city centre and Holbeck.

'If you want my opinion, sir, the best thing would be to cancel the march,' he said. 'We won't be able to keep anyone safe and there's a good chance plenty of our own men will be injured.' They'd asked for his assessment of the route. Now they gave him sour looks as he offered his report.

'Doesn't matter,' Kennedy told him. 'The Watch Committee's said it can all go ahead. Be grateful they're not allowing the Blackshirts near the Leylands.' Letting fascists in uniform parade through the city's Jewish area? That would have been a bloody wonderful idea.

'We'd better prepare for the worst, then,' Raven said.

'We already have,' Inspector Mortimer replied. 'We've drafted in special constables to cover the beats. All the other men on the force will be looking after the march. Leave cancelled.'

'And the chief constable's authorised three marksmen,' the superintendent said. His voice was low and sober. 'But not a word of that goes beyond this office.'

'Yes, sir.' Men with guns? In Leeds? Christ. That terrified him more than anything.

'According to our intelligence, Mosley's bringing his I Squad with him,' Mortimer said. 'They're his hard men. Very loyal. They love a scrap. Most of those who'll be marching won't be from around here. They're estimating a thousand, all told.'

'A thousand? Is that it?' Raven asked in disbelief. 'They'll be eaten alive, sir. I was talking to someone I know from the Communist Party. They reckon there'll be twenty thousand or more out there waiting.'

'Then we're going to have our hands full,' Superintendent Kennedy said with a shrug. He was in his late forties, a major during the war, used to command, battle and sacrifice. He had an easy style, the kind of manner people obeyed without thinking. 'Go home, gentlemen. Be ready for Sunday.'

Two

'LOOK AFTER YOURSELF, Urban.'

'I plan on it.' It was just after six in the morning. Raven was dressed in his old clothes again, the suit with the trousers that were too short, shirt, cap, muffler, prepared for the worst. 'Don't you worry. I'll be back tonight without a scratch.' He smiled. 'It'll be fine,' he told her and tried to read the expression in her eyes.

She stood a pace away, clutching her dressing gown around her body. Lips tight, she nodded. Marjorie Cassy Adelina Raven. A mouthful of a name. But all the children in her family had them. Seven kids, and she was the afterthought, younger than all the others. At least fancy names cost nothing, something to bring a smile when you had no money, and her people had been poor. Not that his family ever had much. His father had been a clerk, a tiny step or two up the social ladder. Raven had left school at fourteen, certificate in hand, and gone to work for the same company as his father until he joined up. But he couldn't face the job again after his long recuperation. He needed something different. And so he'd applied to the police.

'I'll have my truncheon,' he continued. 'There'll be plenty of us there. They won't stand a chance against the coppers.'

Who was he trying to convince, he wondered? Her or himself?

*

He was one of fifty plain clothes officers in the crowd, there to try and break up any trouble before it could become serious. They didn't have a chance, not out here, and all of them knew it. It was like being on the terraces for a match at Elland Road. Thousands upon thousands, so close together that it was hard to move. Even more than the communists had predicted, he was certain of that. And there'd been hundreds lining the route as he walked here from town, all of them ready, all of them with anger on their faces. Mosley and his fascists were going to have a rough ride. He pitied the bobbies who had to march alongside them. He turned to Noble.

'Well, Danny, made your will yet?' He could see the worry in the young man's eyes. That was good; a little fear kept you alert and alive. All around, people were stirring, shouting, singing. They had stones at their feet, an arsenal of weapons. The crowd was primed. And the Blackshirts weren't even in sight yet.

They came soon enough, though. He could hear them long before they were in view. The clatter of marching boots on the cobbles. Even louder, the catcalls and yelling from the crowd. He glanced at Noble. The lad swallowed hard, his face pale.

'Don't you worry,' Raven assured him. 'We'll be fine.'

He looked around, feeling the people stir. Somewhere out there the police had three sharpshooters. He just prayed they wouldn't be needed.

*

Give Mosley some credit, he thought. The man didn't cower behind his supporters. He strode, unafraid, at the head of the parade, back straight, looking like the aristocrat he was. *Sir* Oswald Mosley. A carefully tailored black uniform to match his looks, just like a film star with that little moustache.

The others were right behind him. At the front, the bugle and drum corps, their music drowned out by voices. After them, the shock troops, the I Squad, all of them smirking like thugs who'd done their share of prison time. Then the believers, most of them terrified. A spectacle of ugliness.

Time, Raven thought. It was time.

*

It started almost as soon as Mosley began to speak. He'd just announced that 'the war on want is the war we want' when the first stone arced through the air.

A moment's silence as people followed it with their eyes. It landed short of the stage, catching a Blackshirt on the head. That was the signal. Suddenly the air was full of branches, cobbles prised up from the roads. Bricks. Potatoes with razor blades protruding from the skins.

Raven knew his duty. He was here to arrest those who were disturbing the peace. Sod that; he wasn't even about to try. This lot would tear him apart if he produced his handcuffs.

Bloodlust, that was what it was. Frenzy. Missiles flew both ways. Mosley kept speaking until a stone caught him in the face and he crumpled, his guards quickly gathering around to protect him.

One of the Blackshirt musicians waded into the crowd, swinging his bugle like a weapon and cracking some heads. Too far away to reach, though. Everyone had surged forward, packed so tight that breathing was hard and movement impossible.

Noble was a good six feet away now, shoved around like flotsam by all the bodies surrounding him and looking scared. Never mind, Raven thought, he was trained, he could look after himself. The best thing they could do was try to identify the worst troublemakers. Later, once things had calmed and everyone had gone home, they could go and arrest them.

He glanced up again and the fascists were forming ranks to march away. They hadn't lasted long. Mosley was still there, blood flowing from the cut on his face. The men and women with him looked more ragged now. Stunned, bruised, battered as they left. And the worst was yet to come.

People would be waiting on the route with stones and more. More would be up on the roofs. It was going to be brutal. Here on the moor though, he couldn't do a damned thing about that, and he was glad to be away from it all.

Men were helping the wounded as the crowd began to disperse. Bloody handkerchiefs held to heads, a few carted off unconscious. Weapons lay strewn across the grass. It was like the aftermath of a battle. An air of silence and desolation hung over the Holbeck Moor. All those walking proudly away or just limping – women along with the men – had that curious glint of battle in their eyes. A few sat on the grass, smoking cigarettes and looking as if they weren't sure what had happened.

His part was done. He knelt, picking twigs and small pieces of glass from the turn-ups of his trousers. Noble was talking to a man who stood cradling his wrist, nodding blankly as he spoke. Raven started to walk towards them. Then he heard the sound and stopped.

In the distance, the piercing shriek of a police whistle.

Urban Raven began to run.

Noble was younger and fitter, he had longer legs. He sprinted, following the sound. All Raven could do was trail behind, panting. On the road, the protestors had already faded away like smoke. He could hear angry shouts in the distance, but they might almost be in another county. He breathed hard, keeping Noble in sight as he pounded along before turning onto a street with a Bile Beans advertisement fading on the end of the gable. No motor cars around here, he thought. Tram or shank's mare, that was the choice. A bicycle for the fortunate ones.

People had gathered around a squat brick building. The privies. All the houses here would share outdoor toilets. Breathless, he shouldered his way through the crowd, watching the anger and insults vanish as soon as they saw his face.

A harried constable was trying to keep everyone back. There was dust on his uniform and a small cut on his cheek above a thin moustache. The tall helmet had a dent in the high crown. Caught up in the march, Raven thought.

'What is it?'

'At the back, sir.' He straightened to attention and started to raise his arm for a salute. The sergeant waved it away and marched past, Noble right on his heels.

The body lay in the tight, stinking space between the back of the privy and a brick wall. It must have been dragged there. A man, just beginning to run to fat, he could see that much. One arm was raised, covering his face.

He could pick out the Burton's label in the suit. Decent leather soles on his shoes, not worn through to holes. Not rich then, but not poor either; someone in work. And murdered. Absolutely no doubt about that.

'Get that uniformed copper,' Raven ordered. 'If this is his beat, he might know who this is.' Noble seemed rooted to the spot, staring at the corpse. Of course, his first murder. Death might be common, but killing was rare. There'd been three in Raven's fifteen years on the force. Four now, he corrected himself. He gave Noble a nudge. 'Copper,' he said. 'After that, find a police box and call it in. Tell them we need the crew out here.'

'Sorry, Sarge.'

Alone, he squatted, trying for a better look at the body. They couldn't move him until the evidence boys had been out to take their photographs and measurements and he couldn't reach the pockets to find a wallet. Damn.

Raven breathed through his mouth, small gulps of air, trying to ignore the stench. There had been places like this every day when he walked the beat, but he'd forgotten how bad they stank.

'You wanted me, sir?' the bobby asked.

'Yes.' He stood. 'Is this your manor?'

'No, Sarge. I'm PC 7862, Jones, over in Beeston. They just had me here for the Blackshirts.' A tiny glimmer of envy in his voice as he said the name.

'Have you ever seen this man before?'

The constable squinted and swallowed, Adam's apple bobbing hard before he shook his head.

'I don't think so, sir. Can't see his face properly but he doesn't look familiar.'

'Good. You stay here and keep them all at bay.' Raven glanced at the wall. 'Better watch that, too, or there'll be boys over it before you can say Jack Robinson.'

*

Nothing more to do. An inspector, possibly even a superintendent or chief super, would handle a murder. They had the rank, they could carry the responsibility. Raven gave a grim smile.

At least he'd go home to Marjorie without a scratch, exactly as he promised. He wondered whether she'd be glad about that.

Probably not. Very little seemed to make her happy these days. Her few moments of joy were dotted between long stretches of bleakness, as if she regretted marrying him. Maybe she did. But he'd never pushed her to get wed. With his scarred face he knew he was no prize. He'd been astonished when she encouraged him and said yes as soon as he proposed. They'd met at Beckett Park Hospital after he was shipped home. She was the nursing assistant on his ward. They saw each other every day. They talked. He thought she was beautiful, amazed that someone like her would take an interest in him. The old, old story, Raven thought. Too old. Beauty and the beast.

It hadn't been a lucky marriage. No children. Instead, she'd had four miscarriages, then the advice that they shouldn't try again; another pregnancy could kill Marjorie. And with those words, something had started to wither inside her. Inside both of them, really. A distance that started to widen.

Five years paying off all the hospital bills, setting aside the money every month, was a constant reminder that didn't help the resentment, either. It was no one's fault, he knew that. So did she, he was certain. But he saw it in her eyes, and in his own.

'On their way, sir.' Noble's voice brought him back to the present. He was brooding too much these days. Pointless, a waste of bloody time.

'We might as well get back to the station. This one's probably too juicy for the likes of you and me.'

The detritus of the march littered the road. Scattered stones, shattered glass, small pools of blood. Tomorrow everything would be clean, as if it had never happened. Some men would be back at work, more of them in the dole queue, all of them talking about today until it became another polished memory.

*

He climbed the marble stairs in the library and followed the black-and-white sign to the office. Leeds police had been headquartered here for a few years now, shoehorned in with the books, since they outgrew the space in the Town Hall. There were promises of a new building for them, but words were cheaper than bricks and mortar. And whatever a politician said wasn't worth a damn, anyway.

He wrote up two reports. One covered the events on Holbeck Moor, the other the discovery of the corpse. Raven left them on the inspector's desk then walked over to the depot to wait for the tram to Gipton. He got off past the York Road fire station and walked through the estate. Someone had a window cracked open, a gramophone playing. Al Bowlly singing *Blue Moon*. He hummed along with the tune; Raven had always been partial to the man's voice. A sweet, lulling croon.

They'd been fortunate and moved into one of the new houses when the Gipton estate was built two years before. He'd wangled it through a friend in the housing department; somewhere better than the house full of vermin where they'd been living. A copper made a regular wage, but it wasn't much. Even on a sergeant's pay, he'd never be able afford to buy a home.

When they arrived, everything was brand new, still smelling of fresh paint. Their furniture had gone through the bug van, the same humiliation as everyone else out here. They'd been astonished by all the space and fresh air; it almost felt like living in the country. An inside toilet, bathroom with hot and cold water, a kitchen with a modern gas cooker. Even gardens at the front and back. Too good to be true, that was how it seemed. Sometimes he stood as he approached the place, just to admire it and think he was living like royalty.

As he opened the front door, Marjorie bustled through from the kitchen, wiping her hands on her apron. She was still a lovely woman, he knew that, with her blonde hair neatly styled in a wave, lips red and full. He saw men turn to glance at her as she passed. Who could blame them? He was probably the only one who'd noticed the way her face had hardened and sharpened over the years. She inspected him with a practised look. No injuries, so she gave him a quick hug and a peck on the cheek, then returned to the stove.

He sat with the *Sunday Express*, the BBC *National Programme* playing on the wireless. More talk about the new king abdicating because of his American woman. Love seemed to matter more to Edward than the crown, and for a second Raven felt jealous. What must it be like to have that kind of romance? Even so, to give up the throne for someone… it seemed impossible to believe.

Early evening. They'd eaten, dishes all cleared from the table, and the sun had broken through the thin clouds. He could hear Marjorie humming to herself as she washed up. Maybe he should go and do a little gardening. Some digging would work off all the tension.

*

He hated the telephone: it was never good news when the thing rang. No one he knew owned one. But the force had insisted. Telephones at home for sergeants and ranks above, so they could be contacted in emergencies.

They had the only one for five streets around. A few times a week, people would ask to use it for important messages. Sometimes there was a call for a neighbour and he had to dash down the road and knock on a door. By now Raven was used to it.

He'd just changed into his gardening clothes when he heard the bell, shrill and insistent. With a sigh, he picked it up and gave the number.

'You don't sound in the best of spirits, Urban.' The deep bass voice that didn't need any introduction. Douglas Rushforth, the duty sergeant. 'Missus cut you off, has she?' He chuckled at his own joke.

'What is it, Doug? You haven't called up to natter.' He glanced at the clock. Twenty-five to seven. Still time to go outside and pull the last of the potatoes. This had better be important.

'That body you found today,' Rushforth said. 'The one in Holbeck.'

As if there were more of them around town, Raven thought.

'What about it? That's one for the inspector or the super.'

'Happen it is,' Rushforth agreed. 'But the inspector specifically asked for you. He's even sending a car out to collect you, so you'd better get your skates on and be ready.'

It didn't make sense. He'd been at the scene but that was all. 'Me? What's so important?'

'You don't know who it is?'

'No. I left before they took him away.' He let out a long breath. 'Come on, just tell me what's going on.'

'The dead chap, he was a means test inspector.'

Three

BLOODY HELL. NO wonder they needed him at work. It would be all hands on deck. Raven pulled on his good suit, fastened his collar stud and put on a tie.

A means test inspector.

They were men with plenty of power. They decided whether a family received assistance or starved. A means test inspector could barge into the house of anyone getting money and search it. He could make people sell every possession, every keepsake, no matter how small it was or what it meant. They could say yes or no, and their word was law.

They were hated. Every single one of them. And no bloody wonder.

Christ, finding the killer would be like hunting for a needle in ten fields full of haystacks.

'That was the station,' he explained to Marjorie. She was hanging up her apron behind the larder door.

'They want you in on a Sunday evening?' She wasn't outraged, Raven thought; just surprised and curious.

'There's been a murder.' He wasn't about to tell her more, but he'd never been one to talk about his job. 'I'm not sure when I'll be back.'

She nodded and turned away to put the kettle on the stove. That was it.

*

Outside, a black Humber was idling. He slid into the passenger seat and the constable let out the clutch. Hardly any traffic on York Road, just a single tram lumbering along on its way to Halton and a lorry parked by the pavement while the driver struggled to change a puncture.

He parked on Alexander Street, just behind the library, and Raven hauled himself up the stairs to the CID room. It needed a coat of paint, the high, white ceiling turned nicotine brown by the years of smoke; cobwebs in all the corners.

Inspector Mortimer was there, talking to Noble and two other young men in plain clothes. Detective constables; they had to be, brought in from other divisions. One of them had such a fresh shave that his cheeks glowed pink. Superintendent Kennedy leaned against the wall, watching.

'Raven,' Mortimer said, looking relieved. 'You've heard?'

'Only the bare bones.'

'Here's the file, what we know so far.' He pushed it across the desk. The inspector's face looked ashen, his eyes tired behind a pair of spectacles. He'd turned fifty the year before. Hair that had receded to a monk's fringe around the back and sides of his head made him appear older.

Raven slipped some photographs out of the folder and set them aside, then settled at his desk and began to read.

The dead man was called Frank Benson. Forty-nine years old, married, two grown children. Lived off Kirkstall Lane, close to the suburban railway station, on the cusp of Headingley. He'd been employed as a means test inspector since they reintroduced it back in 1931. A clerk at an ironworks before that, until there'd been no job for him and he'd spent a year unemployed. That was interesting, Raven thought; he'd probably have been willing to do anything and everything to make sure he held onto that new position. Royal Artillery in the war, enlisted in August 1914. No injuries, the usual service medals. There was an addition, pencilled in after all the typing: Benson's territory was Harehills. He covered all the streets between Roseville Road and Harehills Lane, from Roundhay Road to Skinner Lane.

It was a big area, and all of it desperately poor. Had the man been in Holbeck for the march? There was so much they still needed to know. He closed the file.

Still, they had the skeleton, the brief outline. The facts that told him who Frank Benson had been. Now they needed the flesh, to understand what he'd been *like*. They'd build it up slowly, with hour after hour of questions and traipsing around town.

Raven spread out the photographs. Everything he'd seen a few hours before, all there in black and white. The suit jacket rucked up, the arm hiding the face. Light brown hair, he remembered that, curly, thinning. He studied them, seeing nothing new.

More pictures, taken once Benson had been removed from the area behind the privy. The arms down to reveal his face. A thin mouth, bloodless lips, hook nose. Darkness colouring the eyeballs; blood. And the sharp line around the man's throat. Raven moved from shot to shot, comparing one against the other and trying to make it all out. Frank Benson had been garrotted. Slow agony, a long descent into death. Even a means test man didn't deserve that.

He replaced everything in the folder and put it on Mortimer's desk. Noble and the other DCs had vanished; he'd never noticed them leave.

'Is that all we've got, sir?'

'For now.' The inspector took off his glasses and pinched the bridge of his nose. 'I went over to inform his wife. I'd like you to go over and talk to her.'

'Me?' Raven asked in surprise. 'Are you sure, sir?' His face usually scared women and left them silent.

'I'm positive. She mentioned the war twice while I was there. She's very proud of what her husband did in France. Quite the hero, if you believe her.' He raised an eyebrow. Didn't need to say more. The woman would be able to see that Raven had served and been wounded. People were strange…

'Did she say anything about his job?'

'I didn't push it,' Mortimer said. 'She seemed on the edge of hysterics. Her daughter was there, I left her looking after the woman. Maybe she's calmed down a little by now.'

And if not, he'd be the one to handle it. One of the things he hated in the job.

'When's the post-mortem?'

'First thing in the morning. Looks like he was strangled with a piece of wire. I've got men searching around where he was found. Just when we thought we'd escaped lightly with the fascists.' Mortimer took a bottle of Aspro from his jacket pocket and put two in his mouth, washing them down with cold tea. 'The Assistance Board has promised us a list of all the people he's visited in the last three months. They'll have it for us first thing.'

The inspector had been busy. But that was how to do things. Get as much information as possible and begin sifting through.

'We'll have more constables on this once the day shift clocks on,' Mortimer continued. 'In the meantime, see what you can find out from the wife tonight. Take one of the cars.'

'Yes, sir.'

'Report back when you've finished.' A wan smile. 'I'm sure the super-intendent and I will still be here.' He glanced up. 'The newspapers have been round. Stringers from the nationals, too. It's a big story, especially after the march. Everyone's looking, so let's wrap this up quick and clean.'

*

Raven turned the key in the Riley and adjusted the choke until the engine was running smoothly. He eased out onto Calverley Street, then up towards Headingley.

It was a bugger of a duty. He was going to feel on display the whole time, thinking she'd be staring at his face. And he'd need to be gentle. Very gentle. Her husband had just been murdered; he'd probably be lucky to get a damned thing out of her.

But they needed as much as he could learn, and they needed it as soon as possible. God knew there were plenty of questions to ask, about the man's work and what he was doing in Holbeck.

*

Raven sat outside the house for a moment. It was a neat terrace with a postage-stamp front garden and stained-glass borders on the upstairs windows. The lights were on, curtains in the front room pulled to.

He locked the car, buttoned his suit jacket, took a deep breath and knocked.

He hadn't expected a young woman to open the door; he'd forgotten about the daughter. She peered up quizzically at him, frizzy hair held in place with clips. Her eyes were rimmed red and she clutched a handkerchief tightly in her hand.

He took off his trilby, turning it awkwardly in his hands.

'I'm Detective Sergeant Raven,' he said. 'I know it must be a terrible time, but I really need to ask a few questions.'

'I'm Ava,' she told him. 'You want my mum.'

Mrs Benson was in the parlour, sitting in a chair with her arms clasped tight over her belly. She stared as he entered, but Raven wasn't sure she even saw him. She looked like a woman whose mind was years away, lost in better times.

Ava Benson shook her mother's shoulder lightly, until the woman blinked, slowly returning to the here and now. There was something colourless about the woman, sexless, huddled inside an old cardigan. With glasses and mousy hair, there was nothing memorable about her face. But she'd experienced a huge shock, more than anyone should have to undergo.

The room was very clean and spare. A cabinet in the corner, only a few ornaments on the shelves. Antimacassars on the chairs. A cheap rag rug, worn almost threadbare in places. No fire in the grate. Benson might have had a steady job, but means test inspector didn't seem to pay any better than being a beat copper.

'It's a policeman, Mum,' the young woman said gently. 'He wants to talk to you.'

'Yes. Yes.' This time she looked directly at his face. No grimace, none of the usual horror at the scars, just acceptance. 'Please, sit down.' Her voice was hoarse. She gestured at a chair. 'Ava, could you make us some tea, love?'

He introduced himself, then said, 'I know it's a terrible time, but we do need to know more about your husband.'

'Where did you serve?' she asked, keeping her eyes on his face. Her hand rose to stroke her left cheek.

'Western Front,' he replied. He felt as if she was judging him.

'So did Frank. He was in the artillery.' Her face softened for a moment. 'He liked to talk about his time there.'

Now he understood why Mortimer had sent him. He was right; shock or not, she was definitely an odd one.

'I wasn't there long,' he told her. 'Wounded almost as soon as I arrived, then back to Blighty.'

Mrs Benson nodded sadly. He needed to take charge, to get her on track. 'Why did your husband go over to Holbeck, Mrs Benson?'

'Oh,' she answered, as if she was surprised that he needed to ask. 'To hear Mr Mosley. He liked him. We both did. He wants the best for England.'

'Did he go there with anyone? Some friends, perhaps?'

'No, he was on his own,' she answered. 'He never mentioned anyone.'

God, Raven thought. Finding the murderer was going to be impossible.

*

He had to tease information from her, for all it was worth. She didn't know anything about her husband's work. He never discussed it and it wasn't her place to ask. She deferred to him in everything. He'd been low, years ago, after he lost his job, she admitted, and times had been hard. But that was all forgotten once he started working for the Public Assistance people. He was dedicated, put in long hours and he took pride in what he did. He kept people honest, that was what he said.

'Did he have any enemies?'

'Enemies?' She spoke the word as if she'd never heard it before, rolling it round her mouth then slowly shook her head. 'Of course not. Why would he?'

If she really didn't understand, how could he explain it to her?

Finally, after more than an hour, he put away his notebook. At least he had the addresses of Benson's two brothers and a couple of friends.

'Thank you for your time,' he told her. 'I might need to come back and ask a few more questions.'

She nodded. He sensed she was drifting again.

A voice came from behind him: 'I'll show you out.'

He'd forgotten Ava was there. She'd been sitting so quietly on a hard chair by the wall. As she held the front door open, she said, 'Dad was her world.'

'Yes.' From the way Mrs Benson had reacted, he could easily believe that. In her eyes the man could do no wrong. She was distraught. Not doolally, but everything was coloured by her loss. Hardly surprising, really.

He looked at the daughter. She'd been crying, too, but there was a curious sense of control about her. No, not quite that. Detachment. 'My condolences, Miss Benson. It must be very hard.'

'Thank you.'

'It would be helpful if I could talk to you, too.' She might be more open and alert than her mother. Ava Benson seemed bright enough. Aware.

'If you like.' The suggestion seemed to catch her unawares. A moment's pause, then she asked, 'How did my father die, Sergeant? The policeman who came before wouldn't tell us.'

She stared directly into his face, holding his gaze, not repelled by the scars and grafts.

'He was strangled,' Raven said finally. She gave a small, tight nod, no expression showing.

'Thank you. I'd rather know the truth.' She straightened her back. 'I'd better go back. She needs me. I can talk tomorrow, if you want.' As if he'd paid a price that would allow conversation.

'I'll come in the morning.'

Maybe the daughter would be able to shed more light on things, Raven thought as he drove back into town. The roads were empty, the night almost silent.

Four

MORTIMER WAS STILL at his desk, a cubbyhole at the far end of the CID office. Mounds of paper had grown around him. His jacket was draped over the back of his chair, bright red braces showing against his white shirt. The ashtray by his side was full.

'Any luck?'

'A bit,' Raven said. 'Turns out Benson had gone down to Holbeck to hear Mosley speak. He's a supporter.'

Mortimer sighed, lit another cigarette, and shook his head.

'Noble talked to his supervisor at Assistance. It seems Benson was very enthusiastic in his work. Liked to turn the screws on people whenever he could. Between that and his love of Mosley, we probably have thousands of suspects.'

Raven said nothing. They'd keep going, gradually eliminating names and hoping for a break to go with the ordinary police work. One thing already seemed certain: this murder wasn't going to be solved overnight.

'I don't think it had anything to do with the march, though.' The inspector rubbed his belly. 'I can feel it in my gut.'

Hunches. Every copper knew them. They all believed in them, and sometimes they were right. But in this case he could see the sense in it. No one had any love for the means test man.

Mortimer glanced at his watch.

'It's past ten. Why don't you write it up then go home? Early start tomorrow.'

'Yes, sir.' The trams would have stopped running by now. Never mind; he'd cadge a lift in one of the new squad cars.

*

The lights were off in the house. He closed the door softly and took off his shoes before climbing the stairs. Quiet, even breathing from the bedroom. Marjorie was a light sleeper; she'd wake as soon as he tried to settle beside her. Instead, he bedded down in the spare room. He was doing her a favour. At least that was what Raven told himself.

*

A soft, misting rain. It felt soothing on his face as he walked along the Headrow from the tram stop. Somewhere in the distance he could hear a radio, the clipped, smooth tones of a BBC announcer.

Mortimer was in Superintendent Kennedy's office, the door closed. Noble was waiting, smoking a cigarette and nursing a cup of tepid tea.

'The inspector wants me with you today, Sarge.'

'In a bit,' Raven told him. 'I need to see a source first.' It wasn't quite the truth; he was going to talk to Ava Benson. But he didn't think she'd open up with another copper around.

He buttonholed Mortimer as soon as the man appeared. A few quiet words, a nod of approval.

'I've commandeered a couple of cars for the duration. Use one of those.'

'Thank you, sir.' That would make life easier than an endless series of tram journeys. 'Back by half past ten,' he told Noble, and he was on his way back to Headingley.

She opened the door even before he knocked, as if she'd been watching, holding a finger to her lips.

'Mum's still sleeping. The doctor gave her some sort of powder.' Her voice was little more than a whisper. She led him through to a scullery at the back of the house. Stone sink, neatly blackleaded range.

The girl wore a jade green rayon dress with long sleeves and a hem a couple of inches below her knees, pale stockings and shoes with court heels. Today, she'd brushed her hair and tamed it into some sort of order. He could still see the grief and shock on her face, but not as sharply as the night before. Everything dulled and packed down.

'I know this must be hard for you, Miss Benson—'

'Ava. Please, call me Ava.'

'Ava.' He smiled. 'I was hoping you could tell me more about your father. Every scrap is useful. You live here?'

She nodded. 'My sister got married last year. They're down in St Alban's.' He thought her could hear wistfulness and envy in her voice. 'I sent Caroline a telegram last night.'

'What do you do? Do you have a job?'

'I work in a typing pool.'

He glanced around the room. A tiny hesitation. 'What was your father like?'

'He…' she began, then stayed quiet for a long time, looking at the table. Raven watched the emotions cross her face: loyalty, fear, anguish, anger, sorrow.

'It's fine,' he told her finally. 'You don't have to say if you don't want to.' Sometimes that released the pressure and helped them to talk.

'No, no, I want to,' she replied quickly and raised her head. 'It sounds terrible, but my father was a bully.'

Raven cocked his head. 'A bully? How?'

'With mum. Nothing she did was ever good enough for him. He'd complain, shout at her until she cried.' The girl paused. 'Sometimes he'd hit her. Only sometimes, though,' she added quickly.

Raven let the statement hang in the air. He'd seen it often, small men who tried to be big by yelling at home and using their fists where there was no one to hit back.

'What about you and your sister?'

'He never hit us,' she said slowly. A very careful choice of words, he decided.

'Your mother…'

'She loved him.' Her hands were shaking slightly, and she pressed them down on the wood to steady them. 'She didn't think he could do any wrong.'

'But you don't believe that?'

She shook her head. 'No. I was glad for Caroline when she moved away from here. It's never been a happy house.'

'What about you and your father? How did you get along?'

She kept her eyes on the floor and didn't reply.

'Were there other people who disliked your father?' he asked. Would a daughter even know?

'Besides me?' She gave a sad, weary smile and he could see her eyes shining, on the brink of tears. The girl pushed her lips together and shook her head quickly. He wasn't going to press. It must have taken a lot for her to admit this. A betrayal of memory.

'Thank you.' He patted her hand, then stood. 'You've been a big help.'

'Have I?' She looked up, hope on her face.

'Honestly,' Raven said. 'You really have.'

She held onto his fingers for a fraction of a second too long as he pulled away. He heard the creak of a floorboard upstairs.

'You'd better see to your mother,' he told her and left quickly.

Strange family, Raven thought as he drove back into town. Very bloody strange. As he drove down the hill, thick steam rose from a locomotive passing in the cut.

*

'The head of the means test inspectors is called Pearce,' Noble said as they walked into the Civic Hall. Just a few years ago all this area by Great George Street had been shops and back-to-back houses. Now it was a wide square and a big, important building of white stone, a bright, modern contrast to the grand Victorian buildings no more than a stone's throw away and all blackened with soot. That was Leeds, Raven decided, one foot in the present, the other still firmly planted in the past and still not sure which it preferred. 'He sounded terrified last night when I told him one of his men had been killed. Seems a very fussy type,' the constable warned.

Mr Pearce fretted and fidgeted. His hair was shiny, a neatly Bryl-creemed short back and sides, and he wore a tight Fair Isle jumper over his shirt and tie. He was reluctant, but finally he gave them a mimeographed sheet of all the families in Benson's area receiving assistance. It seemed like the perfect place to start.

'What about threats?' the sergeant asked. 'The inspectors must receive plenty of them?'

'Of course,' Pearce agreed with a quick series of nods. 'We keep records.'

'I'd like to see them.'

'Oh,' he replied. 'They're at the other office, where the staff work.'

*

That was in an anonymous brick building near the top of Cook—ridge Street, up on the third floor, the walls on the staircase painted cream and drab green. Their soles echoed on the concrete steps, a steep climb, then the smells of paper and stale tobacco as they went through a door.

A female clerk handed them the threats ledgers. Three of them.

'That's just so far this year,' she said with resignation. 'We tell all the inspectors to note every one. For their own safety.'

'How many have been assaulted?' Noble asked.

'Two.' She didn't even hesitate in her reply. 'Neither of them was Mr Benson. Both on the other side of Leeds. One in Horsforth, another in Wortley. Your lot arrested the offenders. We can't stand for that, you know.'

'No,' Raven agreed. He'd find those files back at the station. In the meantime they had plenty to keep them busy here. 'Is there any index of the names? People who often threaten, things like that?'

'We have our regulars.' She took one of the books and began to leaf through the pages before pointing at a name and address. 'Him. He crops up every couple of months. There are more.'

She picked them out, six men. It was a start.

'Have any of these threatened Mr Benson?'

The woman shook her head. 'Not that he mentioned. He's never reported any threats.'

'Can we take these ledgers?' Raven asked.

'As long as you bring them back,' she told him. 'Sometimes we need them as evidence.'

*

'How do you want to do it, Sarge?' Noble asked once they were in the Riley, the books locked in the boot.

'Back to headquarters. Let's see what previous this lot have. Then we'll pay them a visit and lean on them a bit.'

*

Only one had form. Jack Timms. Back in 1933 he'd done six months for grievous bodily harm and assault, bound over on another occasion for threatening behaviour.

'Sounds like a right charmer,' Raven said as Noble showed him the sheet. The file held a photograph of a man with a battered boxer's face, broken nose, surly expression. Head shaved, scalp shining.

Noble slid brass knuckles out of his pocket.

'Just in case, Sarge,' he said slyly.

'Put those away,' Raven hissed. 'I never saw them. For Christ's sake, lad, make sure the inspector and the super never catch a glimpse. They'll bounce you off the force before you know it, you daft bugger.'

'Right, Sarge.' He reddened, abashed.

'Just be sure you keep your truncheon handy. From the sound of this one, you might need it.'

Just past the Tetley brewery, he overtook a big, lumbering dray and turned at the corner. Timms lived far down in Hunslet, close to Low Road; not much more than a stone's throw from Holbeck Moor, he thought. Half the buildings in the area had been demolished, the ground strewn with rubble. A small area remained, several of the houses already boarded up, most of the cobbles missing from the road. It looked forsaken, the air heavy with decayed industry and despair. No vehicles, just the rusted carcass of a bicycle, wheels gone, lying in the middle of the street. Off in the distance he could hear the raw metal sounds of Hudswell Clarke's Railway Foundry.

Number three was next to the end of the terrace, standing by an empty shop with a faded sign and broken windows. The house needed paint on the woodwork. A crack ran all the way down one pane of glass. Around here no one would bother to replace that. Another few months and all this would be rubble, anyway.

As Raven knocked, the door flew open and Timms stood menacingly in front of them, fists curled and ready.

'Coppers,' he said and spat.

'Good guess.' Raven stared him in the eye, watching for the slightest movement. He could see Noble eagerly tapping his truncheon against his leg. 'A few questions for you, Mr Timms. Would you like to tell me where you were on Sunday afternoon?'

It seemed to catch him off guard. The man frowned and the ugly mask slipped as he seemed doubtful.

'Did you go to the meeting on Holbeck Moor? Mosley and his men?' Raven prompted.

'No.' He snorted. 'Got better things to do, don't I?'

'What, like murder?' Noble asked, taking a step closer. For a long second things teetered on a knife edge. Raven waited, ready; no one would care if Timms took a battering. Just as the situation seemed ready to erupt the sergeant said, 'Enough.'

In a second the tension dropped.

'You have a record of threats,' Raven continued. 'You've been in prison for violence. You don't like means test men.'

'Don't meant I killed one, does it?' His eyes were defiant.

'No,' he agreed. Timms was talking, that was a good sign. It made him less likely to use his fists. 'Who were you with on Sunday?'

'Pub until it closed.' He nodded towards some distant corner; there was no public house in sight. 'Back here and kipped a bit.'

'Was anyone here with you?'

The man shrugged. 'Wife left a month back and took the nippers. Said she couldn't live down here no more. Good bloody riddance to them, too.'

'No one came to visit?'

Timms gave a bitter laugh. 'Take a look around. Who'd come around here? It's like someone blew the place up.'

'Then why don't you leave?' Noble asked.

'It's cheap.' He jutted out his jaw. 'And the council hasn't offered me owt yet.'

Could he have killed Benson, Raven wondered? No doubt about the answer. But Timms wasn't the type to garotte. He'd enjoy using his fists and his boots to get rid of whatever fury he kept inside.

'We might be back.'

*

'Sarge?' Noble asked as they drove away.

'We're not going to forget him, but let's see what else we can dig up. Where next on that list?'

Some had solid alibis. Some had moved on. One other possible, but Raven wasn't convinced.

*

They sat in the car, traffic trundling past, pedestrians moving by, catching snatches of conversations like fleeting moments in the air, and looked at the list that Benson's boss had given them. Two hundred names. More than the pair of them could ever manage to see. They'd need help to go through it all.

'We can make a start,' Raven decided, 'then pass it on. Twenty houses each for now. At least we'll get an idea of the way he was in his job.' He hadn't told Noble about Benson's bullying of his family. He didn't see it was necessary; it wasn't going to affect the hunt for the killer. Let the women keep a little dignity, at least.

*

The first man stood on his step and listened as Raven told him about the murder. He was in his sixties, with a shock of pure white hair and a thick moustache the colour of nicotine stains, with deep lines etched into his face. He spat out onto the cobbles, said, 'About bloody time,' and closed the door.

The next name was three houses further along Kepler Grove. A young fellow this time, with bulging frog eyes and a bouncing Adam's apple. He looked downcast at the news, but nothing more. The same at the next few addresses. No grief. No one here was going to miss Frank Benson.

Round the corner on Gledhow Place, a man named Galloway cradled his infant daughter, heard what the sergeant had to say, then snorted.

'You know what he was like?' the man asked and Raven shook his head. 'A real sod, that's what. He'd dock you for owt. Reckoned he was

God an' all.'

'What do you mean?'

Galloway tucked the girl's head against his shoulder, tenderly stroking her hair.

'About a month back, I were expecting him round. He didn't even knock, just opened the front door and barged right in like he owned the place, looking around, checking in the cupboards and asking if there was any change in my circumstances. No how do you do, no by your leave, no respect. I told him to get hisself right out again. "My wife could have been washing at the sink, you bugger," I said. I picked up the poker and waved it at him. That got him back outside right quick and tapping politely. "Any change in things?" he asked when I let him in. "Aye," I said. "For the worse." He took a glance in the pantry, and when he was leaving, he told me, "I won't forget this." He didn't, neither. Someone told him I'd been making a little repairing boots and they stopped my relief. Five weeks. Still got three to go. Benson relished telling me, too.'

'You realise you've just made yourself a suspect,' Raven said, and Galloway shrugged.

'Arrest me, then. At least you'd have to feed me in jail.'

'Where were you yesterday?'

'Right here. Where the hell else would I be?'

'You're in the clear, then.' Not that he suspected the man; Galloway was far too open, his heart showing loud and bright on his sleeve.

He heard similar tales at other houses. Family members who'd been forced to move into lodgings because they were working and their income would cut assistance to the others.

'The truth is that half of them haven't moved at all, of course.' He sat in the scullery of a house on Anderson Mount, a wooden rack in front of the range with clothes drying slowly. Ernie Haynes was a member of the National Unemployed Workers' Movement. Thoughtful, soft spoken, in his fifties, he seemed to have given up on the idea of ever having a job again. There were plenty more in the same boat. The unemployable. 'They stay out all the hours they can then sneak home to eat and sleep. Benson liked to try and catch them. As if it was a game.'

'No one seems to have a good word for him.'

'How can you, for someone like that?' Haynes wondered.

*

'None of them even said "poor man",' Noble told him as they drove back into town, along Mabgate and past the mills and factories that stood empty and forlorn. Rubbish lined the roads; no one cared. 'Not an ounce of sympathy.'

'He didn't seem to have much of that himself.'

'He's dead, though.'

'We all will be some day,' Raven said. 'That doesn't guarantee respect.'

'It seems wrong, that's all.'

It was the way of the world. Nothing more. People spoke ill of the living, the dead, of everyone. They enjoyed it. Some revelled in it.

In the office, he passed Mortimer the list, telling him what they'd learned and watching him grimace.

'We'll need to get the bobbies onto the rest,' Raven said. 'There are far too many for us.'

The inspector nodded and took a piece of paper from the top of a pile.

'The post-mortem report. Benson was strangled. Whoever it was stood behind him to do it.'

Raven thought of the thin red line on the man's throat.

'What did they use?' he asked. 'Could the doctor tell?'

'An electrical flex, he says. He found some of that fabric they put around the wire in the wound. There was some under Benson's fingernails, too. He must have been trying to pull the cord away from his throat.' He shuddered. 'Bloody awful way to go.'

It was. Slow, knowing you were going to die. It didn't matter how many shades of a bastard Benson had been in his job, that was a terrible death.

*

'We have two strands we need to follow,' Detective Superintendent Kennedy said. He sat back in his chair and blew smoke towards the ceiling. Not a hair out of place. A suit of soft, pale grey wool, the best Austin Reed had to offer. He wore his rank well, easily. 'Benson's job, and his politics.' He looked at Mortimer and Raven with a pair of piercing blue eyes. 'Does that sound fair?'

'Yes sir,' the sergeant answered. He still wasn't going to say anything about the man's family life.

'We need to get his photograph in the newspapers,' Mortimer suggested. 'That might stir things up. His wife gave me one when I saw her.'

'I'll contact the editors,' Kennedy said. 'Someone must have seen him at the march. They might remember his face.'

'We did a house-to-house in the area where he was killed. No one recalls him.'

'He must have been murdered very close to where we found him,' Raven pointed out. 'There were plenty of people around, you couldn't go dragging a body along the street.' The others nodded. 'And there's one more thing we need to think about.'

'What?' Kennedy asked.

'Who the hell walks around with a piece of electrical flex in their pocket?'

A moment's silence, then the superintendent asked, 'What are you saying?'

'I don't know, sir,' he admitted. 'I really don't. It just makes me wonder, that's all: did someone go down there specifically to kill? One thing's for sure; he didn't magic that cord out of the air.'

'You said "he",' Mortimer told him.

Raven nodded. 'I was there. Almost all of them were men, sir. And it usually takes brute strength to strangle someone.'

'Electricians could have flex in their pockets,' Kennedy said.

'So might an odd-job man, someone who's been mending a lamp, sir,' Raven pointed out. 'If it's a clue, it doesn't help us much for now. And there are dozens of electricians in Leeds; we'd need to find one with a grudge against Benson.'

'I'll have some of the uniforms start going through them.'

They were throwing ideas around, looking for any thread that might help them catch a murderer. No thought was too small or too strange: one of them might prove to be right.

'What about his friends?' the sergeant asked.

'Very few and far between,' Mortimer said wryly. 'We interviewed them today. Shocked, horrified, what you'd expect.' He shrugged. 'We haven't talked to his brothers yet. Douglas and Gerard. That's up for tomorrow.'

'You know people in the Communists, don't you, Raven?' Kennedy asked quietly as he put another match to his pipe.

'Only one man, sir.'

'Have a word with him, will you? See what he can tell you.'

'Yes sir.'

*

He knew where he'd find Johnny Harris. Six o'clock on the dot and he'd walk under the Magnet Ales sign into the Pointer in Sheepscar. Harris worked at the boot factory near the bottom of Meanwood Road, operating the machine that attached the upper to the sole. He'd done it for so many years that his skin on his palms was as tough and calloused as the boots he made and he'd never be able to scrub away the smell of leather.

Harris had fought in the war, Gallipoli first, then the trenches, from the Somme all the way to Armistice Day. He'd seen the very worst and come back to a promise of a home fit for heroes, words that were nothing more than lies. As soon as they evaporated into thin air he'd joined the Communists and stayed loyal all through the purges in Russia, never wavering in his belief, working his way up to local party secretary.

Raven had grown up with Harris's younger brother, Paul, the pair of them at school together. The families lived a street apart; he'd known them all his life. But it was only in the last few years he'd had much to do with Johnny.

Harris was a tough man, loud, always ready to argue his point. He read a great deal, his back-to-back house on Manor Road crammed with books. All communist, all biased, but Harris believed with the true fervour and devotion of a convert.

He'd been one of the organisers of the demonstration against the Blackshirts on Holbeck Moor. Harris probably counted the violence as a victory. But Raven hadn't come to argue the finer points of politics as he parked the Riley by the library at the bottom of Roundhay Road. He needed information.

Harris was leaning on the bar, his broad back to the room, savouring his first pint after work. Another half hour and he'd go home to his wife and two daughters and be a loving husband and father when he wasn't doing party work. But this was his time.

'Give him another,' Raven told the barman. 'I'll have a lemonade.'

With a wary look at the policeman's scarred face, the man nodded.

'You must be on duty.' Harris didn't even raise his head. 'You'd be on the pints otherwise.'

'They're slave-drivers.' The drinks arrived. Raven raised his glass. 'Good health.'

'I'll drink to that.' Harris pushed himself upright. He had large hands and heavily muscled arms. At first glance he looked to be a big, dangerous man. But there was a twinkle at the back of his eye and usually a smile playing around his mouth. He sipped the head from the drink with a wink.

'I'll accept the beer because it's depriving the capitalist state of money it might use to exploit the people.'

'Yesterday…' Raven began.

'A success.' Harris interrupted. 'We sent them packing.'

'I was there. I saw it.'

Harris grinned. 'You didn't go on your own time, I bet.'

'Don't be daft. I wouldn't waste a Sunday. But someone else was there of his own volition.'

'That body in the paper today?' Harris asked.

'Yes.'

'Was he one of ours?'

'Not at all. A fan of Mosley. He was a means test inspector.'

The man stayed quiet, tearing a soggy beermat into tiny pieces.

'What are you suggesting, Urban?' Harris asked quietly. 'That we were responsible?'

'No,' Raven answered slowly. 'I'm asking, that's all. Have you heard anything?'

'Not a dicky bird.' He took a long sip, draining half the beer. 'How was he killed?'

'Strangled with an electrical cord.' Raven saw the man flinch and his fingers tighten around the glass.

'None of my lot would do that.'

'You don't know for sure, Johnny. We have to find the killer and we're going to need help.'

Harris pursed his lips. It would be hard for him to help the authorities. It went against everything he believed. But if the killer turned out to be a party supporter and he did nothing to help…

'I don't see it,' he said finally. 'Not a communist.'

'Someone murdered him. And it's a cold-blooded way to die. Brutal.' Raven finished the lemonade. 'I'd appreciate the assistance, Johnny, but

I'll leave it to your conscience.'

'You're a bastard, Urban, putting me on the spot.' He shrugged. 'Let me ask a few questions, all right? But I'm certain it wasn't any of my people.'

'Thank you.'

*

No car for the journey home today; the police would never be that generous. Probably for the best, anyway. He'd only end up with a curious crowd outside the house, staring at the only car on the estate. Jim Green, all the way down on Coldcotes Drive, had a motorbike, but he'd bought it as a wreck and rebuilt it himself.

Raven had to wait for one of the Lance-Corporal trams, half-dozing as it clanked along York Road.

No lights on at home, but there was the smell of cooking in the kitchen. A note on the living room table read: *Gone to the pictures with Gladys. Your tea's in the oven.* At least there was food, he thought. And some peace and quiet.

He ate, then left the plate in the sink. Kettle on the hob to make a cup of tea, staring out over the garden as he drank. There was too much to think about on this case. All they had was a jumble of pieces. He couldn't even see all of them yet.

Maybe Johnny would come up with something. If there was even anything to find. Perhaps a bobby going through the list of Benson's claimants would find a man so torn by guilt that he confessed. Right, he thought as he looked into the growing darkness, and they'd see pigs flying over the Town Hall in the morning. This was going to be slow and difficult and it was going to be painful.

Five

'WAS IT A good film?'

'We only went to the Shaftesbury.' Marjorie came into the living room, pulling off her hat and unbuttoning her coat. 'Fred and Ginger, *Swing Time*.' She gave him a quick smile. 'All that music and dancing, you'd have hated it.'

'How's Gladys?' Her sister: Gladys Queen Victoria Ryan, another cartload of a name. Ten years older than Marjorie, married to a council plumber. Steady work, at least, and a skilled man's wage; they were doing well in a world that seemed to sink year by year.

'She's fine.' Marjorie glanced into the kitchen. 'You could have washed up your plate, at least.'

'Sorry.'

'I'm going to bed,' she said.

'I'll be there very soon.' He looked up from his magazine. As soon as he heard her moving around in the bathroom, he slid over to the table and opened her handbag, hating himself as he did it. Tram tickets into town and back. Make-up, a tiny bottle of perfume. The Shaftesbury wasn't even ten minutes' walk away.

Well, Raven thought, you were the one who wanted to look. You thought to check up on her. You got exactly what you deserved.

In bed she smoked a final cigarette, then turned out the light. A kiss on the cheek and she turned away from him. Urban Raven stared up at the dark ceiling, trying not to think.

*

Douglas Benson was the image of his brother. The same hair, hook nose, and bland features on his face. It was disconcerting, as if the dead had come back to life. He was three years younger than Frank, a dull, pale man who didn't have much to say for himself, a grocer with a small shop in Bramley. Sacks of beans and sugar sitting on the floor, tins on the shelves, bacon and butter under glass. The rich smells of spices and meats and cheese.

'I didn't see him often.' He looked uncomfortable, flushing a little, as if his collar was too tight. 'We had a bit of a falling-out a few years ago, after mother died.'

'What happened, sir?' Noble stood by the door that led through to the shop. Benson pushed his hands into the pockets of his brown overall.

'It was over the will. Father had died earlier,' he explained quietly, 'so she was the only one left. There wasn't much, but it was supposed to be divided equally between the three of us. That was the understanding.'

'Go on.' Raven sat on the only chair, listening intently.

'It wasn't worded very clearly. Frank kept pushing and bullying me and Gerard until we gave in and accepted less.'

'How much money was involved, sir?' Noble asked. He raised an eyebrow at the sergeant. Money was always a good motive for murder.

'Not much. They weren't rich and they'd spent most of what they'd saved. After paying for the funeral…' He shrugged. 'Anyway, since then we exchange Christmas cards and that's it. Say hello if we pass on the street, but nothing more. Bad feelings.'

'Does your other brother feel the same?' Raven wondered.

Benson nodded. 'He does. We still get together all the time, with wives and children, you know.'

'When did you last see Frank?'

'It must be at least twelve months. More: Whitsun last year.' He sighed. 'I feel sorry for his wife and those daughters of his.'

'Why?' The question came out more sharply than he intended and he tried to temper it. 'Why would you think that?'

'They always looked cowed, scared of him.' Douglas Benson grimaced. 'I know, it's terrible to say, but it's true. My brother wasn't a good person. There wasn't an ounce of kindness in him.'

'What are your politics, if I might ask?' Raven asked.

'Mine?' It took Benson by surprise. 'Liberal, why?'

'I'm just curious. Do you know of anyone who might have wanted to harm your brother?'

'I suppose there could have been plenty of people, given his job.' Benson answered with a sad smile. 'God knows, there were times I felt like it myself. But blood is thicker than water. I could never do that.'

*

The answers from Gerard Benson tallied. He was the youngest, with darker, bolder features. Moodier, Raven decided. The kind who seemed to think he had the looks and presence to be a film star. But a butcher's assistant in Chapel Allerton wasn't ever going to end up on the silver screen. He probably had his dreams and underneath he was grateful to be in regular work.

They were standing in the yard behind the shop, the iron smell of blood overwhelming.

'If you're asking whether I killed him, then no, I didn't.' He took a last draw from the Woodbine and tossed it onto the damp flagstones in the corner. 'He wasn't worth hanging for, and that's a fact.'

'Do you know who might have done it?'

'If he treated everyone the way he treated his family, it could be anyone.' He strode back to work.

'What do you think?' Raven asked as they ambled back to the car. 'Suspect either of them?'

'Not really, Sarge,' Noble said.

'Nor do I.' He sighed. 'Pity, it would have been so neat. Come on, let's find some dinner.'

They finally went into a café close to the Roscoe public house near the bottom of Chapeltown Road, the windows steamed over and running with condensation. Inside, the air was hot and damp, the waitress pink-cheeked and harassed as she moved between tables, slapping a hand away as someone tried to pinch her. The customers were mostly working men, labourers in their dirty clothes and overalls, hands black with grease. One old chap, in need of a shave, eked out a cup of tea. And one more who looked out of place in his fancy checked cap and double-breasted suit, leaning back and crossing his ankles to show off gaudy diamond-patterned socks and brown-and-white co-respondent shoes. He was reading a news-paper, yet another headline about the king and Mrs Simpson. What other story was there to grab the nation? Certainly not the damned Depression; that was old news.

Noble ate heartily. Raven pushed his food around the plate and brooded. Was Marjorie seeing someone? It wouldn't surprise him. After all, there wasn't much love at home. He couldn't even begin to guess who it was. As he passed the Shaftesbury that morning on the tram, he'd glanced at the marquee. *Swing Time* was playing. But she'd never make a mistake on something as simple as that.

It was all wrong, that was the heart of it. He didn't understand *why* it had fallen apart, where all the love had gone. He hadn't changed. He didn't think he had, anyway. And everything had been fine in the beginning. Had he been deluding himself all this time, seeing what he wanted to see and not the truth? Was it the gap that had grown between them since the miscarriages? Or had she woken up one morning and noticed him as he really was, with all the grafts and the scars? He didn't know. He'd probably never have the answer and it gnawed at him, took his appetite and soured his mood. But even if her love was over, divorce wasn't an option. Her family would never understand; neither would his. Film stars got divorced. The rich. Not people like them. They were together for life. And he still cared about her. He still loved her.

What was he going to do? Follow her one night to catch a glimpse of her with someone? Discover who the man was and beat seven bells out of him?

Christ, what the hell was he thinking? That would be two seconds of satisfaction and a lifetime of regret. Marjorie would find out, and if the brass at work learned about it… No, he couldn't do it.

What then? Ignore it? After all, it wasn't so much the fact she might have someone else that hurt. It was the hammer against his pride, the thought that he wasn't enough for her.

'Sarge.'

'What?' For once he was glad to be drawn out of his thoughts. They were far too bleak.

'We should get back to work.'

He tossed Noble the keys to the Riley. 'You go out to the car. I'll pay.'

The café was almost empty. Raven left some coins on the table, picked up his trilby, then sat down across from the man with the two-tone shoes.

'Hello Harry. Fancy seeing you here.'

Close to, the material of the man's suit was shiny, the tailoring poor and badly cut. Flash Harry Andrews. He lived up to his name. At least he tried to, doing it all on the cheap.

'Hello, Mr Raven.' He tried to sound surprised, as if he hadn't noticed the policemen. 'I wouldn't have thought this was your type of place.'

'We get everywhere these days. What about you? Staying out of trouble?'

'Always.' The man grinned to show a set of brown, stained teeth. 'You haven't seen me down in the cells, have you?'

Over the years, Andrews had been in and out of jail more often than some people had hot dinners. Pickpocketing, running a con, a record littered with small offences and time in prison. But he was right, nothing recently.

'You can't be going straight.'

Andrews didn't answer, just smiled and tapped the side of his nose.

'I don't care, I've got bigger fish than you,' Raven told him. 'Unless you know something about the murder in Holbeck on Sunday, that is.' He started to rise.

'I might do.'

'Is that right?' The sergeant lowered himself back onto the chair. 'And what do you know, Harry?'

'Just things I've heard, that's all.' He shifted on the seat. 'Nothing specific.'

'Why don't you go ahead and tell me. Think of it as paying back for all those times I didn't arrest you.'

'But—' Harry began, then stopped himself as he saw Raven's grim expression. 'Look, it's just stuff people said.'

The sergeant waited, saying nothing, just staring.

'Someone told me it had to be someone whose money Benson docked.'

'Names?'

Andrews shook his head. 'No one said.'

'Go out and start asking some questions.' He should have known better. Flash Harry was never going to give him anything of value.

*

'I thought you'd got lost,' Noble said. He was behind the wheel, looking proud, a Woodbine dangling from his lip.

'Might as well have. What else do we have?' he asked in frustration.

'Nothing, Sarge. Sorry.'

Of course. Dead ends. No one seemed to like Frank Benson, certainly not the people whose relief he cut. Not even his own family. Unloved; it wasn't much of a legacy. Not that his own would be much better. Anyhow, they hadn't unearthed anyone who seemed like a murderer.

'We might as well go back to the station.'

*

Mortimer was talking to the superintendent, the office door closed. Raven sorted through the papers on his desk. Some came from older cases, items he'd never filed. Bits and pieces. And sitting in the middle of the blotter, an envelope, with his name and the headquarters address in a flowing, feminine script.

No one had ever written to him here before.

He held it with a handkerchief as he slit the top with a letter opener, in case it was evidence. The sergeant pulled out the letter with his fountain pen. A good cream bond, thick, crisply folded.

Dear Sergeant Raven,

I have more information about my father that might be of use to you. I should be grateful if you could call on me so I can give it to you.

Sincerely,

Ava Benson

He read it through again, astonished, then glanced around. No one was watching. Quickly, he folded the letter, slid it back into the envelope and placed it in the inside pocket of his jacket, as if it was a secret he wanted to keep.

She could have telephoned the station and asked for him. That would have been simple enough. He tried to make sense of her. What was she thinking? She couldn't... he stopped before the thought could flower into something awkward. Don't be so bloody stupid. Her father had been murdered, the body was hardly cold. She was probably just feeling lost.

'I'm going out for a while,' he told Noble.

'Want me to come, Sarge?'

'No, it's fine. You write up the report on this morning and tell them about it.' He nodded towards the superintendent's door.

*

She had a cardigan gathered around her shoulders, arms crossed over her chest.

'I got your letter,' Raven said. 'You said you've thought of something else?'

'That's right. Come in.'

He glanced up the stairs. 'How's your mother?'

'Sleeping again. The doctor says it's the best thing for her.'

'What about you?'

'I'll be fine.' She pinched her lips together and dismissed the question.

All he could do was nod and follow her through to the kitchen, watching as she went through the ritual of making tea. He heard the whistle of a train leaving Headingley station and through the window a plume of steam rising off in the distance.

'What did you have to tell me?' he asked as they sat.

'My father... I told you he bullied us.'

'Yes.'

She held his gaze for a long time, as if she was on the edge of something. Finally she looked away for a second, then said, 'He'd argue with our neighbours, too.' She was nervous, fidgeting like a child, unable to keep still.

'Go on,' Raven said. This wasn't why she'd dragged him out here, he was sure of that. But he'd sit and listen; there might be a germ of something in it.

'It was often about stupid little things. As if he had to be better than them.'

The police hadn't talked to anyone along the street. Perhaps they needed men out here to conduct a few interviews. A few more people Benson might have angered. And in the right circumstances, with a good opportunity, anyone could be capable of murder.

'Anyone in particular?' he asked, watching her face and seeing her blush at the attention.

'Mr Dobson, two doors down. Daddy seemed to find fault with everything he did, although it wasn't any of his business. A couple of others, too.'

He took down the details in his notebook, asking more questions. But that was all she was giving. There was something else, he could sense it. Whether she'd ever let it see the light of day was another matter. Still, the information was useful, something new, a fresh avenue to pursue; God knew they needed one.

'Thank you,' he said as she finished, picking up his trilby. 'That's very helpful.'

She beamed. 'I thought of it. It seemed like it might be important.'

'It's possible,' he agreed.

'If I think of anything else, I'll write again.' There was a shrill edge to her voice, and her eyes were oddly bright.

'Yes,' he told her. 'Please do.' A pointed glance at his watch. 'I'm sorry, I need to go.'

He could sense her disappointment.

'Wouldn't you like more tea?'

*

Noble breathed a long sigh of relief as he drove away. At first he'd thought Ava Benson was a kind, sympathetic girl. Now… he was simply glad to be out of there. She seemed to be balanced on a very fine edge. Maybe it was her father's death. Perhaps she was that way naturally. More likely the cause was whatever the darker thing was that she hadn't talked about.

Back at headquarters, he gave her letter to Mortimer, along with a summary of what she'd told him. All in the open, above board. The inspector gave him a long, curious look, but said nothing.

'We should get Noble and the other DCs out there tonight, sir.'

'We will.' He scratched a note on a pad, one more on a long list. Mortimer looked rumpled, surrounded by papers. There were creases in his suit and the collar of his shirt was grubby, a tidemark showing on his neck. He reached into a drawer and drew out a sheet of paper in a cellophane bag. 'Take a look at this. It came in the second post.'

I kilt Benson.

Found him, choked him.

You know were you found him. I put him there.

He had it cuming.

Threw away the cord. It ws from a lamp.

Raven read it through twice then placed it carefully back on the desk. 'Any prints?' he asked and saw Mortimer shake his head.

'Nothing. No clue from the envelope, either, it was sent from the central post office.'

'The spelling mistakes…'

'I know,' the inspector agreed. 'They seem a little too neat, don't they? Look at the handwriting – it's good and firm.'

'There are things here that weren't in the papers.' The use of a flex, there'd been no mention of that; it was one fact the police were keeping to themselves. There'd been no mention of exactly where Benson had been found, either. Anyone with that knowledge had either committed the murder or managed to learn a few things. He gazed down at the note. 'It's him, isn't it?'

'That's what we think. Superintendent Kennedy's over at the Civic Hall with the chief constable right now.' He tapped the letter with a nicotine-stained finger. 'We're keeping very quiet about this. If anyone asks, it doesn't exist, you don't know anything about it.'

'Understood, sir.' He glanced at it again, but the words were already carved in his memory. Taunting them, daring them to try and catch him. How did they even start?

'There was more about Benson in the *Post* this morning. Tips have been coming in. Go through and sort out the possibles, then follow them up.'

*

Twenty-nine of them already, and still counting. He shuffled them into two piles. Sixteen went straight in the bin. Raven took his time over the others, reading and thinking before he discarded half of them.

The remainder looked credible. Nothing definite about any of them, but worth following up. He finished as Noble walked in, still wearing his raincoat.

'Don't take it off,' Raven told him. 'We're going out.'

*

'Where did you go this morning, Sarge?' Noble stared out at the water as Raven drove across Crown Point Bridge into Hunslet.

'A lead. Put those papers into some sort of order, will you? We'll start in Stourton.'

Queen Street. A row of terraced houses, bricks blackened by soot from the railway engines and all the works that stood close by. This had probably been a bustling area once, the sergeant thought as he locked the Riley. Now it barely looked alive, like so many places in Leeds. The city seemed to be slowly running out of breath. It was almost enough to make anyone hope the faint talk of war would grow louder. Maybe then the place would thrive again. But what would the cost of that be?

The small front garden at number twenty-seven was overgrown. Tufts of grass, weeds, vines climbing over flowers and shrubs. Someone had stopped caring. He stood aside as Noble knocked on the door.

The man who answered stood no more than five feet three. A jumper over his shirt and tie, thinning sandy hair Brylcreemed flat, blinking behind spectacles. Easily sixty years old and definitely not strong enough or tall enough to choke anyone.

'Mr Thompson?'

'Yes?' he said suspiciously. 'Who are you?'

'We're from Leeds City Police, sir.' Raven took over, showing his warrant card. 'Peter Thompson?'

'That's right.' He was confused. 'What do you want?'

'I'm sorry, sir. I think we've been given the wrong information. Unless you have a son called Peter who lives here.'

'No.'

Raven lifted his hat. 'I'm sorry we disturbed you.'

One down, he thought as he closed the gate. Five more to go.

Three more tips offered nothing better than Thompson. Dismissed in a moment with an apology. The remaining two had a little more substance, but a few questions and Raven knew they had nothing to do with the murder.

Back to square one, he thought as he shifted through the gears past the football ground on Elland Road. A waste of bloody time, he thought angrily. There'd be more tips waiting back at the office, too. This was the part of the job that he hated, the mundane and the plodding, digging and digging in the hope of finding a tiny nugget of gold.

It all came alive as soon as he had the scent, once there was something to follow. It didn't matter if it was a burglary, an assault, even a picked pocket, when he knew he was on the right track, everything moved faster, every colour seemed brighter. It was stupid, he knew that, but it had been that way since he started on the beat.

*

By half past five he'd had enough. Not a single one of the leads had amounted to anything. The constables sent out to talk to Benson's neighbours confirmed what the man's daughter had said. He was pushy, argumentative. But everyone on the street was in shock at his murder.

The letter they'd received was back in Inspector Mortimer's drawer, carefully locked away. It had come from the killer. He felt it. As soon as he read the words, they buzzed through him like an electric current. That was the man they needed to find.

How they'd do that was a different matter.

*

He was waiting in the Pointer at six when Johnny Harris walked in, rolling his shoulders as he tried to work all the stiffness from his body after a long shift. Raven had two pints of Tetley's bitter waiting on the bar, and pushed one across as Harris flexed his fingers then raised the glass and drank off the top two inches.

'That's better. Wash away the taste of the bosses.'

Raven sipped, enjoying the sharp taste.

'All done for another day,' he said. 'Trying to keep Leeds safe.' He swallowed more and sighed. 'You know why I'm back.'

Harris took out a tin of tobacco and some papers, rolling a cigarette and lighting it before he replied.

'I told you I'd pass the word, get people asking questions.'

'I know.'

'I've done it. It takes time, Urban.' Harris blew out smoke. 'Nothing happens overnight. You'd know that if you had any interest in politics.'

'Murder happens in an instant. Death. Theft…'

'Leave it,' Johnny said angrily. 'It's been a long day. Orders are down. They're talking about getting rid of more people at the factory.'

'I'm sorry.'

'You know capitalism has had its day, don't you?' His voice was serious. 'When the last few years are the best it's given us, how can anyone still believe in it?'

'John…' Raven began, then shook his head. There was no point. Every conversation with Harris always ended up on politics.

'These are people I've worked with for years and they're looking at being unemployed. *That's* real. And it's terrifying. There's a fair chance I'll be one of them, Urban.' Harris gave a small, hard laugh. 'God knows they'd love to be rid of me.'

What could he say? It might not come to that? They both knew the truth. They'd seen it every day over the last seven years. So many men on the dole, haunted eyes on the street corners. An increase in crime, even as hope ebbed away. Any way to feed their families.

Raven drank more. 'I'm under pressure to find Benson's killer.'

'I told you I'd let you know if I heard anything.' There were sparks of worry and fury in his eyes. Urban downed the rest of the beer, clapped Harris on the shoulder, and left. It was better to let it lie. Johnny would do as he promised, and he had enough on his mind at the moment.

Raven just wanted to have some answers.

*

For once they had a pleasant evening. Marjorie had tea ready five minutes after he came through the door. Liver and onions with gravy, a big mound of mashed potatoes. She was in a friendly mood. No snide comments, no digs or innuendoes, and when he searched her eyes for any traces of unfaithfulness, he found nothing.

They played cards, pontoon for matchsticks, laughing at Elsie and Doris Waters on the wireless. For a few hours, he forgot his doubts about her and remembered the happiness they'd enjoyed.

In bed, he watched as she struggled out of the girdle, and those sensual moments as she rolled down her stockings. After that, though, came the reversion to years of being married. The odd, flat intimacies. Cold cream on her face. A hairnet and rollers so the soft curls stayed. The flannel nightgown. A hug and a kiss on the lips. Maybe it wasn't much, he thought as he lay with the light off, but it was more than many had. Perhaps he ought to count his blessings. A sad testament, though, when this was one of their better nights together.

Still, he realised he hadn't thought about Frank Benson.

Six

RAVEN STARED AT the letter again, paper behind cellophane.

I kilt Benson. Found him, choked him.

He sat, he thought, trying to read through the words. On the way to headquarters he'd stopped at the barber's on George Street for a trim, and stray hairs itched against his collar.

Kilt.

'Kilt.'

'What?' Superintendent Kennedy asked. He was going over a list of names with Mortimer.

'The misspelling.'

'What about it?'

'I don't believe it. *Were* for where, *cuming* for coming, *ws* for was. It feels wrong. He's trying to make us think he's stupid.'

'I thought that was what we agreed yesterday,' Mortimer said. 'But I'm not sure exactly why he's doing it.'

'So we underestimate him? To send us looking in the wrong direction?' He didn't really know. The note was anonymous enough, no chance of using it to trace the killer.

'All well and good.' The superintendent took his pipe and fiddled with his matches, blowing smoke into the air. 'How do we catch him?'

That was the real crux of the matter. They had to find the bastard. The sergeant looked down at his shoes. Thick, heavy soles. A copper's shoes. Black, shiny. He'd polished them that morning until the leather glowed.

'I honestly don't know, sir,' he admitted. 'I wish I did.'

'So do I.' Kennedy looked at them. 'Well, gentlemen, let's put our heads together and see what we can do.'

*

'How many more leads from the newspaper story?' he asked Noble.

'Another twenty, Sarge.' He passed over letters, notes, slips of paper with scribbled words, messages taken over the telephone. Raven sorted through them, discarding several immediately. He took time over the others, drinking a cup of tea as he worked. Four remained. He dangled the car keys.

'Ready?'

At first it seemed like a repeat of yesterday. From address to address, criss-crossing Leeds and finding nothing worthwhile. The last was in Armley, a hidden lane off Town Street, cobbles running down towards a park. Six labourers' cottages stood in a terrace at right angles to the road. Raven parked, the engine still running.

'Quite pretty, aren't they?'

'I suppose so, Sarge.'

No more than fifty yards from a busy road and yet all the sounds seemed muffled and distant. The houses were well tended, the windows clean, the paint bright. The kind of place that made coming home a joy.

The place they wanted was at the far end. Raven waited, standing back as Noble knocked, surveying it all. The click of the lock and a tug on the door as it was dragged open, then a young man stood there, a curious smile on his face.

'Can I help you?'

It was nothing strange to find a man home during the day. Too many of them without work and no money to go anywhere or do anything. Their wives might have a job, or their children. This one, though... there was something about him, Raven thought.

'Mr Raymond Gill?'

'That's right.' The man looked from one of them to the other. The coppers were both big, broad men. He was smaller, much younger, no more than eighteen, with glasses and the start of a moustache to try and make himself look older. 'What can I do for you?'

'Detective Sergeant Raven and DC Noble, sir. We're with Leeds City Police. Could we have a word? In private might be best.'

Inside, the house was neat but spare.

'Who lives here, sir?' Raven asked.

'My parents and my brothers.' He blushed with embarrassment. 'They're at work.'

'And yourself, sir?'

Gill shook his head and shrugged, a universal language.

'Can you tell me where you were on Sunday?' Noble said.

'Me?' A small flash of irritation in his eyes. 'Why?'

'If you'd just answer the question, please, sir.' Raven smiled as he spoke, trying to take the sting from the words. But there was still menace in his voice.

'I went to hear Mosley speak.' He straightened his back and set his jaw. 'What about it?'

'Plenty of people there,' Noble pointed out. 'A lot of fighting.'

'I kept away from that.'

65

'Tell me, sir, do you know someone called Frank Benson?' Raven asked.

For a second Gill looked confused, as if he knew the name but couldn't place it. Then his face cleared.

'He's the one who was murdered, isn't he?'

'That's right.'

'Why would I know him? I don't understand.'

'Someone said you were talking to him.'

Gill's surprise was genuine; he was certain of that. But surprise at what? Being seen and reported to the police? Or that he talked to someone who was dead a few hours later?

'I talked to a few people. I was scared. I didn't ask their names.'

Raven took Benson's photograph from his pocket.

'Did you talk to this man?'

'Maybe. I don't know.' He'd barely glanced at it before looking away.

'Mr Gill.' His voice was firm. 'Where were you when you talked to him?'

The man's defences collapsed.

'City Square. We marched out to Holbeck together. As soon as people began throwing things, I ran.' He hesitated, as if he didn't want to admit his cowardice. 'I never even got halfway to the moor.'

'What about Benson?' He waved the picture.

'He left when I did,' Gill admitted. 'He was scared too.'

'Where was this?' he pressed. 'What happened after?'

'I don't know. I've never been over that way before. We didn't get too far. I saw someone bleeding after a stone hit them.'

'Where did Benson go? Was he with you?'

Gill shook his head. 'I don't know. I just ran.' His eyes glistened on the edge of tears. Raven believed him. No amateur could be that good an actor.

They asked more questions, trying to pull out a few details, but Gill had been too fearful to pay attention. Benson might have talked to other people; he didn't remember. Once he started running, he kept going until he was back in the city centre, breathless but safe. He'd seen the newspaper stories about Benson but he'd never come forward because he didn't think his story was important.

There was little Gill remembered about Holbeck and where they might have been. No landmarks in his mind; his only aim was to get out of there unhurt. Still, he'd seen Benson, he'd talked to him – about their admiration for Mosley, the terrible way the country was going – and he could place the man over in Holbeck and still alive. That was much more than they'd had before.

'Did you notice anyone watching Mr Benson?' Raven softened his voice, watching carefully.

'No. Not that I saw.'

Never mind. At least they weren't leaving empty-handed.

'If you think of anything else, get in touch with us.'

*

'I'd say he's telling the truth.'

'I'm sure he is.' Raven made the tight three-point turn, letting out the clutch and easing over the cobbles back to Town Street and the clatter and hum of busy Leeds. The noise, the people, it felt like a jolt. Advertisements for Fry's Chocolate, Carnation Evaporated Milk, and the latest attractions at the music halls were plastered to every wall. The only colours in a drab, sad city. 'I'd love to know how far into Holbeck they got.'

'No one over there remembers Benson,' Noble said. At least the lad was receiving an education in the frustration of CID with this case.

'Someone bloody well does – whoever killed him.'

*

Two notes waited on his blotter in the desk sergeant's neat handwriting. Johnny had rung but refused to leave a message, and Harry wanted to see him. Raven looked at his watch. Twenty-five past eleven. Another hour and Flash Harry would be at the General Elliott on New Market Street. Before that he might be anywhere. And he wouldn't be able to see Johnny Harris until the man's shift ended this evening.

Hurry up and wait. And try not to think about Marjorie and her fancy man.

Noble was writing up the report on the morning. A few more tips from the newspaper article were waiting. Raven leafed through them idly, stopping at the last one, then stuffing it in his jacket pocket.

'Dan,' he called to Noble. 'Leave that.'

*

'Where are we going?' Noble asked as they pulled out of Alexander Street, along the Headrow and down Eastgate. Ahead of him lay the skeleton arch for Quarry Hill flats. Soon enough the buildings would rise, half a mile of frontage following the curve of the road. He'd seen the drawings but he still couldn't imagine it.

'A name I know on one of those tips. He's a bit of a fighter.'

'A strangler?'

'Probably not,' Raven answered after he considered the question. 'Not from behind, anyway. But someone seems to think he knows something.'

The constable pulled the brass knuckles from his pocket.

'I'm still prepared.'

If the lad believed those would make a difference he still had plenty to learn. Raven had lost his idealism – he couldn't even remember when. Probably even before he joined the force. But seeing so much misery day after day you learned just what sods human beings could really be.

'Hopefully he'll co-operate without a fuss.'

*

His surname was White; of course, everyone called him Chalky. A nickname as predictable as the rain in summer. Or at the end of September. The first drops arrived as he parked in Cross Green. Raven grabbed his mackintosh off the back seat, while Noble looked hapless.

'I thought you were prepared?'

The younger man snorted.

The house stood on the corner of East Park Road, above the railway cutting and just round the corner from the smudged, scrubby grass of the park. Raven hammered on the door, then stood back two paces. He knew Chalky White all too well.

The man filled the space, big, heavy. His belly hung over his trousers, the braces straining against his shoulders, feet bare.

'You'd better have a bloody good reason for trying to knock down me door.' He made his right hand into a fist. From the corner of his eye, Raven saw Noble reach into his pocket.

'You know me better than that. I'd never come calling on you unless I had to, Chalky.' The sergeant shook his head sadly. 'If you want to act like a pillock, I'll treat you like one. Your choice.' He hadn't raised his voice. He didn't need to. They'd gone at it once before and White had been the loser. But there was always the chance he'd want revenge…

'Right enough.' The man shrugged and turned away, leaving the door open as an invitation. It was an untidy place, but Mrs White had never been much of a housekeeper. As long as she was working and handed over her wage, why would Chalky care?

'Sunday,' Raven said.

'Eh?' He scratched at his scalp, then examined his fingernails. 'What do you mean?'

'Where were you on Sunday?'

'I don't know.' His fingers hunted around a crowded ashtray, looking for a tab end with some tobacco left. White found one, lit it with a match and blew out a stream of smoke, satisfied. 'Why?'

'Not over in Holbeck?'

A sly smile. 'Well, yes, course. For Mosley.'

'You know someone was killed there.'

'I didn't do it.'

'I know that. It wasn't your style, Chalky,' Raven told him, and the man looked surprised.

'What then?'

'Did you see him?' He brought out the photograph. 'This man.'

'Maybe.' He looked again. 'I don't know, I'm not much on faces. I talked to some people.'

'He ran off once things got rough.'

'No, then,' White said. 'The lads I was with, we were out for a good scrap. No time for cowards. I might have had a word in City Square,' he added, not sure. 'I don't know.'

'Someone says you did.'

'Oh aye?' He cocked his head. Suddenly there was an edge of aggression around him again. 'Who?'

'Anonymous, Chalkie.'

The man nodded, as if he was used to it.

'That it?' he asked.

'Unless you've anything else. Any crimes you want to confess?'

White frowned. 'I never know when you're joking, Mr Raven.' He glanced at Noble. 'Better tell your oppo not to keep his hand in his pocket. Someone could belt him into next week by the time he took it out.'

*

'Take the car.' He tossed Noble the keys. 'I have to see someone.'

'When will you be back, Sarge?'

'Shouldn't be too long.'

A quarter of an hour later, he pushed opened the door of the General Elliott public house. Dust motes fluttered through the air. The place was half dead, a scattering of customers around the small room, the door to the upstairs closed. A thin fire burned in the grate.

Harry had his elbows on the bar, a half of mild in front of him. Raven could remember a time when the pub had been busy every minute it was open, working men out for a cheap pint. How many had the price of a drink these days? Back then you could walk into this place, say you wanted something from the market and five minutes later a boy would deliver it, freshly nicked from a stall. All history now.

'Give him another,' Raven said. 'Lemonade for me.' The landlord's glance made him for a copper and he gave a small nod. After the drinks arrived, they moved to the corner, looking out through a grimy window at New Market Street.

'You rang me, Harry.'

'I heard something. You wanted me to keep my ears open.' He paused. 'Thought it might be worth a bob or two.'

'Tell me what it is and I'll let you know.'

'I was talking to some people I know.' It was the way he always began, as if it was how he learned anything. He glanced around to make sure no one could overhear. 'They said that Benson had talked to the Blackshirts about joining.'

'Who told you that?' Joining was quite a step up from going to hear Mosley speak.

'People I know.' There was greed in its eyes. 'Important, is it?'

'Depends if it's true.'

'Why would I lie?' Harry sounded hurt.

'Because you're a conniving bastard who'd sell his mum for a couple of bob.' It was the truth and they both knew it.

'Cross my heart.'

'Who told you?' Raven repeated.

'Not saying.'

The sergeant shook his head. 'Harry…'

'I can't, Mr Raven. I can't.'

*

Two and sixpence. That was what it cost him, and worth the money if the information was true. He'd claim it back from the force; they had a kitty for paying narks.

Sitting in the detectives' room, Raven told Mortimer, Kennedy, and the detective constables what he'd learned.

'We need confirmation,' the superintendent said. 'I wouldn't take Harry's word on the time if he was staring at the Town Hall clock.'

*

It was beginning to feel like a routine. Six o'clock, waiting in the Pointer, two pints sitting on a table. Harris saw him as soon as he entered, marching over and sitting down.

'Every time I talk to you I feel like I'm consorting with the enemy.' He lifted the glass and drained half of it in a single swallow. 'You enforce the oppression of the masses.'

Raven was never going to be sure just how serious Johnny was with statements like that. He kept his face straight but there was an air of self-mockery in his voice.

'And I keep a certain communist in his evening beer. You left a message for me.'

Harris nodded. 'I put the word out like I promised. But no one said they even saw the man, let alone laid a hand on him.' He held up a hand as Raven opened his mouth. 'I know, none of them are likely to admit murder. But I can hardly go round every one of them and ask, can I, Urban?'

'I appreciate it, Johnny.'

'If I come up with anything, I'll let you know.'

'Heard anything more on your job?'

'Not yet.' Harris had a grim expression. 'Probably a note in my pay packet on Friday. That's how they do it. They can't even look us in the eye like men and tell us.'

'I hope it's not you.'

Johnny grunted. 'If not me, then it's someone else. The only thing that's saved me so far is that I'm skilled. If we owned the factory ourselves...'

'You still couldn't find orders when no one wants boots.'

'Capitalism.' Harris spat the word.

'It's what we've got.'

'For now.'

'If it was going to change, it would have happened a few years ago.' Probably back in 1931, when it seemed like every other man in Britain was out of work and the sense of desperation was so strong that revolution seemed like a real possibility. Things were a little better now. In some places, at least. And where they were bad, a sense of numbness covered everything, of sleepwalking towards death.

'I'm not giving up hope.' Harris finished the drink, went to the bar and returned with two more. 'I was talking to Paul.' His brother, the man Raven had known since they were toddlers. 'He said he hasn't seen you in too long.'

'Police work.' He shrugged. It was always a good excuse, and sometimes it was even true. It hid the fact that he and Marjorie never saw many people these days; it was easier.

'He says you still owe him a drink.' Harris grinned.

'He can keep thinking that.' Raven laughed. They'd had a bet on where Leeds United would finish in the First Division two years before. Paul Harris had predicted eighth, Raven tenth. The club had finished ninth; Paul insisted he'd won the bet. 'Tell him I'll be in touch.'

'Do that, Urban.' He sank his pint rapidly and stood. 'And look after yourself.'

*

He stayed for a third drink, then walked back to catch the tram. The newspapers were still full of the scandal about the king and Wallis Simpson, as if the drama and glamour of royalty could make the reality of poverty go away. Would he abdicate and marry her?

Did it even matter, he wondered? So many out of work and hungry and they wrote about this. Bread and circuses, Johnny had called it. Distractions from the way everything had failed. Raven skipped through the pages. A small item about another planned march of the unemployed from Jarrow to London. He wished them well, but none of the petitions or gatherings had changed anything yet. The government left the North to rot and coppers like him had to clean up the mess that was left.

*

'Don't forget we're going to my parents' house for Sunday dinner,' Raven said as they ate. Polony with salad – a couple of leaves of lettuce, slices of tomato and cucumber, with a dab of salad cream. A summer meal, although the days had already drifted off into autumn.

'How can I?' Marjorie asked. She'd wrinkled her nose when he came home, smelling the beer on him, but still let him kiss her cheek and smiled to see him. 'We go every month.'

It had been that way since their wedding. Edith, Raven's sister, would be there, along with her husband, Ken. He'd done well for himself, rising from salesman to become the area manager for Dunlop. The bad times hadn't touched him. They had a house out in the wide, green streets of Alwoodley, along with a big Humber motor car. A chauffeur to drive it, too, since Ken needed thick glasses to see; his poor vision had kept him out of the war, safe at home as a special constable.

Every time Raven saw him, he felt a twinge of envy. Ken Browning was prosperous, growing pudgy, with two children, both in their teens. No scars on his face and body. But when had life ever been fair? His sister was happy with her husband; that was what counted. He'd forgive Ken a great deal as long as he kept Edith satisfied.

Sunday was still a few days away. Plenty to do before then. It would mark a week since Benson's murder. Like a clock constantly ticking in the background and the longer it dragged on, the smaller the chances of finding the killer.

The murder was still in the papers, but it had moved below the fold. The chief constable kept bluffing in his interviews. The police were following several lines of inquiry. True enough. What he never revealed was that none of them were leading anywhere.

'You're miles away.' Marjorie's voice made him blink.

'Sorry. I was thinking about work.'

'I said there's some fruit salad and custard for a sweet if you want it.'

Raven glanced down. Not a scrap of food left on his plate. He didn't even remember eating.

'Yes,' he answered with a smile. 'I'd like that.'

Reading, slivers of conversation while the wireless played a concert of classical music in the background. They could almost have been a normal couple, he thought. Finally, just after ten, Marjorie put down her copy of *Picture Post*.

'I'm going to bed.'

'I'll join you.'

'Oh,' she said, 'I forgot to tell you: I'm going out with Fran tomorrow night. We're off to the Paramount to see that new Cary Grant film.'

'I'll pick up some fish and chips on the way home.' Was that the reason for being so pleasant tonight? So she could nip off to see her fella tomorrow?

In the bedroom he watched her undress and slip into the nightgown, not sure what was going through his mind and not trusting his emotions. He was a policeman, a detective; it was his job to be suspicious. But… Marjorie could be telling the truth. She might simply be enjoying a trip to the cinema with Fran.

He saw the pale skin on her back as she removed the blouse, the red marks from the girdle. A moment later the nightgown fluttered over her head and covered everything. Soon enough her breathing settled into a gentle rhythm. But Raven stayed awake, asking himself questions and discovering no satisfactory answers.

*

'So the communists say it wasn't one of theirs who killed him.'

'That's right, sir,' Raven told the superintendent. 'But my contact knows that doesn't mean a thing.'

'Just as well.' Kennedy lit his pipe, raising a fug of smoke around his head. He turned to Mortimer. 'Anything more on this idea of Benson joining the Blackshirts yet?'

The inspector sighed. 'Not yet, sir. I'm working on it.'

'Push people if you have to. I want to know if it's true.' He looked at his watch and walked out.

Sometimes the police never get their man. There was a murder back in 1927 that was still on the books, more if he went back further. They were the failures that they all tried to forget but everyone remembered. Time to go and do some work. With a nod, he signalled Noble to follow him out of the office.

'Where are we off to, Sarge?' he asked as they walked out to the car.

'We'll do some digging and see what turns up.'

He was just starting to unlock the door of the Riley when a shout came from the back door of the building. The inspector, face so pale it was almost white.

'I've just had the Bensons' neighbour on the blower. The daughter's vanished. Didn't sleep in her bed last night.'

Seven

A UNIFORMED COPPER stood outside the house. In the kitchen, a woman police constable was sitting with Mrs Benson, trying to find out the details. Raven beckoned to her.

'What's she told you?'

'Not much, Sarge,' she said. 'The girl, Ava, was here yesterday evening. The mother went to bed at half past ten. The daughter stayed up to listen to the wireless. Everything seemed fine this morning. An hour ago, Mrs Benson went to wake the girl so she wouldn't be late for work. Bed was made, nothing disturbed, but no sign of the girl. She's not gone into her job. We've checked.'

'Any clothes missing?'

The WPC blushed. 'I haven't got to that yet. Sorry, sir. But Mrs Benson's upset.'

'Take her to check,' Raven ordered. 'Also see if any suitcase or bag is gone.'

'Yes, Sarge.'

'We're going to do all we can,' he assured Mrs Benson. 'Don't you worry, we'll find her.'

'Look around,' he told Noble as soon as the WPC had escorted the woman upstairs. 'See if you can turn up anything down here.'

Five minutes of going through the rooms, the detective constable checking the cellar, and they'd come up with nothing beyond a snapshot in an album. A year old, he judged, but a fair likeness. Raven slid it into his pocket and climbed the stairs to see Mrs Benson sitting on the single bed in the back room, the wardrobe door wide open. The female constable raised an eyebrow and gave a small shake of her head.

'I need to ask you a few questions,' he said softly as he touched the woman's arm. She recoiled quickly, then looked up at him.

'I'm sorry.' Mrs Benson squinted, trying to place him. 'You're the one who was in the war.'

'That's right. Do you know where Ava might have gone? Or why?'

'No.' She blinked, confusion and fear in her eyes. Hardly surprising. Someone had killed her husband and now her daughter had vanished. And she'd been on a precipice when he saw her before. 'She's always been a good girl. Always home at night.'

'What about her friends?' Raven asked.

'I've got some names,' the constable said. 'Ava's suitcase is still on top of the wardrobe and Mrs Benson says there don't seem to be any clothes or underwear missing.'

He could ask more questions, but he knew he wasn't likely to get much information from the woman. Almost half past nine: Ava Benson had last been seen eleven hours earlier. She could be almost anywhere in Britain by now. A sudden thought made him stop.

'How much money did your daughter have with her?'

'I don't know. She hands over most of her wages.'

'Is there any other money in the house? In a jar, something like that?'

'We keep a little in the biscuit tin.' Mrs Benson frowned. 'It's never more than a few bob. For emergencies.'

When he checked it was empty.

'Stay with her,' he said to the WPC. 'I don't expect you'll get anything, but do what you can.' He gave her a sympathetic smile. 'Maybe the girl will just come home.'

'Do you believe that, Sarge?'

'Not really,' he admitted. 'But it sounds better than saying we have no idea where to look.' He turned away, then back. 'You'll get a few reporters sniffing around once word gets out.' He raised his eyes to the bedroom and Mrs Benson. 'For God's sake keep them away from her.'

'Yes, Sarge.'

*

'Where do we start?' Noble asked as they drove back into town.

'I don't know. I wish I bloody did.' He banged his hand against the steering wheel. 'Damn the woman. Now we have to find her as well.'

'She's of age, Sarge. You don't think she's a suspect, do you?'

Raven shook his head. 'No. But it doesn't matter, does it? Not in this case. Can you imagine the outcry in the papers if we do nothing? *Murder Victim Daughter Vanishes.* They'd hang us out to dry. We don't have any choice.'

As soon as he had the photograph and the facts, Mortimer sent out the uniforms. Railway station, bus station, the girl's friends. Waking the ticket office staff who'd been working the night before to see if they recalled Ava Benson's face. Noble went with another detective constable to talk to the girl's colleagues at work and see if they had suggestions.

'What about me?' Raven asked.

'You're with me again,' the inspector said. 'Nothing much you can do about the girl until we know more. I've got an address for one of the head men from the local Blackshirt branch. Andrew Reynolds.'

'Who?'

'He was a businessman,' Mortimer answered. 'Insurance, I think. Something like that. Retired now.' He started the Riley and adjusted the choke until the engine sounded solid. 'Lives in Alwoodley.'

*

The inspector drove as if it made him uncomfortable. He was wary, slow, too cautious by half. Going through Sheepscar, they passed a group of men in old clothes standing around a fire in a metal barrel on a corner, nowhere better to go.

'The dead on leave,' Mortimer said, so softly he could have been talking to himself.

'What, sir?'

'Something my wife heard on the wireless.' He gave a quick smile and a shake of his head. 'Someone was talking about all the unemployed. Said they were like the dead on leave. It struck me, that's all.'

It was good, Raven had to agree. But it wasn't just those without jobs. What about the fools and the cuckolds? They lived in that same sad, shifting world, too.

He glanced up the hill to Little London. That was what they called the area, but none of the streets were paved with gold. Instead, plenty of the cobbles were missing and fully half the houses were slums. Dilapidated, in need of knocking down, like so much of Leeds. Happen somebody would drag the whole city into the twentieth century before it was halfway over.

*

Reynolds had money, no doubt about that. His house was hidden behind a glossy privet hedge and a gardener marched up and down the grass with his lawnmower. Mock Tudor beams fanned across the front of the building, trying to give a sense of history and solidity. This was another world. Insulated and moneyed. Untouched by poverty.

A maid to answer the door. A parlour to receive visitors. And finally Mr Reynolds himself. His hair was smooth and expensively cut, and he wore flannels with a sharp crease, with a blazer that came from a good tailor. But the effusive, welcoming manner didn't match the black eye and the scrapes on his knuckles; his souvenirs of Holbeck Moor.

'I'm not sure what I've done to warrant the police calling,' he said with a wary smile.

'Just a matter of a couple of questions, sir. We'd appreciate your help.' Mortimer said politely. 'I understand you work with the British Union.'

The British Union. The simple, ambiguous name for the British Union of Fascists. A polite title for Mosley's followers.

'I do, Inspector.' He was still genial, the gracious host. 'Is there a problem of some kind?'

'I understand you look after the details of local membership.'

'That's correct. Why?' Reynolds was on his guard now.

'We're looking into the murder on Sunday—'

'Poor man. It was nothing to do with us, you know. I trust no one says it was.'

'Of course not.' The inspector sounded astonished at the idea. Good acting, Raven thought. 'We've been told that the victim had expressed interest in joining the Union. He was a supporter of Mr Mosley.'

'Really?' A hint of surprise in his reply. 'I see.'

'We know he was in City Square and joined the march over to Holbeck, but he didn't go all the way to the moor.'

'What was his name again?'

'Benson,' Raven said. 'Frank Benson.'

He hesitated for a second. 'Give me a minute, please, gentlemen.'

Reynolds left the room without another word, returning a little later with a notebook, a pair of spectacles perched on his nose.

'Benson.' He read out an address. 'Is that him?'

'Yes.' Raven nodded.

'It's my writing, so he must have approached me about becoming a member. A lot of them were quite keen.'

'Do you remember him?' Mortimer asked.

'Not especially,' Reynolds replied. Gingerly, he rubbed the bruise around his eye. 'No. But it was a hectic day, of course.'

'What's the procedure for membership?'

'I probably said I'd send him something about the party and a membership form so he could join and pay his dues.'

'Did you?' Mortimer asked.

The man shook his head. 'Haven't had a chance. I never even put two and two together, the man who was killed and the one who approached me.' A small pause. 'Do you think his murder was political?'

The note was there in his voice, somewhere between sorrow and hopeful.

'We've no idea at this point.' The inspector began to turn away. 'Thank you for your time, sir.'

'Can you keep me informed, please?'

'It'll be in the papers,' Raven told him. 'You'll be able to read all about it.'

*

'Loathsome man.' The first thing Mortimer did in the car was light a cigarette. 'Vile.'

'At least we know one more thing about Benson, sir.'

'What does it really tell us, though?' He turned to look at Raven. 'Fine. Benson was interested in joining the fascists. But he hadn't become a member yet. And he scarpered before the violence began. Not very committed, was he?' He gave a grim smile. 'Do you know what he sounds like to me? Someone who likes the idea of control and order, but not the messy reality.'

It seemed close enough. Benson probably imagined himself in one of those black uniforms, thought he'd look good in it. But he'd see himself as a leader, not one of the foot soldiers. A cut above, the type who believed he was born to command. Still, the inspector was right; it might be one more fact, but didn't tell them anything useful. It didn't help catch a murderer or find Ava Benson.

Eight

'THE GIRL.' SUPERINTENDENT Kennedy sat behind his desk. He steepled his fingers and placed them under his chin, looking at Mortimer, then Raven. 'What are we doing and why haven't we found her yet?'

'We've got men looking everywhere,' the inspector answered and marked off the list with his fingers. 'No boyfriend that we know about. So far we haven't had a sniff. Nothing from the train or bus stations. The problem is that she had hours to vanish.'

'She might well still be in Leeds,' Raven suggested. 'Hotels; we should look at those. Guest houses. Lodging houses, too. She didn't have anything with her. It doesn't sound as if she was going permanently.'

'Good idea.' Kennedy nodded. 'What else?'

That was the problem: there wasn't anything else. Ava Benson had a full night's start on them. She could be anywhere.

Raven shook his head as he left the meeting. Why hadn't they found her? It wasn't as if they hadn't been looking. Right now Leeds City Police might as well change their name to the Benson Police. Half the force was trying to discover who'd murdered the father; the other half was searching for his bloody daughter. If she really wanted to disappear with very little money in her purse, where would she go?

'Sarge?' Noble said, but he barged right past, leaving the man to run and catch up. No car this time, but a walk through Leeds, down to the empty open market, across New York Street and Kirkgate to Wharf Street.

It led to a parade of empty warehouses set along the river. Abandoned, windows smashed, slates tumbled here and there from the roofs. Whatever business they'd once done was just an echo of history now. The barges that had travelled along the Aire were outdated, and there was nothing for them to carry, anyway. All the orders had dried up.

But down here, where hope trickled down the drain, stood a pair of lodging houses. Too grand a name, Raven thought as he pushed open a warped wooden door. Doss houses was closer to the mark. Hannigan's and Turnbull's. If money was very tight, Ava Benson could have ended up in one of them. No one would expect a girl like her in a place like this. It would throw everyone off the scent.

'Bloody hell, Sarge, look at that.' Noble pointed. A rat the size of a tomcat sauntered lazily between two buildings, the king of all it surveyed.

'That's one of the babies,' Raven told him and hoped he was only joking.

Inside, Hannigan's was as bad as any slum, with cockroaches, vermin and God only knew what. But maybe it was better than sleeping in a doorway. Maybe. Old, piss-stained mattresses, the constant threat of theft. Crooks loved it. They could disappear here.

It didn't seem a likely place to find Ava Benson. But that was what made it attractive.

The owner took his time, expression changing as soon as he saw the sergeant and the constable. Raven looked like a copper and he was proud of it. And the scars caught people off guard.

'Who are you looking for?' The words came out like a weary sigh.

'A young woman. She'd have come last night. Late.'

'We only take men here.' He turned and aimed phlegm at a spittoon. 'Wouldn't have a lass. Too dangerous. Try Turnbull. He's not fussy.'

It was a handful of yards away, where the street met High Court. Another fragment of Leeds' past gone to rack and ruin, mortar crumbling between the bricks.

'Yes, she was here,' an old, exhausted man said when he saw her photograph.

'Was?' Noble asked and the man turned his long, heavy face towards the detective constable.

'Out by seven sharp. Them's the rules. We're not a hotel, we're not going to wine and dine them and give them bloody room service.'

'Did you see her leave?' Raven asked.

'No, but the rooms are all empty. I went and checked. Sometimes they try to hide.'

'Was she alone?'

'Course she was. No couples. Don't allow it.'

'How did the girl seem?'

'Nervous.' The man shrugged. 'They always are the first time in here.'

He could understand that. Coming to a place like this was scraping bottom, an admission of defeat.

He'd been lucky, or maybe he understood Ava. What did she want – to become a missing person or to be the centre of attention? At least they knew she was alive; that was something to report.

*

Superintendent Kennedy looked relieved at the news. One less worry.

'Now we know she's here, we'll leave it to the bobbies to catch her.' He tapped his pipe gently against the desk. 'Chances are she's still somewhere in the city centre.' He looked at Raven. 'Good thinking. But I want you back on the murder.'

'Yes, sir.'

'What made you think she'd be in one of those places?'

'I don't know, sir. They were so unlikely I just thought they were worth a shot.'

Kennedy raised an eyebrow, not sure whether to believe him.

'Either way, well done.'

*

Raven sat at his desk and read through Frank Benson's file again, making notes on a pad. Facts, more facts. All the things the constables and detectives had learned about the man.

Like every life, it was a jumble. A bit of this, plenty of that, a smidgen of the other. Still, it gave him a few ideas. He glanced at the clock. Ideas he'd follow up in the morning. For once, he wanted to leave the station on the dot of five.

Marjorie was surprised to see him so early. She was standing in the hall, gazing in the mirror as she applied bright red lipstick.

'I hadn't expected you yet. I told you I'm off out with Fran.'

'I remember.' He held up the fish and chips in their newspaper.

She adjusted her hat until it looked just right. 'I don't know what time I'll be back. Probably not too late.'

'Enjoy yourself.'

She gave him a smile and a wave; he heard the front door close behind her. Quickly, Raven went into the kitchen and put his food on a plate. A change of jacket, a cap instead of the trilby, then he was locking the door and walking down the path, head down.

He shouldn't be doing it. The only thing this would bring was suffering. But he wanted to know. He *needed* to know. It was stupid, but he couldn't stop himself.

Don't be a bloody idiot. For a moment he hesitated then kept on moving. Raven was still a hundred yards from the stop when the tram rattled down York Road. Marjorie was already there, two others waiting.

He halted. If he ran, people would notice; the whole point of following someone was not to be seen. Raven waited until it pulled away, the pavement empty, then turned and ambled home. Maybe it was for the best. And there were fish and chips waiting.

*

'Frank Benson.' Kennedy tapped the newspaper open on his desk. The dead man's picture was on the front page again, under the headline *Killed For His Politics?* 'I want an explanation.'

Raven had read the article on his way into town. Reynolds, the man from the British Union of Fascists, had contacted the paper, claiming that Benson had been targeted for murder because he'd wanted to become one of Mosley's men.

'Hot air,' Mortimer said. 'He didn't even know Benson had applied until he checked his records for us.'

'I see.' The superintendent pursed his lips. 'I still want you to follow up on it. We're going to have reporters all over us today.'

'I still think it most likely has to do with his work,' Raven insisted. 'Look at it. He was a means test inspector, for God's sake.' The others nodded; it was perfect sense. 'But a couple of things throw me off.'

'What?'

'The electrical flex, for one. Who on earth walks around with that in his pocket on a Sunday?'

No reply. How could there be? If they had the answer, then they'd have the killer.

'And there's that letter.' *I kilt him.* That was provocation, a taunt. Catch me if you can. It didn't ring true with someone seizing the chance of revenge for the means test. But stranger things had happened.

'Follow up on it all,' Kennedy ordered. 'Let's see if we can get somewhere today.'

'What about the daughter, sir?' Raven asked. 'Ava. Has she been found yet?'

'First thing this morning. She'd gone to a guest house. Step up from Turnbull's, anyway,' he added wryly. 'She's downstairs talking to a WPC.'

'I'd like a word with her, sir.'

It took Kennedy a moment to make up his mind. Then he nodded. 'If you think it'll help.'

*

Raven stood by the window, looking at the traffic going by on the Headrow. Another grey day with autumn dampness heavy in the air. He couldn't even remember the last time the sun had shone.

Marjorie had returned just before eleven o'clock. He'd been lying in bed, brooding, when he heard her key turn in the lock. She came straight upstairs, full of chatter and merriment when she saw he was still awake. Her eyes glittered and he could smell the alcohol and cigarettes on her breath.

Had she really been with Fran, he wondered? With the lights off, and the soft snuffle of her breathing next to him, the question niggled and tugged at his brain.

A tentative knock on the door, then a voice: 'Sarge?'

He turned. It was the woman police constable who'd been questioning Ava Benson.

'How is she?'

'Quiet. Honestly, I'm not sure if she fully knows why she ran off.'

Astute, he thought and gave her a smile. She turned her head away slightly. Of course. Who'd want to see ugly scars stretched into a grin?

'Why do you think she did it?'

The WPC pursed her lips. 'I think she wanted some attention. But it's hard to be certain.'

'I'll have a word, then you can escort her back to her mother's house. What's your name?'

'WPC Sheldon, Sarge.'

'You just stay in the corner, Sheldon.' That was the rule when interviewing a female. Never alone in a room with her.

*

Ava Benson looked bedraggled. She'd slept in beds while she was gone, but rest hadn't been kind. Her thick hair flew every which way and she had dark circles under her eyes.

'You led us quite a dance, Miss Benson.'

'Ava,' she answered. 'You were going to call me Ava, remember?'

'I do.' He settled on a chair. 'You must have known you'd worry everyone, running off like that.'

She smiled. 'You were all asking about Daddy. I told you, he bullied us. He was always angry with the neighbours.'

'Of course we're asking about him, Ava,' he said gently. 'Someone murdered him.'

Her fingers fidgeted with the handle of her bag.

'He'd been murdering us for years.' Her voice rose a little. Not shrill, but with a strange edge.

'We talked about that.' Raven kept his voice calm and level. 'I still don't see why you needed to run off.'

'You don't *understand*.' She slammed her palm down on the desk and Sheldon started to move forward. Raven motioned her back.

'Understand what, Ava?'

'It was him. With me.'

He was silent for a long time, trying to weigh up if she was telling the truth. She was strange, no doubt about that, but… this was what she'd really wanted to say when she wrote and asked him to visit the house. Something she'd kept bottled up for too long.

'Why didn't you say so before?'

'I tried, but I just couldn't do it.' She sounded desperate.

'What about your mother?'

'She doesn't know. I can't tell her. Especially not *now*.' She fumbled in the handbag, brought out a handkerchief. 'I just needed... I needed to be on my own for a while.'

Was it the truth? Or all in her imagination? He could believe it, everything fitted with the oppressive nature of Frank Benson. But standing on its own, a stark statement, that didn't make it real. He needed something more.

'I want you to tell WPC Sheldon all about it. Everything you can.'

'Why not you?' Ava asked, tightening her shoulders.

'Because it would be better if you talked to a woman. She'll look after you.' Before she could argue, Raven was already walking out of the room.

If it was true, he began... then stopped himself. Even if it was, did it affect the investigation into Frank Benson's murder? It painted an even uglier picture of the man. But Ava Benson had been with her mother when Frank was killed. She hadn't done it.

He sighed. Christ, the whole thing was a mess.

*

'Sarge?'

He turned away from the window. WPC Sheldon stood in the doorway. She had an uncertain expression.

'What do you think? Do you believe her?'

'Yes, sir.' She didn't hesitate. 'She's telling the truth. She's given me the outline. I can find out more but it hardly seems worthwhile, does it? Since her father's dead, I mean.'

'No,' he agreed. 'Probably not.'

'We usually suggest they speak to someone about it,' Sheldon continued. 'The thing is, we've no reason to keep her here. Unless there's anything else, we'll take her home.'

'Go ahead.' Between the mother and the daughter, that house would be a dreadful place; the ghost of the father would never leave. 'And thank you.'

*

'Hardly surprising someone killed him, is it?' Noble said. 'Means test inspector, supported the fascists, molested his own daughter.'

They were walking along Commercial Street, dodging between the people on the pavement and the lorries and cars on the road. Music began to play and Raven paused to glance in a shop as they passed. Someone was demonstrating a new gramophone. Ambrose and His Orchestra, with Jack Cooper singing *Bye-Bye Baby*, blared out of the speaker. Something else to stick in his head for the rest of the day.

They passed Betty's Café, then the entrance to the old private Leeds Library, the tune still rippling through his mind. Raven didn't even notice the people stare at his face then quickly avert their eyes. It had gone on for so long. Most of the time he could brush it off. There had only been one instance when it had bitten deep. 1923 and he'd been in Matthias Robinson's, waiting to buy something for Marjorie, when a woman shook her screaming child, pointed and said, 'If you don't shut up, your face will end up looking like his.'

He'd turned and walked straight out of the shop, chest so tight he could hardly breathe. After that, he knew he daren't allow words to touch him if he wanted a normal life. But what was normal?

'You go on,' he said to Noble. 'Follow up on whatever needs doing.'

'Are you all right, Sarge?'

'One or two things to do,' he lied. What he needed was time to think, to try and put it all together, to make sense of everything. Not just the Bensons. *Everything*.

The memory of the woman's words to her child jarred him, the way they always did when they sprang into his mind. One more bloody scar and it still hurt as much as the ones on his face.

On top of all Ava Benson had said, he needed to be somewhere quiet for a while, no people around, nobody talking to him. He caught the tram to Woodhouse Moor, finding a bench as far from the road as possible.

Frank Benson was a bastard, pure and simple. No real loss to mankind. The kind who loved his tiny bit of power, who squeezed all he could from other people. His daughter, his wife, his brothers, his neighbours, the poor sods on assistance. Anyone he could bully and torment.

He'd have been a perfect recruit for the Blackshirts. But the man had no courage. How had he managed in the war, Raven wondered? No one survived that without some grit at the core. The artillery had been behind the lines, but they'd still received a pounding sometimes.

That was something worth looking into: if he could find someone who served with Benson back then, he might be able to shed a little extra light on the man's character. Worthwhile, yes, although it still wouldn't help them find the man's killer. The more he learned, the more he thought the murderer might have been doing mankind a favour.

The letter that claimed to be from the killer was the best lead they had. The line about the flex, only the murderer could have known that. But… no more notes, no way to trace it. Just words waving in the wind.

And then he had to work out what to do about Marjorie…

He sat for an hour, hands in his pockets, his mind far away from the world. Finally, a chill in the breeze roused him. Nothing seemed any clearer but all the noises in his head had grown quiet again.

In hospital, between the endless operations and grafts, a doctor had suggested that Raven talk to someone; said it might help. He knew what that meant: one of those trick cyclists probing deep into his mind. He didn't want that on his record; employers wouldn't like it. He turned the man down and never regretted it. Moments came when he felt as if the world was pressing down on him. But after a little solitude they passed and he was fine again. As long as he could keep it all pressed down he'd get by. He coped.

Raven stirred from the park bench. Autumn, and the leaves were falling. Conkers from a horse chestnut had dropped onto the path. He stopped and picked up a few, assessing them for shape and smoothness. One worth keeping, then another. Raven weighed them in his hand then let them drop. Too many things had happened for him to ever reclaim that innocence.

Nine

SUNDAY. RAVEN WAS off duty and glad of the rest. A week of searching had brought them no closer to Benson's killer. Bobbies kept questioning those on assistance in the area the man supervised, and pressed those whose money he'd docked. A few suspicions, but no one who seemed like a juicy suspect.

He'd seen the tight looks of frustration in the CID room, the tempers beginning to fray as every street became a brick wall in front of them. He felt it himself. But today he could try and forget.

Marjorie had her arm through his as they strolled through Cross Green. Street after street of houses, piled one on top of the other, terraces, back-to-backs. Black was the colour everyone saw, soot and grime from the years when Leeds made things and countless chimneys spewed out smoke. No trees, just paving stones and grey cobbles, the only patches of faded colour over in the park.

He could walk around here in a blindfold and still know exactly where he was. He'd grown up in this neighbourhood, covered every inch of it as a boy. Soon enough they'd see the top of St Hilda's church, gazing down over the valley. Then they'd knock on the door of his parents' house.

Edith and her husband would already be there with their son and daughter. Ken liked to arrive early and leave as soon as was polite, as if he couldn't wait to be away.

Every month it was the same thing. Raven's mother would fuss about the Sunday dinner. His father would sit quietly and smoke his pipe. The women would chatter and he'd make small talk with Ken.

Then, finally, as they washed and dried the pots, Edith would suggest that her parents come and live with them in the big Alwoodley house. And each time her mother would refuse. This was their home. She knew everyone around, and life wouldn't be the same without meeting people for a gossip at the shops.

He could have played a gramophone record of it and the words would barely change from month to month.

'You've looked like death warmed over all morning,' Marjorie hissed as he knocked on the door. 'Smile or they'll start wondering if something's wrong.'

'I will,' he promised. Who wanted questions? They only had to be answered.

*

His father talked about yesterday's football match. Leeds United had lost again. A neighbour had gone to Elland Road and given him a full report over a glass of beer the evening before. Retired and trying to eke out his pension, they took their small pleasures where they could.

Ken didn't care about football or rugby, or any of the things that roared through the blood round here.

'Business good?' Urban asked.

'So-so.' It was never excellent, sometimes terrible. 'That must have been quite a to-do last Sunday.' He pursed his lips and shook his head. 'Were you there?'

'In the thick of it.' Right there with the pushing and the shoving and the shouting. The smell of men, sweat and fear. And afterwards, the body…

'What about that murder?' Behind his spectacles, Ken's eyes were sharp.

'I can't say much. Sorry.'

And then the call to eat. Six of them squeezed around the table, Edith's son and daughter, both in their teens, sitting on pouffes like infants with plates on their knees.

Happy families. They might annoy him, but deep down he knew he wouldn't swap these Sundays for anything.

The same routine of leaving, slipping threepence each to his nephew and niece, then the long goodbyes and the march home.

'We should have them all over for Christmas,' Marjorie said as they crossed York Road. 'My family, too.'

He stared at her in astonishment. The last time everyone had been in their home was two years before, just after they moved in.

'Are you sure?'

'Yes.' She smiled to herself. 'It might be fun.'

Well, Raven thought as they turned the corner to their street, knock me over with a feather. What was going on in her mind?

*

Monday, and he felt it as soon as he sat down with Inspector Mortimer and Superintendent Kennedy. Tension so tight it might snap.

'Did you see the *Post* this morning?' Kennedy asked.

'Yes, sir.' He'd read it on the tram, only glancing away to watch a line of women going into York Road baths to do their weekly washing.

The headline had been about the bashing the Blackshirts had endured in London. Somewhere called Cable Street, and so many people out and angry that they'd been forced to cancel the march. Enough to make him smile. That marked two Sundays and two black eyes in a row for Mosley's men. Maybe they'd get the message that Britain didn't want them.

The other piece was a complete contrast, a vicious piece of writing, condemning the police for doing nothing to catch Frank Benson's killer.

The editors could complain all they wanted, he thought. They didn't have to do the bloody job. Scare up evidence, follow whatever leads arrived. He noticed that the reporters hadn't managed to come up with any suspects.

A third article had caught his eye, too, hidden away on page two. Men from the Holbeck Moor riot had been up before the magistrates. Guilty, but they were given fines, not the prison sentences everyone expected. The fix had to be in. Someone high up must have given the magistrates their orders: be lenient or we'll have insurrection on the streets.

Johnny Harris and the communists would see it as one more victory, of course. The Blackshirts would be smarting at the injustice.

Raven didn't care. He had his own job to do.

'What are we going to do about it?'

Mortimer took out a cigarette, turning it over and over in his hands before lighting it.

'We're doing everything we can,' he said. 'That letter we received is from the murderer; we're as sure as we can be about that. But we can't trace it.'

'And the more we look into Benson, the worse he appears,' Raven added. 'At this rate it'll be easier to find people who didn't want to kill him.'

'What about this fascist connection?' Kennedy asked.

'There isn't one,' the inspector replied. 'He'd talked to the local chap about joining but nothing more had happened. And an eyewitness has him running away long before the march reached Holbeck Moor.'

Kennedy brought his palm down hard on the desk. The slap rang through the room.

'Well, there has to be something.' He stared at Raven. 'What are you looking into?'

'I'm going to dig up some of Benson's old pals from the war, sir. They can tell me what he was like.'

*

'He was a pure bloody skiver.' The man sank his pint and pushed the glass forward half an inch. Raven signalled for another.

He'd found Andrew Cardigan at the British Legion. He was unemployed now, in his early forties and with the weary, stoop-shoulder walk so many men possessed. Years of looking for work and finding nothing had ground down his spirit. His cap and muffler were neatly folded on the table.

'What do you mean?'

'Did as little as possible and liked to order everyone around, never mind he was just a gunner, same as the rest of us. Bullied where he could.'

'Bullied?' He'd bought a packet of Woodbines before coming into the Legion. Now he offered one to Cardigan who sucked the smoke down eagerly.

'Most of the lads, they'd tell him where to go. But he'd find the weaker ones, you know. Acted like an officer around them, he did, like he should have special privileges.'

'Did anyone knock him down a peg or two?'

Cardigan sipped at the beer and smacked his lips in satisfaction.

'A few times. He learned quick enough what he could get away with. Brown-nosed the NCOs and the officers.'

'The men didn't like him?'

'We couldn't bloody stand him. If the shells began falling anywhere close, he was out of the way. Said he had orders to deliver a message or some bollocks. Coward, nothing more.'

'How did he last out the war?' Raven might have only spent a fortnight on the Western Front before he was wounded, but it was long enough to see the way of things. Without thinking, his fingers moved to the scars on his face, the network of lines and hard, shiny skin.

'Dodging, diving. After a few months, about the only thing we cared about was getting home in one piece.' He drank a little more; Raven offered a second cigarette. 'Must have been the same for your lot.'

'Yes.' He remembered the soldiers from his platoon who'd spent months in the trenches, seeming more corpse than human. The dead on leave.

*

Mortimer made a few quick notes as Raven recounted what he'd learned.

'If we went back to his school, we'd probably find he was a bully there, too,' the sergeant said.

'Even if he's rotten to the core it's still our duty to find his murderer,' Superintendent Kennedy reminded them.

'Being out of work must have shattered his confidence,' Raven said. 'When he was taken on as a means test inspector he must have relished having some power again.'

'So we're back to looking at the people whose money he cut,' Mortimer said.

'I'm not sure we ever stopped, sir.'

'These theories are all well and good,' Kennedy said. He pushed tobacco into his pipe, struck a match and a fug of dirty-smelling shag filled the air. 'But we need names.'

True enough, Raven thought, but he couldn't magic them out of thin air. Noble was out, following some more leads. It was the way, shoe leather on pavement and endless questions until you caught the end of a thread and began to tug. Until then it was all hope and perseverance.

He'd put on his mackintosh and was just picking his trilby off the desk when a young constable knocked nervously at the door.

'Sir?'

'What?' He could see the horror on the lad's face. 'Spit it out.'

'We've just had a telephone call from Golden Acres, sir. Out along Otley Road,' he added, as if there was another in Leeds. 'One of their groundsmen has found a car. There's a body in it.'

'Call the pathologist and tell him. Leave it with us.' He was surprised he sounded so calm. Raven ducked into Kennedy's office. 'Dead man in a car up at Golden Acres.'

'You drive,' Mortimer told him.

No talk, no speculation. There was no point until they knew what had happened; there were too many possibilities. Once he'd passed the ring road, Raven accelerated out into the countryside.

Golden Acres was popular with families. It had a lake, a train that chugged around the grounds, swimming pool, a good café and plenty of walking. Even a new hotel close by. He'd come out here with Marjorie a few times in the summer, taking the tram to the terminus at Lawnswood, then the shuttle bus. It took up a huge stretch of land, God only knew how large, stretching almost all the way to Alwoodley. Clean, fresh air, amusements, ice cream; during summer it was bursting with people every weekend.

Raven swept into the car park. He could hear the engine ticking as it cooled while they looked around. Off near the railway platform someone waved frantically and they started to run.

A single glance told them all they needed. An Austin 7 sat by itself near the bins behind the kitchen. The window on the driver's side was open, a man slumped over the steering wheel. Flies were black around the bullet hole in the side of his head.

'The doctor should be here soon,' Raven said.

Mortimer nodded. 'Better get the fingerprint bods, too.'

*

Another hour and they knew more. The bullet had caused the death, the physician confirmed, probably around four in the morning. The shot had been at very close range but not self-inflicted. He refused to offer more details before the post-mortem.

Photographs, the car dusted for fingerprints. The plain black van from the coroner's office arrived to take the body to the infirmary. Mortimer checked the pockets of the corpse's suit as it lay on the stretcher. A wallet, keys, a packet of Gold Flake cigarettes, almost ten bob in change, a fresh, unused handkerchief.

Raven had spent his time on the telephone in the park manager's office, checking the car's number plate. It belonged to Alwyn Davies, with an address in the Romans off Street Lane.

'No weapon in the car,' Mortimer told him when he returned. 'Can't see one nearby.' He looked around at the expanse of park. 'I'll have some uniforms start scouring.'

But it could be anywhere. Tossed in the lake. The killer might have taken it with him.

He started to go through the dead man's wallet. The name matched the vehicle's owner.

*

'No one would have heard a shot out there,' Mortimer said as Raven hit fifty miles an hour on the ring road. 'Not at that time.'

'The killer must have had a vehicle,' Raven pointed out. 'Golden Acres is out in the middle of nowhere.'

It looked like an assassination, he thought. Cold-blooded. Two murders within a couple of weeks. Leeds was starting to seem like an American gangster city.

'We'll know more when we've seen his house,' Mortimer rolled down the window and tossed out his cigarette end. 'He must have had some money if he owned a car, though.'

Ten

IT WAS PART of a series of terraced streets hidden in a well-to-do-area off Street Lane. They tried to look like villas, but the postage-stamp front gardens and tiny flagstone yards behind the back doors gave them away; these were the poorer relations. A few people had planted buddleia or clematis. Someone had tried a tiny lawn but these places would never be grand.

Davies had done nothing to the outside of his house. A few weeds crept between the stones. Mortimer knocked on the door and waited. No answer. He tried again.

'Let's talk to the neighbours,' the inspector said.

The woman wore a pinafore, hair caught up in a turban. Her eyes widened with astonishment when the inspector raised his hat and showed his warrant card.

'Do you know Mr Davies next door?'

'Why?' she countered. 'Has something happened to him?'

'I'm afraid so.' He didn't give an explanation. 'Is there a Mrs Davies?'

She eyed them coolly. Raven could almost hear her mind working, deciding how much to tell them.

'No,' she answered after a few seconds. 'He's a bachelor. What's happened? You've not arrested him, have you?'

'Is there a reason we should?' Raven jumped on her question.

'No. I just wondered. He lives alone, if that's what you want to know.'

Mortimer smiled at her, showing nicotine-stained teeth.

'Thank you, madam. We're going to take a look in his house, so if you hear anyone moving around, don't worry.'

He tipped his hat again and turned before she could ask more.

*

Davies kept a neat home. Clean white antimacassars on the armchairs by the fire. Dishes washed and put away in the scullery.

'I'll look upstairs, sir,' Raven said.

The stair runner was nearly new, a brightly coloured rug on the landing. He started in the bedroom that looked like Davies'. Double bed, with candlewick and counterpane. A table with hairbrush and small tools to manicure his fingernails. A fastidious chap, Raven thought.

Three suits hung in the wardrobe, a sports jacket, two pairs of trousers. He went through the pockets: all empty. Shirts folded, but nothing hidden between or under them.

Finally, he reached the bottom shelf, and found something carefully folded away at the back in a brown paper bag.

'I think you'd better come and have a gander at this, sir.'

Mortimer's big boots clumped up the stairs, then he appeared in the doorway. Raven opened the bag.

'There are black trousers on a hanger, and there's this.' He pulled the shirt out of the bag. Black as pitch, high neck, buttons across to the shoulder and down, like a fencing shirt. The uniform for the British Union of

Fascists. He tossed it on the bed and reached into the bag again. A BUF armband with its red, white and blue lightning strike.

'Benson wanted to become a Blackshirt and now someone's killed a fully fledged one. Makes you wonder, doesn't it, sir?'

'It makes me do a lot more than wonder,' the inspector answered. 'Come on, let's give this place a thorough going-over.'

It took an hour and a half, sifting through papers, checking under rugs, going in the attic and the cellar, opening the cistern and looking in all the obvious hiding places. They learned that Davies had a sister in Filey, had never been married, no children. He had an account with Yorkshire Penny Bank, in the black to the tune of fifty-four pounds, seven shillings and sevenpence, and he was the manager of the insurance company founded by Reynolds, the local secretary of the BUF.

'Probably makes sense he'd join,' Raven said as they locked the door behind them.

'Worth another trip to Alwoodley,' Mortimer said. 'Once we're back at the station I'll ring Filey. They can go and tell the sister.'

*

Reynolds looked surprised to see them again. He was just coming out of his front door, carrying a bag of golf clubs, as they opened the gate.

'Is there something wrong?' he asked. 'Something you forgot?'

'I'm sorry, sir,' Mortimer told him. 'Can we go inside, please?'

'My,' Reynolds said after they told him. He sat down sharply in the chair, face white. 'My. Alwyn?' He shook his head as if he couldn't believe it. Raven poured a glass of brandy and handed it to the man. He drank it down in a single gulp and slowly some colour returned to his skin.

'Murdered?' he asked. His voice was a raw croak.

'I'm afraid so.'

Reynolds looked as if he'd aged a decade in two minutes.

'What can you tell us about him, sir?' Raven asked. 'Did he have any enemies?' Silly question. If the man was a Blackshirt, no matter how carefully he hid his loyalties, he'd have plenty of enemies.

'No, of course not.' He sounded as if the question astonished him. 'He's worked for me since the war. As reliable as they come. Honest and trustworthy.'

'I believe he followed you in other ways, sir.'

'Eh?' Then understanding dawned. 'He was a believer, if that's what you mean.'

'How much of a believer?' Mortimer asked quietly.

'A foot soldier. But a good one.'

And a dead one now. They'd have the post-mortem report later in the day, but it was unlikely to tell them much they hadn't seen for themselves. They stayed and questioned Reynolds, hoping to find any kind of lead. But he had nothing to give them. Davies didn't have any women friends that he knew of. He wasn't one to boast of his conquests. No real hobbies. He kept an allotment but it wasn't the centre of his life.

The man worked hard and well, he'd been manager of the insurance agency since 1933, when Reynolds retired.

'I knew he'd look after it properly,' the man said. 'After all, I'm relying on it for income in my old age.'

He'd drunk a second brandy but still looked like someone who'd taken a hard knock. When he showed them to the door his back was stooped and his fingers shook and fumbled with the lock.

Mortimer sat in the car and lit a cigarette.

'What do you think?'

'The surprise seemed genuine,' Raven answered. 'I don't think he's trying to pull the wool over our eyes.'

'If you believe him, Davies was as pure as the driven snow.'

'Unless he was messing around with someone's wife, I'd say he was killed for his fascist connections.'

The inspector pointed his cigarette towards the house.

'That probably wouldn't be much comfort to the gentleman in there.' He turned the key and the engine came to life. 'We'd better go and find some answers.'

*

The pathologist had been quick with his work. Davies had been shot at very close range, six inches or less, from the right-hand side. The bullet had taken off most of the left side of his skull as it exited. No cuts or bruising, no sign of a struggle.

The lab boys had found the bullet buried and bent in the passenger door of the car. A .45 calibre, probably from a Webley VI.

'That doesn't help,' Mortimer said. 'Must be hundreds of them floating around. Most of the officers in the war carried them. I had one myself.'

Raven had been given a rifle when he was a Tommy, for all the good it did him. It couldn't defend against a shell and thousands of gallons of petrol.

Noble had gone to the Reynolds Insurance Agency to discover what the victim had done on his final day alive. They had Davies' address book. Detective constables were calling on everybody in it. Someone he knew and trusted had murdered him; that much was obvious. Someone who could make him go out late at night to a deserted place and roll down his car window.

'Go and talk to your communist friend again,' Superintendent Kennedy ordered.

'This doesn't sound like them,' Raven warned him.

'Maybe not. But they'll have their hard men, too. And we've seen what they can do in Russia.' He took out his pipe and filled it from a leather pouch. 'See if you can get some names.'

'Yes, sir,' he answered, although he knew Johnny Harris would never give up one of his people.

Still, he was at the Pointer Inn just after six, putting a pint glass in front of Harris.

'I know why you're here. The murder's been on the wireless.'

'An insurance man—'

'Who also happens to be a Blackshirt.'

That part hadn't been released by the police.

'Go on,' Raven said.

'Come on, Urban. You think we don't know our enemies? The police have files. Maybe not you, but you can bet good money that Special Branch does. On us, on them. So do we. We like to know who we're up against.'

'Then you'd better tell me what you know.' He sipped his beer. He was off duty, as much as any CID man ever could be.

'Not much to say.' Harris cracked his knuckles and lit a Woodbine. 'Davies wasn't important in their outfit. Paid his shilling a week membership. Not a thug, not one of the brains.'

'Just did what he was told?'

'More or less.' Harris nodded. 'Hardly someone to be feared.'

'Cannon fodder?'

'We all are in the end, Urban.'

He didn't want to start on political philosophy. Not now.

'Anything else?'

'That's it. We certainly didn't kill him,' he said in earnest. 'Whatever you might think, we don't do that.'

If someone in the party was murdering fascists, Harris didn't know about it, he was certain. Time to change the subject.

'What about your job? What happened?'

'I'm still there.' His voice was grim. 'That's more than you can say for the thirty people who got the chop last Friday.'

'Are you safe?'

Harris shrugged. 'No one's safe. It's how the bosses keep us all down. If you're scared, you'll keep quiet and you won't make trouble. They have you under their thumb.' He paused. 'Have you seen Paul yet?'

'Johnny, I'm working on two murders. When do I have the time?'

'Just make sure you don't forget.'

There was something in his voice that made Raven narrow his eyes. 'Why? Is there something wrong?'

'I'm not saying a word. Go and visit him, Urban.'

*

'I had tea with Gladys in town today,' Marjorie told him as they ate. Cottage pie, the meat dry and the potato crust dark brown from too long in the oven; with the trip to the Pointer he'd been later than usual. But it filled him, and that was all that mattered. He clattered the knife and fork down with satisfaction onto the empty plate.

'What did she have to say?'

'The usual. Their Eddie is acting up. She asked if you could have a word with him.'

He'd talked to Eddie before. Fourteen years old and all the makings of a little thug. Clouted round the ear a few times by the bobby on the beat, for all the good that seemed to do. Told off regularly, belted by his dad, none of it seemed to work; he was teetering on the edge of crime.

'It won't help a damn.'

'He respects you, that's what Gladys says.'

And if Gladys said it, it had to be true. Except that Eddie didn't respect anyone. If another war did come and he was conscripted, the boy was going to get a shock.

'I'll see,' he told her. 'Too much on at the moment. Another murder.'

'I heard on the wireless.' She cleared the plates away and returned with a bowl of tinned pineapple.

'Aren't you eating?'

'I'm full.' She took a few coins from her purse. 'I'm just popping to the shop, we're out of tea.' She glanced at the clock. 'It'll still be open.'

He gave her two minutes, long enough to wolf down the pudding, then followed towards the parade on York Road.

Marjorie didn't look back once; there was no reason she should. Raven barely kept her in sight. The Gipton estate was still so new that there were no bushes or trees for cover.

He watched as she reached the shops and ducked into a telephone box. No point in waiting. They had a working phone at home. He turned away and strode back to the house.

*

Raven sipped his tea and turned on the wireless. The BBC Military Band playing naval marches. He turned the dial again: an orchestra. It still wasn't the music for his mood, but better that than anything martial.

Marjorie was in the kitchen, humming to herself as she washed the dishes. She'd returned with a quarter of tea as if nothing had happened.

He wasn't going to cause a fuss. What would that serve? More than that, he knew he might hear some truths that were better left unspoken. Just stay quiet, he decided. It might all blow over.

Marjorie came into the living room, cup and saucer in her hand, smiled and kissed his cheek before she settled in her chair with a sigh.

Eleven

'WHAT DO WE know about Davies so far?' Superintendent Kennedy crossed one leg over the other and waited.

'Beyond the fact he was a Blackshirt, there doesn't seem to be much to him,' Mortimer replied. 'I had people looking at his work and friends; there's nothing unusual there. No one mentioned anything odd.'

'Is the murder tied to Benson?'

'It's possible,' Raven said. 'There's a connection but it's very thin. Benson hadn't joined the fascists yet. Davies was there when Mosley was in town, so he and Benson were both in City Square and on part of the march to Holbeck Moor. But Benson ducked out early. So there's hardly anything. Certainly no report of them together.'

'Two murders in just over a week, gentlemen.' Kennedy brushed some invisible lint off his trousers. 'We've never had that, as far back as anyone can recall. How do we solve them?'

If they knew, they'd be out doing it, Raven thought, not sitting on their arses reminding each other that they had no idea.

'I think we need to look at each one separately instead of trying to find links,' he said. 'Maybe something brings them together, maybe it doesn't. Don't forget, Benson was a means test inspector. That's a guarantee of hatred.'

'So far that hasn't brought us any results, has it, sergeant?'

'No, sir, but we're still looking. The letter we received hasn't helped us, either. It muddies the waters.'

'Then we need to look harder.'

He admired the super. The man had worked his way up, the same as everyone except the very top brass. He'd put in time on the beat before his promotions, he understood the problems. But the chief constable would be putting pressure on him. Scotland Yard was probably itching to come and teach the provincials how to solve crimes. Kennedy needed results from his men. Not the ignominy of London smartarses coming and showing them up.

He was right. They needed to look harder.

It had been all over the papers, of course. Murder was always big news, especially when the victim was a respectable man and the killing was like an American gangster execution. A tide of outrage rippled under the words. No mention of the man's membership of the BUF. They probably didn't know; it wasn't common knowledge yet. And it would only sully the picture of an upstanding citizen.

*

'Where are we going, Sarge?'

It was a good question. Raven had spent an hour looking through all the papers they'd accumulated on Davies. In just a day, they'd managed to dig deep into his life. Apart from his membership of the fascists, he was as ordinary as a million other men.

The killing had something to do with the Blackshirts. It had to. It was obvious. He could feel it in his gut, a copper's instinct.

Benson, though, that was a different matter. There was something in there. Just out of reach now, but he'd find it. The man they needed was the one who'd written that letter. And he was out there, somewhere in Leeds.

Simmering away at the back of his mind was the problem of Marjorie. Everything screamed at him to let it lie. She wasn't going to leave him, not after all these years. What would be the sense in that? All the scandal and the gossip. He knew her well enough; she'd want to avoid that.

Yet some small part of him couldn't blame her for looking elsewhere. It was bad enough looking at his own face in the mirror every morning when he shaved. How must it be for her? Not just that, but not being able to have children.

'Sarge?'

'Hold your bloody horses.'

He shifted down and the car accelerated up the hill from Churwell towards Morley. It stood not even five miles from the centre of Leeds, but it was a fiercely independent little town, determined to keep its own identity even as the city kept drawing closer.

It had been on its uppers since most of the mills had closed. That showed everywhere. Litter on the pavements and neglect in the air. The stuffing had been knocked out of the place. A heavy, dead sense of defeat hung over the buildings.

Raven found King Street and parked halfway along. A row of terraced houses that had been smart half a century before; now they were in decline. Except for one. He knocked on the glossy black door of number twenty-five and waited.

The woman who answered was slim, wearing a pale cream twinset above a skirt in muted checks. Everything about her seemed softly under-stated. In her forties, but with an easy grace in her movements and few lines on her face.

'Sergeant Raven.' She stared at Noble. 'And a new boy, too.'

'Hello, Agnes. I could use a word.'

She looked into his face for a moment. 'You'd better come in, then.'

Agnes Woods knew people. Her husband had run one of the mills that went bankrupt after the Crash. He'd died of a heart attack in 1932, leaving his widow with a small annuity and a thick address book. She had enough to support herself, but little to spare. The car, the chauffeur, the maid, all those luxuries had gone. So had the large house. Now she lived here, alone and quite content. Even in her poverty she still had more money than many.

Raven had met her three years before. He'd arrested a burglar who was trying to sell his loot in a pub. Some of it had come from Agnes's house. He'd arrived to take her statement and they'd struck up an odd friendship.

She was a social woman, asked to cocktail parties and charity events. She mingled, she met, and she listened. And from time to time she'd proved to be a very useful source.

The parlour looked onto a small, overgrown garden. Books and newspapers littered the room and there was a thin patina of dust on the table. Her housekeeping was a chore, not a skill.

Agnes Woods perched on the edge of an old club chair and smiled.

'It must be something important to drag you all the way out here, Urban.'

'Do you know anyone in the BUF?' No point in beating about the bush; their meetings had never involved small talk.

'One or two, I suppose,' she answered after a moment. 'There's Arthur Reynolds, of course.'

'I've met him.'

'What did you think?' Woods took a cigarette from a box and lit it.

'He probably believes in empire and the kind of Britain that hasn't existed since before the war,' Raven said.

'That's more or less right.' She smiled and nodded. 'Good at organising and paperwork, that sort of thing. He has the time and a bob or two to put in the kitty. That never hurts.'

It fitted with the impression he had of the man.

'Who else?'

'Let me see.' She held a finger against her lips. Suddenly her eyes brightened. 'Roland Harding. Do you know him?'

'No.'

'He's one of the brains of the operation, really. At least around here.'

'How do you mean?' Raven asked.

'Comes up with all the ideas, things like that. Why on earth are you interested?'

'Something that's come up.' It was his turn to smile. 'Confidential.'

Her eyes glittered. He knew how much she liked secrets, even being at the edge of them.

'My, my, my.'

'Where would I find Mr Harding?'

'You should try the Leeds Club. I would imagine he's there most days. Robbie knew him a little.' She turned to Noble. 'My late husband.'

'What's Harding like?'

'I think he's sort of the power behind the throne. I've only met him a few times. Let's just say I didn't take to him, shall we?' She stubbed out the cigarette. 'Those are the only two I know who are part of the Union.'

'Thank you.'

At the door she bussed him very lightly on the cheek.

'Will I read about it in the papers?' Suddenly realisation dawned. 'This is about the chap who was killed near the march, isn't it?'

Raven tapped the side of his nose and winked.

*

He'd never heard of Harding. That was no surprise. Unless the man had a criminal record, their worlds would never have touched.

The Leeds Club. He'd walked past it many times, but inside wasn't for the likes of him. It was Leeds' version of a London gentlemen's club. The rich and the quietly powerful gathered behind the doors on Albion Place. How would they react when a copper turned up, he wondered?

*

'I'll come with you,' Mortimer said. 'My brother's a member; I used to go quite often.'

'Very good, sir,' Raven said. He'd relished the idea of intruding, but this might be easier. The inspector could smooth the way, and he was a good copper.

From their office at the library it was close enough to walk, pushing their way through the crowds in town, crossing the Headrow outside Lewis's between the stream of trams and lorries and cars that passed along the road. The Leeds Club stood behind an impressive sandstone front, with tall, shining windows and double doors.

Inside, an old soldier, medals proudly displayed on his jacket, moved forward to meet them. Everything was neat, subdued and tasteful. The atmosphere was as hushed as a church. A hallway led away towards the back rooms, and a staircase with a polished walnut banister rose sharply.

Mortimer showed his warrant card and mentioned his brother's name. The man nodded, then once more when the inspector asked for Mr Harding.

'He's probably in the billiard room, sir. There's a small parlour if you'd care to wait.'

Five minutes became ten, then twenty, until half an hour had passed. At first Raven wondered if Harding had been given the message. But of course he had. The man was simply putting them in their place. They were policemen, something lesser. He hadn't even met Harding yet but already he despised him.

Finally the door opened and he bustled in, looking as if he'd rushed to meet them. He was small, with a full head of thick silver hair, dressed in a suit that fitted him perfectly, a white shirt, and a tie with discreet stripes.

'I'm sorry to keep you waiting.' The eyes gave the lie to the words. 'How can I help you, gentlemen?'

'We're hoping you can give us some information, sir,' Mortimer told him. He had the proper accent and the bearing for this interview. Raven stood and watched.

'About what?' Harding took out a cigar, clipped the end and lit it, blowing a wide plume of smoke towards the ceiling.

'I believe you're a member of the British Union.'

He eyed them for a while. 'What of it? It's perfectly legal.'

Of course it was. Mosley himself had veered from political party to political party before founding the BUF. And he was a baronet; you could hardly be more respectable.

'So you're confirming it, sir?'

'Yes. As I said, there's nothing wrong with it.'

'I know, sir.' Mortimer smiled. 'What's your position in the local branch, if I might ask?'

'I work with Andrew Reynolds. He's the secretary. I'll ask again: what's this about?'

'Do you know a man called Alwyn Davies?'

'I did.' A small nod. 'And you're here because he was one of ours.'

'More or less,' Mortimer agreed. 'We're wondering if you can tell us more about what he did in the branch.'

'You should ask Andrew about that. Davies was his man – worked for him.' He gave an elegant shrug. 'As far as I know, he was just a member.'

'Were you on Holbeck Moor, sir?'

'Just the first part, on City Square.' He gave a wry smile. 'I'm too old for marches and violence. Andrew and I discussed it beforehand.'

Not such a fervent supporter, Raven thought. The man put himself first. Harding was probably seventy. Too old for the last war. He'd probably never fought anywhere.

'You're aware of what happened there, sir. The murder.'

'Of course. Everyone knows about that. But he wasn't one of ours.'

'He'd spoken to Mr Reynolds about becoming a member.'

'I heard that. But he hadn't joined us yet.' The man studied the tip of his cigar. 'It's awful, though.'

Words, nothing more. No emotion behind them. He didn't give a toss. The inspector asked a few more questions with answers that went nowhere. Finally Raven said, 'What's your role in the branch?'

Harding turned and stared at him.

'I told you – I work with Mr Reynolds.'

'Yes, sir, you did. But *what* do you do?'

'This and that.' He made it sound modest. 'I organise things. I arranged Mr Mosley's visit.'

'I see.'

Mortimer was ready to leave; he could see it in the man's small stirrings. Harding wasn't going to give them anything else. Not that he'd offered a scrap of value. Every statement had been bland.

Outside, a bitter gust of wind pushed at their faces, a reminder that autumn was here.

'What did you think?' the inspector asked.

'He's very smooth, isn't he?' Raven answered.

'Very,' Mortimer agreed. 'The question is whether he's hiding anything. There's probably a great deal that he'd rather we didn't know.'

Probably? Definitely.

'I'd trust him as far as I could throw him.'

'So would I. But I can't see what he might have done.'

'I've been thinking about that letter we received, sir. From Benson's killer.'

'You're not suggesting they were behind it, are you?'

'Just something that came into my mind.'

'Then get rid of it,' Mortimer agreed with a small sigh.

'We still need to do more about the letter. It's the best thing we have.'

'Feel free. I've been racking my brains. It's the only good lead we've got and it's worth nothing.'

*

Raven sat and read the letter over and over, the cellophane envelope that held it crackling under his fingertips. What he wanted was some sense of the man who'd written the words. *I kilt him*. Try as he might, though, it wouldn't come. All he saw in his mind was a blank face.

No fingerprints that the lab boys could find. The sender had been careful. He knew what he was doing. If there was anger behind the murder, then the killing, the leaving of the body, and the sending of the letter had all been carried out very coolly.

And there was still no answer to the question he'd asked back at the beginning: who carried a length of electrical flex with them?

By six o'clock, all he had was a list of questions in his head. Tomorrow he'd see about finding some answers.

Twelve

'COMMUNISTS BEHIND MURDERS! Read the news!'

The boy knew how to catch attention, marching up and down the road by the tram stop. Raven took a couple of coins from his pocket and bought a copy of the *Yorkshire Post*.

There it was, in black and white.

The Communist Party might be behind the recent murders of two men in Leeds, a member of the British Union of Fascists has alleged. Roland Harding, 71, a BUF member, claims that members of the Communist Party of Great Britain could well be responsible for the killings of means test inspector Frank Benson and the shooting of insurance agent Alwyn Davies.

'We know the communists don't believe in the rule of law as we understand it. This brutal, deadly thuggery is typical of their style. You simply have to look at the Stalinist purges in Russia for that. The elimination of any who disagree with their way of thinking is the way the communist mind works.'

Harding stated that he'd been visited by two policemen, and from their

questioning he believes that Leeds City Police suspect the communists are behind
these terrible crimes. The police refused to speculate on rumours.

Raven folded the paper and tossed it onto the seat. He didn't want
to finish the article. Harding had been busy, getting his lies out before
any truth could emerge. And it *was* all lies, every single word. But if a
reporter asked whether any police had talked to the man, a confirmation
would play into his hands. Denying they had any suspects simply made
them look bad.

He'd be hearing from Johnny Harris today. No doubt at all about that.

*

Superintendent Kennedy had his office door closed. Raven could hear
the murmur of the man's voice. Mortimer was intent on some paperwork.
He could feel the anger simmering in the room but no one was saying
a word. They'd been had and they knew it. But their hands were tied.

How long before the explosion?

Not five minutes; closer to ten. He heard the crash of the phone
receiver onto the cradle, then Kennedy's door opened and he waved
them in.

The superintendent's face was red.

'I've just been talking to the editor of the *Post*. Before that I had a
reporter from the *Mercury* on the line asking me if there was any truth
in the rumour that we were going to have a communist revolution in
Leeds.' He packed his pipe as he spoke, then swept a Swan Vesta match
along the box and began puffing angrily. 'Well?'

'Harding's sly,' Mortimer answered. 'Yes, we went to speak to him.
We were bound to; he's high up in the Blackshirts, although he didn't
quite admit that. The most he said was that he organises things. We never
mentioned communists.'

'Harding certainly did.'

'You know he's using this as ammunition, sir,' Raven said.

'Of course. I don't give a damn about that. But I don't have anything to fire back. What do we know about either murder? We need some suspects, gentlemen. The papers are wanting to know. It's been over a week since Benson's death.'

He didn't need to say more. Get the evidence. Find the killer. Shut the fascists up.

*

He guided the Riley around Benson's patch. Another means test inspector had probably already been assigned to the area. The car rattled over the cobbles. Up and down from Roseville Road, desperate streets, an area just like the one where Benson had been found.

Washing lines had been strung high up over the road. But this wasn't Monday so nothing was hung out to dry. A few kids who should have been in school were starting to stack wood for a bonfire on a piece of scrubland that might have been a park. Not long until Guy Fawkes Night. Soon enough they'd be begging for a penny for the guy and planning what they'd do on Mischief Night.

Was Benson's killer somewhere in here? The man who wrote the letter? He parked at the top of the hill, close to Harehills Road, looking down over the district. Apart from that letter – the taunt – they hadn't had a sniff of a suspect.

Did it connect to Davies' death? It must, but he couldn't find the link. The only common factor was the fascists and that seemed to be stretching things. Benson had come no closer than the edge. As soon as the violence began, he'd fled.

He put the car in gear, drove through town and out towards Holbeck Moor, glancing left and right at the streets that ran off the main road. He was starting to believe they wouldn't find the murderer here. It didn't feel right. Nothing more definite than that. No evidence, nothing more than that awkward copper's hunch.

Raven parked by a fence covered with posters, the only splash of colour he could see in the neighbourhood. Nestle's Milk, Bird's Custard Powder, a newer one pasted over the top: *Horlicks Helps You Sleep*. He took out his notebook and scribbled a series of questions:

Where in Holbeck did Benson leave the march?

How was someone able to strangle him and dispose of the body without being seen?

Where did the killing happen – couldn't have been far from where he was found?

The police had no similar murders on the books; it was one of the first things they'd checked. He thought for a minute, licked the tip of his pencil and added two more questions:

Why electrical flex?

Who carries that with them?

Had there been any luck going through the electricians? There couldn't have been or they'd be scrambling to bring the man in for questioning. But it might be worth his time to look further.

*

The street was empty. Only the sound of a radio from one house. He walked along, thinking. The privies, standing separate from the block of homes, stank. Behind them, newspaper had gathered where Benson had been. A pile of dog dung, sitting long enough to turn white. Nothing to show a body had ever been there.

On the pavement he brushed the cobwebs and dirt off his suit, stopped and looked around. Plenty of bedrooms overlooked this spot. The bobbies had gone house-to-house, but how far had they walked? This street, yes, and the next. But he could see one home, three roads away, where an upstairs window offered a clear view of the scene. It was unlikely that anyone had been standing there… but if you didn't try, you never knew. Sometime the dice had to roll in his favour.

*

'I might have seen something.'

Her name was Mrs Witham. In her late forties and scrawny, her dress covered by a long pinafore. There was no sign of Mr Witham, or any children. Just a spotless house that smelt of carbolic soap where she'd been scrubbing; her hands were still pale and wrinkled from the water and her ankles bulged in a pair of thick stockings.

It had taken him three attempts to find the right house. Now they were standing in the bedroom staring through a clear, sparkling window at the scene in the distance.

'Did you or didn't you?' Raven asked and turned to glare at her.

'I did.'

'What did you see, Mrs Witham?' It was like pulling teeth to make her admit anything. Not suspicion of the police, just... he didn't know. The typical reticence to own up to anything, perhaps.

'One man was holding up the other. Like he was drunk or summat. I thought they was two mates who'd been down the pub. I saw him put the man down, then I couldn't see much 'cos of the brick wall behind the khazi. A bit later he walked off on his own, dusting himself down.'

Of course, supporting the body like someone too drunk to stand on his own feet. No one would give that a second glance.

'Which way did they come?'

'Over there.' She pointed to the far end of the street, away from the main road. A network of streets. Benson must have gone that way when he ran, thinking it would be safer.

'What did he look like? The man who walked away.'

'Mackintosh. He had a hat like yours.' A trilby. Round here most wore caps. That was something.

'How big was he?'

'Tall,' Mrs Witham replied. 'He looked it, any road. But not broad.'

'What about his face?'

She shook her head. 'Couldn't see it. The hat.'

Benson had been hatless when they found him. The killer could have taken his hat to hide his face. A question to ask the family.

That was it. She'd given him what she knew. But he had one last question.

'Why didn't you come forward when you knew about the murder?'

'Didn't want to be involved. Nowt good comes from that, does it?'

*

At least he had some solid information. The first glimpse of the killer. He walked back into the streets. Somewhere along here Benson had been strangled. Not far, he was sure of that; a body was too heavy to move any real distance.

It was close. Suddenly he could feel it. He'd never find the spot, it didn't even matter, but suddenly the thought of finding the murderer seemed possible again.

*

Ava Benson looked pale, almost like an invalid. She showed him through to the parlour as if they'd never met before. Nothing but distance in her eyes.

At least Mrs Benson seemed more a part of the world. The woman saw his face and remembered.

'Have you found something?' she asked. It was the voice of a woman whose hopes had been dashed so often that nothing remained but wreckage.

'I'm sorry, no. All I have is a question: did your husband wear a hat?'

'Of course.' She blinked, astonished he even had to ask. All men wore hats.

'What type of hat?'

'A trilby. Like yours.'

'Thank you.' And he left before she could ask him to explain.

*

Superintendent Kennedy said nothing, puffing steadily on his pipe as Raven went through what he'd learned.

'Why hadn't we found this woman before?' he asked Mortimer.

There could be a hundred reasons: pressure, speed, not asking the right questions. Simple human error. But Raven wasn't going to say. He wasn't leading the investigation.

'We simply hadn't,' the inspector answered.

'Let's do a proper sweep of the area, see if we can find the killing place.'

'With respect, sir, I don't see the point,' Raven told him. 'Benson was strangled. There's not going to be any blood. We could walk over the spot and never know. Maybe a house-to-house to ask if anyone saw one man supporting another who might have been drunk. We might get a better description.'

He didn't expect anything – who'd remember a drunk at the fringe of a pitched battle? – but it was worth the shot.

'Good idea,' Kennedy agreed with a nod. 'Put some uniforms on it.'

*

Raven knew Johnny Harris would be in the Pointer. He hadn't expected to find someone else leaning on the bar next to him. A similar broad back, but brown curly hair on the head. Harris's brother, Paul, the man Raven had known since they started school together.

'What are you drinking?' he asked.

They settled at a table away from everyone else. Johnny's eyes were blazing. The first thing to do was put that fire out, Raven thought.

'No one in the police said the communists were responsible for those murders,' he began. 'I was there when we talked to Harding. There wasn't even a hint of it. He's using the idea as a stick to beat you with, that's all.'

'Typical of the bastard,' Harris replied. 'He's never met muck he didn't like.'

'We're not looking at you for it.'

'I don't care about that,' Johnny told him. 'We've been called worse before.'

'Then don't worry about it. But,' he added, 'if you hear anything at all about the killings, I want you to tell me immediately.'

Harris nodded. The angry heat was still rolling off him. He swallowed the rest of the pint and stood.

'I'm going home.' They watched as he stalked out of the public house.

'He'll calm down,' Paul said as the door closed. 'A few minutes and he'll be right as rain. How are you, Urban? I haven't seen you in ages.'

'Up to my neck in a pair of murders. Other than that...' He shrugged. 'What about you?'

'Getting by. The kids are growing.' He'd been the clever one at school. Good at English and Mathematics. Good at anything that involved the brain. Like everyone else, though, he'd never had the chance to develop it. His family needed the wage he could bring in.

Paul Harris clerked for a lawyer. Suit and tie, ink stains on his fingers. Not much, but it was a living, and that counted for a lot these days. He'd served in the war and been gassed in the trenches by the Germans. Mustard gas. Even now, all these years later, he'd have choking fits of coughing.

'How's Jane?'

'She's blooming. But when isn't she?' Harris's wife was round, with a face that was always smiling and hopeful. Never a bad word about anybody; one of life's eternal optimists, no matter the circumstances. 'What about Marjorie?'

'She's fine.' He didn't want to talk about his problems. What good would it do? They'd still be there once the conversation was done. And no solution in sight.

It took a couple of uneven minutes, but soon enough they fell into easy conversation. This and that over two pints. Paul Harris didn't share his brother's politics, but he was aware – funny, too, when the mood took him.

A third drink and a few memories. Boys they'd known at school – their faces trapped in amber as they'd been when young – and what they were doing now. Some had died in the war, more ground down by the Depression.

Paul had three children. He lived along Meanwood Road. In blissful love with his wife, a girl who'd attended their primary school. It was something close to a match made in the cradle.

Finally he glanced at his watch and said, 'I'd better get going. Jane will have the dogs out searching for me. Just something I wanted to tell you. The doctor's suggested I go into hospital. I've been having more problems. It's always worse when winter's in the wings. Apparently there's a new treatment that might help my lungs.'

'That's good news, isn't it?' He looked into his friend's face and saw the trust.

'I'm banking on it.' Harris held out a pale hand. 'It was good to see you again, Urban. We need to do this more often.'

Every time they met, one of them said that. But somehow, it rarely happened.

*

The drink left him restless, not ready to go home yet. He prowled back into town. It was a week night, but the pubs were busy with workers who'd stayed on for an evening out. No faces he knew as he moved from place to place.

Raven ducked into a dance hall just past Leeds Bridge. It was little more than a long room with a low stage but it was full. A small combo played the popular tunes, jazzing them up a little. *I'm In The Mood For Love, Love Walked In.* The musicians looked young, barely in their twenties, but the crowd loved them.

He stood in the shadows, out of the way, all too aware of his face.

People were out to enjoy themselves; no need to remind them of reality. For five minutes he watched. The band took a break, but the pianist kept going, turning *Love For Sale* into a long wandering solo that had the dancers crowding round the upright piano to listen.

Very good, he thought. Then he caught sight of Roy Simpson coming out of the Gents, glancing down to check his flies were buttoned.

Time for a quiet chat.

Simpson was in his forties, still wearing the cropped haircut of the Tommy. He was a bantam of a man, no more than five feet four and thin as a rail, but he had three convictions for assault. Raven moved up quietly and took him by the elbow. He turned, startled, then a guilty grin spread across his face.

'Hello. Mr Raven. Haven't seen you in a long time.'

'Outside. I want a word.'

The air had turned chilly. Rain was coming. Simpson pulled a packet of Park Drive from his jacket and lit one. A sheen of sweat covered his face.

'What can I do for you, Mr Raven? Only I've got a bird waiting in there and the band will start again in a minute.'

'You're a Blackshirt, aren't you?'

'What if I am?' He had a note of defiance in his voice. 'Mr Mosley's the only one telling the truth about Britain.'

'I'm not here to argue politics, Roy. Were you down on Holbeck Moor?'

'Course I was.'

'There was a man killed down near there that day.'

'I know. I read the bloody papers.'

'And another of your lot was shot to death a couple of days ago.'

He saw Simpson wince. He knew the man had been on the Somme, up there on July the first and seen God knew how many die. Strange that the mention of a single killing could have that effect.

'Mr Davies. He was a good bloke.'

'What's going on, do you think?'

'It's them commies. Got to be. It was there in the *Post*.'

'I don't care what any reporter writes,' Raven told him.

'It's got to be true. Those Bolshies hate us.'

'If you know anything…'

Simpson gave him a withering gaze.

'Come on, Mr Raven, who'd tell *me* anything? It's like the army that way. We just get us orders and we do what we're told.'

'And what's the word on this?'

The man looked around. 'Keep shtum, that's what they're telling us.'

'About what?'

'Everything.'

'Why?'

The man shrugged. 'Don't know. It's just what they say.'

'A word to the wise, Roy: if you know anything, you'd better tell me.'

'I don't know a thing. Honest.'

'You hear any whisper, I want to know. Got it?'

Simpson nodded. 'Can I go now? I don't want someone else walking off with my bird.'

'Who gave you the order to keep quiet?'

'Come down from the top. But it was Bob Hoyland 'as said it to me. He's like…' he fumbled for a phrase. 'Like an NCO.'

'Who's in charge? The kingpin?'

'Mr Mosley, of course. But round here there's Mr Reynolds and Mr Harding.'

'I know them.'

'And Mr Gilbert. He's more the political one.'

'I haven't heard of him,' Raven said. 'I thought Harding took care of all that.'

Simpson looked around and leaned close enough for Raven to smell the beer on his breath.

'Mr Gilbert, he stays out of sight.'

'What's his Christian name?'

'Ian, I think. I'm not sure.' He looked at his watch. 'I've got to go, Mr Raven.'

He waved the man away. A third man at the top. Mortimer might know him. Not that it helped with the Benson case, though.

*

'You stink of beer.'

'I ran into Paul and then I went to find some information.' He'd kissed her cheek and that was it. She pulled her face away from him.

'You could have rung.'

She was right. He'd been thoughtless. But was it any worse than having a fancy man on the side?

'Brush your teeth well,' Marjorie told him. 'It's like being in a brewery.' The short snap and she returned to her book.

In the kitchen, he cut a couple of slices of bread and slathered on butter and jam. Not a meal, but it would do. He ate where he stood, gazing out into the darkness. This weekend he needed to get into the garden; he'd left it for too long.

Ian Gilbert. He'd never heard the name before, but he hadn't paid much attention to the local Blackshirts before Mosley came to town. He dealt with crime, not politics. This time the two had met.

Thirteen

'WE KNOW WHO he is,' Superintendent Kennedy said quietly. 'Inspector Mortimer's been looking into him.'

'Why did the name even come up?' Mortimer asked.

'I ran into a BUF member last night,' Raven told him.

'I don't know what you're thinking, but it's a dead end. He does work for them, but he wouldn't have anything to do with a murder.' He cocked his head to the side. 'Besides, what would he have to do with Benson's killing?'

'No idea, sir. But we need every lead we can get, don't we?'

'Don't worry about Gilbert,' Kennedy said. 'Other people are keeping an eye on him. Concentrate on Benson.'

'Yes, sir.'

He left them in the superintendent's office. That was him told. Keep your nose out of things too grand for you. Raven sat at his desk and fumed until Noble came over.

'Sarge? I had someone on the blower while you were in there.'

'What did they want?'

'They wanted to talk to someone looking into the Benson case.'

Raven sat up straight. 'Go on. Man or woman?'

'A woman,' Noble replied. 'She must have been in a telephone box. I could hardly hear, she was whispering.'

Get to the meat, he thought. Spit it out.

'Anyway, she said we ought to take a look at the boyfriend of a mate of hers.'

'Why? Who is he?'

'He's called Stan Dyer. She thinks he's been dropping hints that he's the one who did it. Boasting without boasting, she said.'

'Where do we find him? And is there anything in Records?'

*

Dyer was shaking. He couldn't keep control of his legs. They seemed to bounce up and down slightly as he sat. The man was terrified.

Maybe he was cocky with the girls, but sitting in an interview room with a pair of coppers, all his confidence had fled. He was like jelly. He'd turned pale as soon as he saw Raven's face with its shine and scars.

He worked in the stockroom of a company in Hunslet, wearing a brown overall over his old clothes. About twenty-five, thin as a rail, looking more like an overgrown boy, with jug ears and a bumfluff moustache, than a man.

'Why would I kill someone?' he asked, and Raven believed him. There was no file on him, he'd never been arrested. Dyer pulled a packet of cigarettes from his pocket, barely able to hold the match straight enough to light it. He looked like he wouldn't have had the strength to shift Benson's body.

The sergeant glanced at Noble and gave a small shake of his head.

'We won't trouble you any further,' Raven said.

'Who gave you my name?' Dyer asked. 'I'll do for them.'

Raven turned in the doorway.

'No you won't. Not unless you want us back again. And if that happens, we'll bring the handcuffs with us.'

*

'Sorry, Sarge. The woman who tipped the wink must have been having a joke.'

'Doesn't matter. It's always worth a try.' He put the Riley into gear. 'We'd be in clover if the tip had been good.'

'What now?'

It was a good question. Back to the beginning, maybe.

'Have another go round your narks,' Raven said. 'Maybe they've come up with something.'

'What about you?'

'I think I'll go back and talk to Benson's daughter.'

*

'I've given up work,' Ava Benson told him. She was wearing a thick woollen coat, a hat over her unruly hair. They were climbing the hill, walking to the shops on North Lane. She'd answered the door when he knocked at the house and whispered, 'Wait a minute,' then reappeared dressed for the outdoors. 'I need to be there to look after mum. She's taken it badly.'

'I'm sorry.'

She shrugged, as if it was just one more burden.

'We have a little money. Not a lot.' She turned her head to look at him. 'Have you found him yet?'

There could only be one 'him': the killer.

'No,' Raven told her. 'That's why I'm here. To see if you or your mother might have remembered anything else.'

'Mum's…' she groped for the words. 'Not very well. Always down.'

'What about you?'

'I cope.' She gave a weary smile. 'I suppose I'm stuck here now.'

A father who'd molested her, a mother who was falling apart. The poor woman had a shabby life.

'I'm going through it all again. Maybe something's come into your mind.'

'Not really.' She caught a wisp of hair and pushed it behind her ear. 'I'll only be a minute.' She ducked into the chemist and he waited on the pavement. Raven stared around. It was a copper's habit, taking everything in, looking for something rum. Fifteen years and it was second nature.

She also needed bread, a piece of skate, a visit to the greengrocer, everything going in her string bag. And she still hadn't given him a proper answer. If he'd wanted a bloody trip to the shops he could have stayed at home with Marjorie, Raven thought. Finally she was done and turned to him with a smile.

'Home now. And there was one thing I thought of.' Her low heels clumped quickly on the flagstones.

'What's that?'

'My dad liked Mr Mosley.'

'I know. Your mother told me that. Both of them believe him.'

'We were having tea a few days before he went to... he said he'd been talking to someone from that party. You know, the one he leads.'

'The British Union of Fascists.'

'Yes. That's it.'

'Did he say who?'

'I don't think so. I don't remember, really.'

A dead end. He tried another tack.

'What about communists? How did he feel about them?'

'Couldn't stand them.' She stood by the front door, the key in her hand. 'He said most of the people he saw every day were probably Reds.'

'What about you? What do you think?'

'I don't know,' she answered. 'I've never really thought about politics. I'm sorry, I need to go. I wish I had more to tell you.'

'You've been very helpful,' he lied and raised his hat. 'Thank you.'

*

That had been a waste of time. There weren't too many members of the BUF around. Enough, though, that they couldn't talk to every single one. And there were probably plenty more who gave silent support.

As he pulled into Alexander Street, he saw uniformed coppers filing quickly into a van. It sped away, bells ringing sharply.

'East Parade, Sarge,' the man on the desk told him. 'Robbery. The super's over there now. There's a bloke dead, by all accounts.'

'Does he want me?'

'He's got the inspector and three detective constables with him. Said you should keep on your cases. He'll phone if he needs you.'

That was fine. Raven already had enough juicy murders on his plate.

He spent the afternoon going through his notes with a fine-tooth comb, hoping there might be something he'd missed. By five, though, it was time to admit defeat. He wasn't going to pull anything more from what he had.

Raven heard the reports on the robbery as they came in. One man had gone into the bank. He'd shot an ex-serviceman who tried to stop him. There'd been an accomplice, waiting outside in a Morris. At least witnesses had given a good description of the killer and taken down the number plate.

The car belonged to a man in Bramhope. His son and a friend had taken it out earlier. He'd had no idea they'd think of doing anything like this. Of course. Now the murderer and his friend were on their way to God knew where.

But none of it concerned him. He could go home.

*

Marjorie seemed surprised to see him.

'I thought you'd be out after the pair who killed that man in town. It was on the wireless.'

'Not my case, and I'm glad about it.' He sat down with a long sigh. He'd never imagined that going through papers could be so draining, the dragging weariness that dropped down made him feel as if he weighed twenty stone. 'The inspector took it. Looks like they've fled. What's for tea?'

'Egg and chips. It won't be a minute. Can you lay the table?'

Raven pushed himself to his feet and set out cloth, knives and forks.

'Do you fancy doing something tonight?' Marjorie called from the kitchen.

'I'm exhausted.'

'All right. It's just that I've been inside all day.'

He knew he should make the effort; she'd asked, after all. But he was drained.

'I'm sorry. It's been rough. You go ahead.'

'I'll give Helen a ring. She might want to go somewhere.'

He'd met Helen once, a loud, brassy woman.

'If you like.'

Any hope of a good mood between them was broken. They ate in near silence, just the voice on the radio filling the room. The bank robbery and murder was the main story; what could be bigger? A description of the men and the car, urging people not to approach them but to call the police.

Marjorie hurried through her food, washed the pots, then vanished upstairs while he drank his tea. Let her go, he thought. Even if she's meeting her fellow. Give her time and she'd get all that out of her system. After all, they had fifteen years of marriage behind them...

He almost convinced himself.

He was tired, weary right through to his bones. But even at the best of times, he didn't like going out at night. He always felt people were staring at his face. When he was working it didn't matter as much; he could hold his authority like a shield. Off duty, a civilian, things seemed different. He was aware of every eye that noticed him.

Marjorie came through, buttoning her coat and checking her hat in the mirror over the fireplace.

'I won't be late.'

'Enjoy yourself,' he told her, and didn't mean a word of it.

Fourteen

'WE GOT THEM.'

Mortimer's smile was so broad he might have caught them himself. Raven had barely had chance to take off his mackintosh.

'Where?' he asked. 'When?' It hadn't been in the paper.

'About an hour ago, near Liverpool.'

'That's excellent, sir.' It was. A pair of killers off the street, co-operation between forces. A perfect operation. And solved within twenty-four hours. 'Was anyone hurt?'

'They gave up without a fight. Still had the gun on them.' The inspector was fizzing with victory. Let him enjoy it. Soon enough he'd remember that their other big investigations were both stalled and he'd be back to earth with a bump.

Raven sorted through the papers that had arrived. Nothing important. He needed something, some piece of luck that didn't turn into a dead end. He was about to leave when the desk sergeant put his head round the door.

'Telephone for you, I'll put it through.'

*

'It's Harry,' the voice on the end of the line whispered. Flash Harry.

'You've got something?'

'Yes, but not on here.' Noises in the background. He must be in a telephone kiosk. 'I'll go stony if I keep putting money in the box.'

'Where?' Raven asked.

'Kardomah. Upstairs.'

'When?'

'Soon as you can.'

*

The Kardomah stood on Briggate, the stone front as grimy as everywhere else in Leeds. Raven walked through the shop, breathing in the rich smell of coffee. In the restaurant, he looked around. Harry was in the corner, out of the way. Hardly any customers this early in the day. He took a seat at the table and ordered tea.

They waited until the waitress set out the cups and pot.

'What have you got?'

'Depends what it's worth.' Today Harry was wearing a cheap blue pinstripe suit, double breasted, the material thin and shiny, with a wide, colourful tie.

'You know how it works,' Raven said. 'I can't tell you that until I know what you've got. Don't be a bloody fool.'

'This is good. Top quality information.' He had a thin, feral face, the moustache little more than a line above his lip. But he wasn't Clark Gable. Not even close.

'Spit it out. If it's as good as you say, I'll pay.'

'It's about Frank Benson.'

'Go on.' Raven tried to sound casual.

'You haven't got whoever did it, have you?'

'You already know that.' He sipped his tea.

Flash Harry lit a cigarette and blew smoke towards the ceiling.

'Happen I know someone who can help with that.'

'Then stop buggering around and tell me,' Raven told him quietly. 'I don't have all day to sit around and gossip.'

'Ever heard of Carl Todd?'

Raven shook his head. 'Should I have?'

'He works for an electrician. Just a helper, not qualified or anything.'

Electrician. He tried not to let his face show anything.

'What makes you think he did it?'

'I was in a pub last night and someone was dropping hints he'd done something. A few pints in him, wanting to seem a bit of a lad.' Raven knew the type. 'I started talking to him.'

'Did he come out and admit it?'

'Course not.' Harry picked a strand of tobacco off his lip. 'He was three sheets, not daft.'

'What did he say?' Raven asked casually.

'The usual, how he's a dangerous man, he's done someone over badly. Laughing to himself, you know. Took some electrical cord from his jacket.'

'How did you know about the flex and Benson?'

Harry grinned and tapped the side of his nose. 'Least said...'

It didn't matter; word was bound to spread. Very little stayed secret for long.

'Where do I find Carl Todd?'

'What's it worth?'

'If it's him I'll give you a couple of quid.' Big money, but the force would spring for it if he was the killer.

'Five.'

'Don't push your luck, Harry.' His voice was quiet but there was a steel edge to it. Their eyes met. Harry broke the stare first and nodded.

'You're getting it cheap.'

'I'm not and we both know it. Where?'

'He works for a bloke called Pilton. I found him drinking in the Duncan.'

'Good enough. If it works out, I'll pay you.' Raven sorted a shilling from the change in his pocket and put it on the table.

*

'Carl Todd,' he said to Noble. 'See if there's anything in Records on him. And find the address for an electrician called Pilton.'

'Do you have something, Sarge?'

'I bloody hope so.'

He told Mortimer and Kennedy, seeing their expressions sharpen as he mentioned the words 'electrician's assistant'.

'Noble's seeing what he can find out. Then I'll bring him in.' He paused. 'One thing, though. My nark knew about the strangulation with electrical flex.'

He left them to think about that; leaks weren't his concern.

'A couple of drunk and disorderlies,' Noble said. 'Nothing since '33. And Pilton's is near the bottom of Roundhay Road.'

Very close to the area Benson covered as a means test inspector.

'Where does Todd live?'

'Burmantofts, Sarge.' Still near to that area.

'Come on. We have a few people to see.'

Pilton's house was his office, a terraced place with a yard at the back just off the main road. His wife answered, wiping her hands on a tea towel.

'He's out on a job.' She looked at them suspiciously. 'What do you want him for?'

'Does Carl Todd still work for him?'

'Him, is it?' she said. 'Might have known. He's a sly little devil. Has he been light-fingered?'

'I'm sorry, I can't say,' Raven told her. 'Is he with your husband?'

She nodded, checked a thick notebook and wrote down the address where the men were working. 'I warned him about Carl, said he looked like a wrong 'un.'

*

'It's one of those streets off Harehills Lane,' Noble told him. 'Up towards the cemetery.'

Raven knew it, the big plot of land at the top of the hill. He'd been to a few funerals there.

'Turn here, Sarge. It should be down on the left.'

Dark terraced houses. The small yard at the front looked dank, as if it never received the sun. He parked the Riley behind a blue Austin 7 van. The door to one of the houses was open, voices coming from inside.

'They won't be expecting us. If he tries to run, I want you on him hard.'

'Yes, Sarge.' Noble grinned.

A quick knock on the wood and they were in the place, then through to the kitchen. Two men stood there, holding mugs of tea and smoking. The older one looked up in surprise.

He wore a shirt without a collar, sleeves rolled up, a pair of stained trousers and boots.

'What do you think you're doing?'

But he wasn't the one who interested Raven. The other man was putting down his tea, ready to run. Noble moved swiftly to the back door, cutting him off.

'Are you Carl Todd?'

'He is,' the older man said.

'I'm Detective Sergeant Raven with Leeds City Police. I'd like you to come with us to answer a few questions if you would, sir.'

'What's he supposed to have done? The lad works with me.'

'It's all right, Tony,' the young man told him. 'It must be a mistake or summat.'

He was probably twenty-two, maybe twenty-three. Wiry, as if he hadn't grown into his body and filled out yet. A thin face with hollow cheeks and deep-set eyes.

'How am I supposed to finish this job?' Pilton complained. 'I need someone to help me, we're rewiring the whole place.'

'Sorry, sir,' Raven told him and took Todd lightly by the arm. If he tried to bolt, he'd do it as soon as they reached the pavement. Without thinking, he tightened his grip just as Todd started to pull away.

'In the car, son.'

He bundled the man into the back seat, Noble beside him. No handcuffs; Todd wasn't under arrest yet. It had gone smoothly, quickly. If Harry's tip was right, they could have the Benson killing wrapped up in another hour.

At headquarters they escorted him to an interview room.

'You're Carl Todd?' Raven asked.

'Who the hell did you think I was? The king?' He'd discovered a little fire hidden away in his belly. 'What do you want me for, anyway? I haven't done anything.'

'All in good time, sir. Do you remember Sunday, September twenty-seventh? It's not that long ago.'

'No. Why should I?'

'Mosley and his Blackshirts went out to Holbeck Moor.'

'I read about that,' Todd admitted.

'And where were you that day?'

'I don't know. At home, probably.'

'Was anyone with you?'

'My parents.'

Raven nodded at Noble. The detective constable left the room; he'd talk to Todd's family and check. A uniformed officer remained inside the door.

'Turn out your pockets.'

'Eh?'

'I want to see what you have in your pockets, Mr Todd.'

Slowly, he complied. First, his trousers. A handkerchief, some coins, a wallet. Then the jacket: cigarettes, matches, a screwdriver, wire strippers, a couple of other tools, and lengths of wire covered with fabric.

'Quite a haul,' Raven told him.

'You know what I do.' He glared. 'What's this about, anyway?'

'The day of that rally on the moor, someone was murdered.'

'You don't—' He started to rise.

'Sit down,' Raven ordered. Very slowly, Todd took his seat again, staring. Not so confident now. 'He was strangled.' Raven gestured to the pile on the table. 'With flex.'

'What?' The man stared as if he couldn't believe what he'd heard. 'You think I...'

'Did you?'

'No!' He almost shouted the word.

Raven took a cellophane bag and scooped the pieces of wire and flex in with the tip of a pen.

'I'm going to have our boffins take a look at these. It's amazing what they can find these days.'

He left the room. The bobby at the door would watch the suspect. Todd wasn't the killer. He'd stake his pension on that. But he'd let the lab check, anyway, do it all by the book.

'Well?' Mortimer was hovering by the door of the CID room.

'This was in his pocket. Noble's checking his alibi.'

'What do you think?'

'Probably not. But I'll sweat him to make sure.'

The inspector made a sour face.

'Pity. A good arrest right after that East Parade shooting would help.'

'I'll see what I can do.'

*

'You've had a little time to think about where you were that Sunday,' Raven said as he sat down in the interview room. He'd stopped to get himself a cup of tea. Nothing for Todd.

'I told you, probably at home.'

'Probably?'

'I don't have a social secretary or you could check with her.' His mouth turned down at the corners. 'I didn't do it.'

'Maybe you did, maybe you didn't.'

Todd was drumming his fingers on the wood. Good, he was growing nervous. That was when things came out.

'You've had a couple of arrests, Mr Todd.'

'Drunk,' he said. 'And not for a long time.'

'Maybe you'd been drinking that dinnertime. Maybe you and Benson got into an argument.'

'I never met him.'

'We only have your word for that. Why don't you have a think about it? I'll come back again in a little while and you can give me the truth.'

'I've been telling you the truth!' Todd shouted as the door closed.

*

'What are your politics, Mr Todd?'

He looked up as if he'd never been asked the question before.

'Me? I don't know. Who gives a toss about politics?' He said it like it was a badge of honour.

'Do you know who's Prime Minister?'

Todd shook his head and Raven believed him. Too many took no interest in who was running the country. The young were always the worst. There'd been an election the year before. The man might have been old enough to vote then.

'Doesn't make any difference who runs things, anyway, does it?' Todd said. 'Always the same for the likes of us.'

Raven decided to switch tack.

'Why did you kill Frank Benson?'

'I didn't kill anyone.' He took out his packet of Park Drive and lit one. His hands were shaking. 'You know that.'

'I don't know anything,' Raven said. 'All I see is a man with the same type of flex in his pocket that was used to strangle someone. A man with no alibi.'

'My parents. I told you. You sent that bloke—'

'He's not back yet. And we'll want to take a proper look at those cords under the microscope. You won't be going anywhere for a while. If you're guilty, you won't be going anywhere ever again.' He paused for a fraction of a second. 'Except the hangman's noose, of course.'

'It wasn't me.' There was desperation in his voice. 'You've got to believe me. It wasn't me.'

'The only thing I have to believe is the truth, Mr Todd.'

*

'His parents say he was there, Sarge.' Noble was out of breath. 'Had to chase them down, they were walking the dog.'

'Do you believe them?'

'Yes,' he answered simply.

'Do we have anything back from the lab yet?' Raven asked Mortimer. The inspector shook his head.

'Keep him until we have the results,' Superintendent Kennedy ordered. 'I'm not going to risk losing a good suspect.'

'Yes, sir.'

*

Raven came out into late afternoon sunshine, bright enough to make him blink and rub his eyes. Todd was down in the cells, belt and shoelaces confiscated. Still protesting his innocence. He was probably right, but they couldn't take that chance.

He caught the tram, and stared vacantly out of the window, slowly returning to the world.

Fifteen

'SIMILAR, BUT NOT an exact match.' Mortimer slid a piece of paper onto his desk. 'The results on the flex. You'd better let Todd go.'

'Yes, sir.' He was disappointed, but hardly surprised.

He watched as the man checked all his belongings and signed for them at the desk.

'I told you it wasn't me.' That cockiness had returned. 'You should have believed me.'

'I like evidence,' Raven told him. 'Now you have to convince your boss you were innocent.'

Todd's face began to fall. The sergeant turned away. The best suspect they'd had and he was free.

*

'The uniforms didn't find anything when they checked through the electricians, did they, sir?' he asked Mortimer.

'No. Nothing they reported.'

'Can you let me have a couple of DCs to help? We'll give them a proper sorting.'

*

Seventy-three electricians in the city directory. Raven and three detective constables to go through them all. Hard work, but they had nothing else to follow now. He told them what he wanted: find the names of all the employees, including anyone who'd left in the last few weeks and check them against the records. It might work. He'd hoped Carl Todd would be the killer, but… at least he didn't have to fork out money to Flash Harry.

It was all shoe leather and time on the telephone. Anything to stop the investigation grinding to a halt. Mortimer was having the same poor luck with the Davies shooting. Apart from his membership of the BUF, the man had lived a completely respectable, sober life. Constables were sifting through it all, talking to everyone the man had known.

Dead ends, both of them. But murder could never be shuffled away to obscurity. The police had to do their damnedest to solve every killing. You couldn't let people feel they might get away with it.

The force had expected a rise in crime after the war. That was what an old copper told him while he was training. All those men coming home and finding things no better than when they left. All of them trained to kill, with the souvenir weapons they'd brought back. It never happened, but only because the police came down hard.

Now, after years of having nothing, who could be surprised when men became desperate and dangerous? He'd arrested people for stealing food to feed their families. There was no justice in that. He'd let one or two go with a warning; the others he'd taken into custody.

Murder was the extreme, it was where it all ended. As bad as it got. These two cases, though, weren't about passion or arguments. Davies' shooting had been carefully planned. Benson… he honestly didn't know. The fact that he was a means test inspector still seemed the likely motive.

He left the Whip as the landlord called last orders for the afternoon, letting the door close on the smells of cigarette smoke and stale beer. He'd been hoping to check out a tip in there, but it had turned out to be another waste of bloody time. Back at headquarters, a list waited on his desk.

'We don't have the names of all the people working for the electricians yet, Sarge,' Noble said. 'Those are what we've come up with so far. Checked against records. The ones with stars have convictions. You might want to take a look at that one.' He pointed, finger bright with nicotine. 'Joseph Miles. The day after Benson copped it, he didn't show up for work. Hasn't been back since.'

'Bloody hell, why didn't you say so before?' Raven asked. 'Let's pay him a visit.'

The address they had was on Quarry Hill, but the home was rubble now, making way for the new flats. A telephone call to the housing department, bullying the clerk for information. Out on the Gipton estate. The Miles family lived no more than half a mile from Raven's house.

It was a semi-detached, with a square of dirt in front where a lawn would grow if anyone gave it some care. He hammered on the door until he heard footsteps inside and a tiny woman glared up at him.

'What do you want? If you're selling owt, we're not buying, so push off.' She tried to close the door on him, but Raven used his weight to keep it open.

'I'm Detective Sergeant Raven and this is DC Noble.' He waved his warrant card. 'We're looking for your Joe.'

'Not here, is he?' Nothing softened in her gaze.

'Where is he, love?'

'Don't know. Come home just over a week ago and said he was jacking in his job and going away.'

'Why? Where?' The feeling started to rise inside. That tingling, the buzzing in his veins.

'Didn't say. We told him not to be so daft. Who chucks a job these days? They don't grow on trees. But he wasn't having any of it. Put some clothes in a holdall and left. His dad came close to clouting him.' She pursed a hard mouth. 'What's he done?'

'Maybe nothing,' Raven told her. 'That's why I need to talk to him. Have you heard anything since he left?'

She shook her head. 'It's something bad, isn't it?'

'The day he left, where had he been?'

'That rally, the whatchacallits. You know, Blackshirts.' It was Miles. It had to be. He knew it.

'Does he support them?'

'Not that I know. He just wanted to see it. Went down with a couple of his pals.'

'Have they vanished, too?'

'No. Only Joe. I went round and asked them what had happened but they acted like butter wouldn't melt. You'd better tell me what you reckon he's done.'

But all he had for now were more questions.

'Have you ever been on relief? Or Joe, maybe?'

'Course not,' she snorted. 'My fella's always had a decent job. Joe did, too, till he scarpered.'

'I need the names of his friends.'

Her anger had given way to fear. Worry clouded her eyes.

'Mrs Miles…' he prompted.

*

They left with the names and a photograph of Joe Miles. He still hadn't told the woman that her son might be a murderer. Inside, though, he felt sure of it; finally, they were on the right bloody track.

'You talk to those pals of his. Push them as hard as you like, but I want some answers.'

'Yes, Sarge.' Noble smiled.

'Report back when you're done. I'm going to headquarters to get this circulated. It's him.'

*

'Vanished at the right time, out of the blue. No word since,' Raven said. 'Joe Miles. Got to be.'

'It's damning,' Superintendent Kennedy agreed. 'All right, get that out to all forces. Newspapers and radio, too. We should never have trusted uniforms to do the job. Be careful how you word it, though. We don't have any evidence yet. Any motive?'

'Nothing from the mother. We'll see what his friends say.'

'Better than I've managed on Davies,' Mortimer said.

'Still nothing, sir?'

'Not a dicky bird.'

'Right. Let's see what you can find out,' Kennedy said. 'We've got that pair of killers back from Southport. They're up before the magistrate tomorrow. Straightforward, committed for trial. Their lawyer isn't even asking for bail. Let's get these two done and dusted and we'll be looking good again.'

He left the office, a trail of pipe smoke behind him.

'Easier said than done, wouldn't you agree, sir?' Raven said.

'We'll get there in the end. These are murders.'

*

He wasn't putting all his eggs in a single basket. He'd done that once before and looked a right fool when his suspect was innocent.

The rest of the afternoon vanished in a haze of pubs and clubs, long after opening hours had ended. Walking past men with hopeless eyes on the street corners. Some sold clothes pegs from a tray. A couple were busking, harmonising well; truly singing for their suppers and touching their caps whenever anyone tossed them a coin.

Nothing. Raven might as well have sat at his desk. But he knew that was impossible. He had the excitement of the chase racing through his body.

Noble was waiting at headquarters.

'Well?'

'His mates said they all went to watch Mosley's march,' Noble began. 'They had a few pints then stood just on the Holbeck side of the bridge. They'd been there about ten minutes when Miles said he needed to go. Reckoned he'd slipped off for a piss somewhere. That was the last they saw of him. He didn't even tell them about leaving his job and vanishing.'

'Do you believe them?'

'I don't think they're bright enough to be lying, Sarge.'

'No trouble at home or at work that anyone's saying and he ups sticks. Miles must have had a reason for going.' He sighed. 'Good work. Now we hunt him down.'

And he'd show his face soon enough. Every newspaper would carry the item tomorrow and it would be on the wireless – *If anybody knows the whereabouts of Mr Joseph Miles of Leeds, please contact the police as soon as possible. They need to speak to him urgently in relation to their inquiries.*

A waiting game. He hated those. But there was no choice.

*

He could hear the rain against the bedroom window. It had come on about ten o'clock, lashing down. He felt sorry for the coppers out on the beat. At home, with the covers up around him, he felt cosy.

Marjorie was making her usual preparations at the dressing table. Rollers in her hair to keep the bounce, a net over the top of it. Some smears of cold cream on her cheeks, rubbed in until her skin seemed to shine a little. Raven half-watched, half-read.

He knew they should talk, to settle whatever had grown between them. But words were dangerous. Once they'd been spoken they could never be taken back. It was safer to stay silent and let things carry on. The evening hadn't been too bad. Small talk, a magazine and the wireless. She'd spent the time ironing and darning. And then, finally, bed.

It seemed as if he'd just turned out the light when the telephone began to ring. The bell seemed dangerously shrill, loud in the darkness. Raven padded down to the hall and lifted the receiver.

'Got a car on the way for you, Sarge,' the voice on the line said.

'What is it?' Not another murder, for God's sake. Or had they caught Joe Miles?

'A fire.'

'I'm not the bloody fire brigade—'

'It's down at the BUF office.'

'Right.' Damn it all to hell.

'Inspector Mortimer's already there. He told me to ring you. The car should be with you in five minutes.'

Christ, didn't Mortimer ever sleep? He rummaged for a clean shirt and collar. No time to shave. He glanced over at the clock, the hands illuminating the time. Twenty to two. Marjorie hadn't stirred; she was too used to him being woken in the middle of the night.

The Humber was idling on the road, the driver sliding it into gear as soon as Raven sat down. No talking. Windscreen wipers moving from side to side. The roads were empty, the wet surface reflecting the street lights. The only noises were the roar of the engine and the hiss of tyres on the wet surface.

Upper Basinghall Street, just twenty yards down from the Headrow. The fire engine blocked the road. He could smell the smoke and feel the heat as soon as he stepped out of the car.

Flames licked up to the night sky. Hoses were pouring water on the blaze. He spotted Mortimer, a dark figure silhouetted against a wall.

'Doesn't look good, sir.' He didn't understand why the hell the man had dragged him out of bed in the middle of the night for this.

'I don't know.' The inspector gave a nasty grin. 'A bag of chestnuts and some parkin and this could be quite entertaining.'

'How bad is it?'

'They won't be salvaging anything. Still, the firemen say they have it contained. It should be out in half an hour or so.' He ground out his cigarette on the pavement and lit another. 'The man in charge says it's arson. He could smell petrol when they arrived.'

Now it made a little more sense.

'The communists, do you reckon?'

'Could be anyone, but yes, they're the obvious candidates, don't you think?'

Raven couldn't imagine Johnny Harris allowing this. Still, there were hotheads everywhere.

Someone was pushing through the crowd. In the light from the fire he could make out Andrew Reynolds, the branch secretary of the BUF.

'I'm sorry, sir, you can't go any closer.' Raven moved to intercept him.

'But—'

'Too dangerous, sir.'

'Everything we have is in there.'

'You'll be able to take a look after they've put it out and the building's cooled down.'

The man was unshaved. He looked as if he'd thrown on the first clothes he could find.

'It'll all be gone then.' He paced back and forth, a few steps each way.

'The fire brigade is working as hard as they can, sir,' Raven said. 'Let them do their job, please.'

Reynolds looked haunted, as if all his life's treasures were going up in smoke. But he said nothing, finally stopping and staring, as transfixed by the fire as Mortimer.

A few minutes later the flames seemed to dampen. From there it was a short time until they were gone completely. Firemen moved carefully into the ruins of the building to douse the last remnants of the blaze.

The night air was heavy with smoke and the smell of destruction. A photographer moved around taking pictures, his flash bulb illuminating the darkness. Too late for the morning edition, Raven thought. Too late, period. He still didn't understand why the inspector had wanted him here. It didn't need another copper standing round like a spare part. This damn thing could have waited until morning.

A shout caught his attention. One of the firemen darted out and spoke to his commander. Just a quick exchange then he edged back into the building, the other man behind him. Raven glanced at Mortimer. The inspector shrugged.

Even Reynolds was standing still, hands deep in his pockets. A few seconds later the commander reappeared, removing his helmet and wiping the sweat off his face. He looked around until he spotted Mortimer.

Raven edged close.

'We've got something in there.'

'What?'

'It's hard to be certain at the minute, but it could be a body.'

Sixteen

NOTHING TO BE done until daylight and everything was safe.

A uniform to guard the place and keep the gawpers at bay. Not a word to Reynolds. Let him keep the night watch in front of the place if he wanted. If there really was a body, they'd be talking to him in the morning.

The headquarters in the library was quiet. Time seemed to slow down. It was that way in the small hours, Raven remembered. He'd worked nights for six months and the clock always crawled towards the end of shift. It didn't help that daylight came later, either.

Men reported for the morning shift, the stamp of boots in the corridor. Finally, at half past six, Mortimer said, 'Come on, I'll buy you some breakfast.'

There was a café close to the market that the traders used, open early, runnels of condensation sliding down the windows. An egg with black pudding and bacon and three cups of tea brightened his mood. All his paperwork was up to date, everything signed, ready to pass on.

The inspector smoked three cigarettes, one after another, watching the daylight growing outside.

'We should be able to see now.'

*

He could smell the building from the bottom of the road. The hard, dead tang of burning and charred wood. No sign of Reynolds. The fire engine had gone, leaving wide pools of dirty water. A constable stood at ease.

'Any trouble?' Mortimer asked.

'Not yet, but it's still early, sir. They'll all be wanting a gander on their way to work. The fire investigator's in there. You'd better mind how you go – he says it's dangerous.'

Inside was devastation. The remains of a few beams that held up the second floor had crashed down. The fascists wouldn't be able to use this again, Raven thought. The stench of smoke and burning was so strong and acrid that he put a handkerchief over his mouth.

The fire investigator was close to the back wall, training his torch beam down on the ground.

'Be careful,' he called out. 'It's tricky back here.' He moved the beam to trace a path for them.

'What is that?' Mortimer asked once the three of them stood together.

'I think it's the remains of a human being,' the fireman said. 'Hard to tell with all this rubble on top. But look there; I'm positive that's an arm.'

It could be, Raven thought. He reached out to move some of the debris.

'Don't!' The warning came loud and sharp. 'It's still hot. And it could be evidence.'

'When will we know what's under there, Desmond?' Mortimer asked.

'Later today, once it's cooled. Get your scientific bods up here. I want this done right.'

'Was it arson?' Raven asked. 'Your fellows seemed to think it was.'

'No doubt about it. Knew it as soon as I walked in. Started over there.' He directed the light to a corner where a back door had once been. 'Petrol, by the look of it. You can see that darker patch where it started.'

All Raven saw were scorch marks and burns. But the fireman knew his job.

'I need to get to that body as soon as possible,' Mortimer said. 'If it is one.'

'I'm ninety per cent certain. Give it while this afternoon.'

'How much of him will be left?'

The fire investigator shrugged.

'Depends. If all this fell before he burned you should have most of the corpse.'

'If not?'

'Burned meat.'

*

'We could bring Reynolds in for questioning, but I'd rather wait until we're certain about the body,' Mortimer said as they walked back to headquarters.

'True,' Raven agreed. Could the Union have set the fire themselves? No, he decided. It would be too stupid, especially with someone inside.

'It'll probably be tomorrow before we get the pathologist's report.' The inspector kicked at a stone and sent it bouncing along the pavement. 'In the meantime I'll get someone digging into who owns the building. Have you had any word on that man for the Benson murder?'

'Joe Miles? Nothing yet,' he answered calmly. 'He'll show up soon enough. I started calling round local forces yesterday. I don't think he has the gumption to go far.'

'Let's hope so. The super needs results. Even more if that really is a body in the building.'

*

It took twenty-four hours for things to really begin moving. By then, photographs of the destroyed office were pinned to the wall of the CID office. The mounds of plaster and burnt floorboards. And the charred corpse.

The pathologist's report arrived. The body belonged to a male, but he hadn't died from the smoke. His life had ended before the blaze began. A blow to the back of the skull with a blunt object. The doctor had managed to take a print from the only finger that had survived intact; he'd sent it on to Records.

'Time to have Reynolds and Harding in for questioning,' Mortimer insisted. 'No pussyfooting this time.'

Superintendent Kennedy nodded his approval.

'What about this other chap?' Raven asked. 'Gilbert. You warned us off him before.'

'Special Branch are watching him. They want us to keep our distance from him.'

'Begging your pardon, sir,' Raven continued, 'but once this news is out, won't he think it's odd that we don't interview him?'

'Good point.' Kennedy took out a gold propelling pencil and scribbled a note. 'I'll ring them in a minute. You know what they're like, though.'

He did. Brute force and no brains. The type of copper all the others despised.

A knock on the door and Noble entered.

'We've got a response from Records on that fingerprint, sir.'

'Well?' Mortimer asked.

Noble took a deep breath.

'It seems like the body in the fire is Joe Miles, sir.'

For a moment the office was completely silent. It didn't seem possible. How? What did it mean? Raven was thinking furiously.

'Sergeant Raven, take Noble and pick up Mr Reynolds,' Kennedy ordered. The superintendent turned to Mortimer. 'Ewart, go and see the parents. Break the news. See if there's anything else they can tell us. Have some uniformed officers collect Miles's friends. I'll bring in Harding myself.' He cracked the knuckles on each hand. 'That's all, gentlemen.'

*

Reynolds insisted on telephoning his solicitor. The man would be waiting for him in town.

He kept asking questions but Raven never gave him information.

'They'll tell you down at the station, sir.' He repeated it so often it began to feel like a recording.

They escorted him through to the interview room where his lawyer was waiting.

'Harding's the same,' Mortimer said with a sigh. 'Brief here before he showed up.'

But rich men knew the law and how to use it. Raven would rather be outside, asking questions and seeing where they took him.

'How were the parents?' Raven asked.

'In tears.' He sighed and lit a cigarette. 'They don't understand it. Whatever's going on, they didn't know a thing about it. What do you think the story is?'

'I haven't a clue.' He perched on the corner of his desk, took off his trilby and wiped his forehead. 'But I'll tell you this: I've got the feeling we're being played for a bunch of bloody mugs, sir.'

'Why?'

'It's too pat, isn't it? Everything in the Benson murder seemed to point to Joe Miles. He vanishes at the right time. But does he run off somewhere? No. He stays in Leeds and turns up dead in a fire that the brigade said was arson. Doesn't that seem fishy?'

'Maybe.' He smoked furiously, a cloud above his head. 'But...' He raised a finger for each point like the schoolmaster Raven had known when he was twelve. 'It's blind luck we were able to get a fingerprint and identify the body. Without that, we'd have been searching for Miles until kingdom come. All we'd have had would be an unidentified body at the fire. Second: the simple explanation is usually the right one. You've been doing this job long enough to know that.'

That was sensible. But Raven knew he was right. He felt it. This wasn't just events happening one after another at random. Even that letter they'd received had a purpose. Someone was behind it all, pulling the strings. And the force was jumping. Riddles within bloody riddles. And now they had to wait while Kennedy talked to Reynolds and Harding.

The super was good, but he'd be hard-pressed to get anything from that pair. Not when they had their solicitors in the room.

Perhaps it was all getting on top of him. Not just work, but Marjorie, too. He tried not to think about that, but it was there, simmering away on the back burner. He needed to resolve things between them. But later, later… once everything else was done. Then he could give it the attention it deserved.

There were times he considered throwing up his hands and walking away from everything. Turn in his warrant card, pack a suitcase and go. Marjorie would probably be glad to see the back of him.

Nothing more than a pipe dream, though. He was one of life's stickers, a stayer. Another ten years and he'd qualify for his police pension. Ten more years and he'd be secure. Maybe the pension wasn't much and he wouldn't be ready to retire for years yet. But he'd have a cushion.

Anyway, if he took to the road, who'd want someone with a face that scared children? No one would hire him. No one would care about him. He was better off exactly where he was. Family, a few friends, a job he enjoyed. Maybe he even had a wife who still loved him.

Better the devil you knew. It made sense.

*

'The problem with the fire is that any mug with a can of petrol could have started it,' the arson investigator explained. He was sitting in Kennedy's office, with the superintendent, Mortimer and Raven listening. 'What we look for is a signature. Your proper firebugs have their own methods, it makes them dead easy to spot. But this...' He shook his head. 'It's the kind of thing any amateur would do to get a blaze going. He even left the can.'

'Any chance of prints from it?' Mortimer asked but the fireman shook his head.

'Only a few bits of twisted metal left.'

'Is there anything you can tell us?' There was frustration in his eyes and on his tight lips. But his voice was relaxed.

'I'm afraid not, sir.'

'Could the body in the office have been responsible?'

'Not unless he brained himself after he lit the match. That place would have gone up fast. In seconds. You'd have thrown the match in from the doorway and scarpered. Anyway, the post-mortem says your man was dead by then.'

A few seconds of silence while they all thought about it. Confirmation of what they already knew. Someone else was there with Miles. Someone who'd planned to murder him and make it look like he was a fire victim. One killer down, another on the loose. And no idea of who he might be.

Nothing from Reynolds or Harding, of course. Only to be expected. The frustration was so thick in the room that Raven felt he could have sliced and sold it in the market. Mortimer smoked cigarette after cigarette and Kennedy chewed the stem of his pipe.

'So Reynolds insists all the doors were locked when he left on the evening of the fire,' Mortimer said. 'But how do we *know*?' He was about to continue when a hand rapped on the door and a uniformed constable appeared.

'Sorry to interrupt, sir, but there's a telephone call for the sergeant.' A brief frown. 'It's urgent.'

*

What the hell was so important, he wondered as he lifted the receiver and said hello.

'This is Sister Nolan at St James's Hospital. Is this Sergeant Raven?'

'Yes.' He could feel fear creeping up his spine. No call from the hospital was going to be good news. His mum? His father?

'Your wife is here, sir. Marjorie Raven.'

'My wife?' he echoed dumbly. It was the last thing he'd been expecting. She'd been perfectly fine that morning.

'She was hit by a van, I'm afraid. She's in the operating theatre now.'

'How...' He didn't dare complete the sentence.

'Her leg's broken and there's some damage internally.' The nurse sounded cool and professional. 'I don't know how much. The doctor will have to tell you.'

'Yes.' He dragged the word up from his stomach. Suddenly he felt cold, as if he was buried in ice. His hand was shaking as he hung up.

'I'll get someone to drive you to the hospital, sir,' the constable offered. 'You don't look in any fit state.'

'Yes. Thank you.'

*

He didn't remember the trip. A squad car? It must have been. He didn't know much until he was in the waiting room. Even then, they'd only say that Marjorie was still in theatre. All he could do was sit and try not to think the worst as he watched the hands turn on the clock. He daren't even go for a cup of tea in case someone appeared with news.

Finally, almost two hours later, the surgeon appeared. He looked grave, his mouth turned down under a grey moustache. Christ, Raven thought, it's bad.

'Sergeant Raven?'

'Yes.' His voice was hoarse and he was gripping his hat so tightly that his knuckles were white. His belly ached.

'I'm Mr Hare. First of all, your wife is going to be fine.'

The wave of relief soared through him. The silent thanks to God, the shuddering in his muscles.

'How bad is she? Nobody would tell me anything.'

The surgeon had a ghoulish smile.

'Her leg's broken in two places, nasty fracture. We've mended that and put her in plaster. There was some internal bleeding, that's what took the time. We were trying to stop it. I think we found everything.'

'Can I see her?'

Hare shook his head.

'She's still out – going to be for a while yet. Leave it till this evening, let her rest. Being cut open is a shock to the system. I daresay you know that.' He inclined his head slightly. 'The war?'

Without thinking, Raven reached for the shiny scars on his face.

'Yes. And after.' He didn't want to talk about that. He needed to know about Marjorie. 'Are you sure she's going to be all right?'

'I promise you.'

'Thank you.'

Raven turned on his heels and walked out. Thoughts sparked like electricity in his brain, going everywhere and nowhere. The woman deserved it. No, she didn't, no one deserved that. Dammit. He didn't know what he was thinking. Without even realising it, he found his way back to headquarters, sitting in the CID office.

'How is she?' The voice roused him.

'They say she'll be right as rain.'

Kennedy put his hands on the desk and leaned forward.

'Go home, Urban,' he said quietly.

'I'd like to work, sir. It'll keep my mind off things.'

'In the morning. Look, it's three o'clock now. Go home, rest, see your wife, and then come in tomorrow.' He smiled, but there was steel behind the kindness.

'Yes, sir.' He stood and picked up the trilby.

'I'll get a car to take you.'

*

One stop first. The police substation on York Road. He wanted the details, to know how it had all happened.

'A van was coming along when a dog ran out into the road,' the sergeant at the desk told him. 'The driver swerved and hit a patch of oil. Your wife was on the kerb and the front of the vehicle clipped her. It was the back wheel that ran over her leg.' He paused. 'The witnesses all said the same thing. It was an accident, pure and simple. I'm sorry.'

Raven nodded and left. The truth seemed like a poor consolation.

*

It felt strange to be home during the working day. Wrong, somehow. He wandered through the rooms in a daze, half expecting to hear her voice at any second.

Finally, for something to fill the time, he changed into his old gardening clothes and went outside to dig up the last of the potatoes. Pushing his fork into the soil, the mechanical push and pull; that helped. By the time he'd finished he'd worked up a thin sweat.

Once the first frost arrived, he'd dig over the garden properly and put down some manure. But every thought was no more than a distraction.

At seven, he was waiting outside the surgical ward with a bunch of flowers in his hand. Bathed, shaved, dressed in his best suit. His lips were dry. He licked them apprehensively.

As soon as the nurse opened the door, he walked inside, gazing around, searching for her face. Down at the far end. His footsteps echoed sharply on the floor.

She was sitting up in bed, wearing a hospital nightgown, her hair brushed, a metal cage over the broken leg. Her face was a mass of bruises.

'You've been in the wars, haven't you?' He looked around for a vase, then left the flowers on the table beside the bed.

'Could be worse.' Her voice sounded hoarse and strained.

'They tell me you'll be fine.'

'I hope they're right.'

'What on earth happened?' Raven asked. He reached out and took her hand lightly. 'I know you were hit by a van.'

'I was minding my own business at the parade, ready to cross the road, and the next thing I knew I was on my back looking at the bone coming through my leg and screaming blue murder. Then the ambulance arrived.'

'Seems they're looking after you here.'

'The nurses are lovely. And they've given me things so it doesn't hurt.'

'You'll be back on your pins in no time.' He smiled.

'Longer than that, Urban.' She shifted slightly in the bed and he saw the pain flicker over her face. 'Who's going to do for you while I'm in here.'

'Don't you worry about that,' he told her. 'I can fend for myself.'

Marjorie stared at him. 'As long as I don't come home to a tip. I know what you can be like.'

He stayed until the bell announced the end of visiting hours. A quick kiss and he left the ward behind. At least she wouldn't be gallivanting anywhere for a while, he thought, then loathed himself.

As he left the hospital, he heard someone in the distance whistling *Goodbye Dolly Grey*. Christ, he hadn't thought of that one in years. They'd been singing it as they marched to the Leeds station, off for training and war. So young, so full of patriotism and bloodlust, with absolutely no idea what was really ahead of them. Almost nineteen years before. A lifetime and what had it brought them all? Death, pain, and the Depression. Disfigurement. It didn't feel like much of a bargain.

He bought fish and chips on the way home, eating them from the paper so there wasn't a plate to wash. The house was eerily quiet, just the soft clang from the water pipes. An old pan on the stove where Marjorie had been boiling face flannels before she went out.

He emptied it and hung them up on the rack to dry.

*

'Why didn't you ring me earlier?' Gladys's voice was a mix of shock and outrage.

'I'm sorry,' Raven said and meant every word. The day had dashed everything out of his head. He'd been about to lock up the house for the night when he remembered he hadn't told anyone about Marjorie's accident. Her sister was the place to start. She could spread the news.

'You're sure she's going to be all right?'

'Positive,' he said for the third time. 'The doctor told me himself.'

'They lie to make you feel better, everybody knows that.' God, she'd drive him barmy. No wonder he'd forgotten to ring her.

'Go and see her tomorrow afternoon,' he said. 'She'd be glad to have a visitor.'

'I will, don't you worry. And I'll make sure they tell me the truth.'

For a moment he was tempted to ask if she'd met Marjorie at the cinema recently. But he was too tired, and maybe it was better not to open that particular can of worms. Not right now. As it was, by the time he put down the receiver his ear had started to ache. He was in bed by ten. All the fear and tension had left, replaced by exhaustion. Raven set the alarm clock and drifted quickly to sleep.

Seventeen

'SORRY ABOUT YOUR wife, Sarge,' Noble said.

Raven grunted. He'd had a bad night, tossing and turning and waking every half hour. Guilt and anger, pain and sorrow: they wouldn't leave him alone.

'What happened yesterday?' the detective constable asked.

'You know that the super didn't get anything from Reynolds or Harding?'

Noble nodded his head. He was still young enough to only shave every two or three days.

'Well, he was never likely to, was he?'

'What about Miles's friends?'

'The inspector had a go at them.'

'Anything?'

'No. I was there. He put the fear of God in them but they didn't know anything. They were shocked when he told them Miles had died in the BUF offices.'

Another bloody dead end. Raven let out a long breath.

'The lad must have some other mates. What about them? There must be more than the two he was with at the march.'

'Mr Mortimer got a few more names. He's looking into that.' Noble paused for a heartbeat. 'He's pulling in your commie friend, too, Sarge. They went to pick him up a few minutes ago.'

Christ. Johnny hadn't anything to do with this. Not himself. And he wouldn't cover for any of his members who did, Raven would stake his pension on it. Pulled away from work like that, it could cost the man his job.

The desk sergeant poked his head round the door.

'Someone to see you, Urban.' He raised his eyebrows. 'A woman.'

*

Ava Benson was sitting on a hard wooden chair, staring down at her lap. She wore a brown wool coat and a felt hat that tried to tame her wild hair.

'Can I help you?'

'Oh?' She raised her head quickly, eyes wide. 'Sorry. Yes. I don't want to be any trouble, but I found something.'

It looked like a small book as she held it out. Raven looked at her questioningly.

'It's my father's diary,' she explained. 'I was going through some of his things and found it. I thought it might help you. Although I know you've found the man who killed him. That's what the papers say.' Her voice held an accusation.

'We might have. It's not one hundred per cent.'

'I see.'

He took the diary from her fingers. It was for that year, 1936, and well thumbed. He flicked through the pages. Plenty of entries in pencil.

'Thank you,' he said. 'It could be useful. Whereabouts was it?'

'In an old jacket of his. I thought we could get rid of his clothes, they were just a reminder for mum. I didn't even know he kept a diary.'

'Have you looked at it?'

She nodded. 'It didn't mean much to me, but I thought…'

'Thank you,' he said again.

'Like I said, I don't want to be any trouble.'

Raven smiled. 'I'm very grateful.' He was eager for her to leave so he could sit at his desk and read properly.

'I'd better go. Mum will be wondering where I am. She's become very nervous since Dad died. I didn't tell her about…' The woman nodded at the diary. 'She'd only become upset if she thought Dad had been keeping secrets.'

'We'll be in touch, Miss Benson.'

*

It was scrawls and scribbles in pencil, half of them smudged and faded. All in a type of personal shorthand. Trying to make sense of it was like breaking a code. People referred to by a single initial, locations abbreviated.

After half an hour Raven had begun to work it out. He started with the day Benson died. *To hear M speak finally*. That was clear enough. M for Mosley. Working backwards he muddled through a mix of work and the personal. Benson kept a private record of the men whose benefits he docked, noting them with an asterisk and exclamation marks, as if each one was a triumph. There were more than he'd imagined; the man had obviously relished his work.

But plenty of entries remained mysteries: What did *D, 1.30* mean? Dentist? Doctor? He'd never know.

An hour and he was coming to think it was a waste of time. Nothing that could help identify his killer. No Joe, no Miles, not even close. He was about to throw the diary in a drawer when he came on an entry for early August. *Meet K. Interesting young fellow.* On a Sunday; nothing to do with work.

But that was the only reference. Maybe it didn't mean a thing; it was impossible to be certain.

'Sarge?' Noble called from his desk. 'What are we doing today?'

'I don't know yet. Do any of Miles's friends have a name that starts with a K?'

The constable opened his notebook.

'There's a Keith. Why?'

'Let's go and have a word with him.' He let the diary fall onto the desk and picked up his hat.

*

'Course Mosley's right. We can't be having Jews and foreigners coming here willy-nilly and taking over the place.'

Raven tapped a spoon in his saucer and watched the young man take a drink of his tea. A café, a good, safe place to talk. Keith Hardisty wouldn't feel threatened here. If he seemed to be hiding something they could always bundle him down to the station and put the frighteners on him.

'Is that what Joe Miles believed, too?'

'Joe?' Hardisty laughed. He had small scars flecked across his knuckles and the backs of his hands. A foundry worker until the foundries closed down. Now he scuffled through life, doing this and that when someone offered to pay him. This was enough of a treat to start his tongue wagging. 'I don't want to speak ill of the dead and that, but if it wasn't football, girls, or money, Joe didn't give a toss.'

'Did he have a girlfriend?'

Hardisty laughed. 'Joe? Not bloody likely. Played the field. He was working, he had money. He'd take them out, show them a good time and they'd be grateful. You know what I mean?'

He knew. Things didn't change from generation to generation.

'Was he a fighter?'

The young man shrugged. 'He didn't run away if it started. Didn't go looking for it, mind.'

'How did he like to fight?'

'You what?' Hardisty stared at him.

'Was he a brawler? Fists and feet?'

'Nah, he was clever, was Joe.' A finger tapping against his skull. 'He fought dirty. Fast. Always said a hand on the throat'll stop 'em.' He grinned.

Now that *was* interesting. Did Hardisty just happen to mention that or was he planting it deliberately? There was something shifty about the young man. He didn't meet a gaze, eyes roving around, never settling on anything.

'Or a piece of cord?'

'Never seen him do that.'

'Why did you think he vanished?'

'Wondered if he'd got some girl up the spout.' Hardisty laughed. He didn't seem too distraught at his friend's death. 'Good reason to do a runner, isn't it?' He gazed around the empty café. 'Anyway, you can't blame anyone for taking off from here, can you?'

'When did you see him last?'

'The night before he went. He was in the pub.'

'How did he seem?'

'All right.' He smiled at the memory. 'He'd been paid. He was standing rounds.'

'Did he do that a lot?'

Hardisty shook his head. 'Said he'd won some money.'

'Did he bet on the horses?' Raven asked sharply. It was illegal, but so many did it that few coppers cared any longer.

'Not that he ever told me. I didn't ask.'

'When did you meet Frank Benson?'

'Who?' It was a quick response. Too fast. It was a lie; Raven knew it.

'Frank Benson.'

Hardisty shook his head. 'Don't know him.'

'Right you are, sir.' Raven stood and picked up his hat. Let the boy think he was clever. But anyone who read the papers knew Benson's name after the murder, and Hardisty had the *Daily Sketch* in his pocket. 'One thing, if you don't mind.'

'What's that?'

He gave a small nod to Noble, so he positioned himself on the other side of the man.

'We'd like you to come down to the station with us and answer a few more questions.'

He was ready. How many times had he seen this? Hardisty pushed back from the table and stood, ready to run. Instead, he found his arms gripped hard by a pair of policemen; he never had a chance. He didn't even struggle for two seconds before he gave up. No real fight in him at all, Raven thought. Good; that would make the questioning easier.

He tossed a shilling on the table and smiled at the terrified waitress.

'Right, my lad,' he said to Hardisty. 'Let's be having you.'

*

No tea this time. Just an hour of questioning. He wouldn't let Hardisty smoke; that would keep him on edge. Time and again Raven went over the friendship the young man had with Joe Miles. Always the same answers until he was satisfied they were the truth. Then, finally, on to Frank Benson.

'Look, you met him. It's in his diary. Start of August, wasn't it?' If it seemed like you already knew, they'd sometimes confess; it was a good trick.

'Don't know him. I told you. Must be some other bloke.'

Raven brought his palm down hard on the table. The crack resounded like a gunshot.

'You lied earlier. Don't do it now, son. I'm not in the mood.' With his face, that seemed like a real threat. 'Now, when did you meet Benson?'

But Hardisty wasn't quite ready to crack yet. He'd need a little more persuasion. The smallest of nods and Noble took the brass knuckles from his pocket, stroking them and sliding them over his fingers before clenching his fist. If Mortimer or the super came in now…

But nobody knocked on the door. There was just the growing silence in the room.

'Last chance,' Raven said. 'Then I'm going to let my friend ask the questions.'

'All right. It was early August,' Hardisty admitted. His voice was dry and husky. He'd spill it all now, and not even a mark on him.

'Where did you meet?'

The words came in a torrent. They'd met in the Palace, a pub on Kirkgate. Both of them admired Mosley and everything he stood for. He was the one who could keep the Empire and make sure Britain was a power again.

A week later they met again. This time Joe Miles had come along. He didn't have much to say, he wasn't interested in politics, but he listened. Benson talked about joining the BUF, becoming a part of it all. Hardisty didn't want to do that. A few words in a pub was one thing, all the palaver of becoming a member of a party – that wasn't for him. During the evening Benson started ordering Joe around, sending him off to buy another round, making fun of him for being so quiet. Little things, but Hardisty could see they niggled.

Finally they had a connection between the two men. About bloody time, as well.

'Did you see Benson again?'

'The week after. But Joe didn't come. He thought Frank was a bloody idiot. Got right up his nose.'

'But you didn't think he was daft?'

A shrug. 'He was all right, if you didn't let him get to you. If he tried to start lording it, I slapped him down. He said he was going to the rally and he was going to join the party. Good luck, I told him.'

'Did you see him there?'

'No. But I didn't expect to, did I? Not with all them people.'

'What about Joe?'

'Don't know. He was there and then he was gone. You reckon he did it?'

'Do you?' Raven asked.

'He kept going on about what a bastard Benson was. Didn't let it drop. But killing him?' Another shrug. 'I don't know.'

'Someone murdered Mr Benson. And someone killed Joe. You might want to think about it.'

'It wasn't me.' He gave a cold, hard stare. 'That's all I know.'

'Who else was with you at the rally?'

'My neighbour. He just came down for a laugh.'

He took Hardisty through it again and again, listening for the slightest inconsistency. They'd found a spot in Holbeck with not too many people and seen Miles with two other men that Hardisty didn't know. That fitted with what Raven had learned. They had a good view, easy to get into the ruck that was bound to happen. Miles hadn't even stayed long enough for that. Said he'd be back and took off. That was it.

'Are you going to charge me?' Hardisty asked when he'd finished.

'Why?' Raven asked. 'Done something you want to confess? Detective Constable Noble will type it all up. You sign it and you're free to go.' He stood, then leaned across the desk. His face was close enough to Hardisty's to make the young man flinch. He knew the effect his scars had. 'But next time, if you have any information, don't make us find you. Understand?'

He nodded.

*

It wasn't perfect, it was shaky as buggery, but now they had a reason for Miles to kill Benson. Motive… opportunity? Most likely he'd seen the man in the crowd and decided to take his chance. It would certainly explain why he'd fled straight after.

Thin, only circumstance. But they didn't have to make it stand up in court.

'It's as close as we're ever likely to get,' he told Mortimer and Kennedy, then took a sip of tea.

The superintendent took the pipe from his mouth and pursed his lips.

'I'll accept that. But there are still two glaring questions, aren't there?'

'I know, sir.'

The big one. How did Joe Miles end up dead and burned in the BUF office? The other: what about the letter? Miles seemed more like a frightened rabbit than someone who'd gloat and taunt the police.

'A friend of mine at the *Post* rang earlier. One of their reporters was out interviewing Roland Harding today.' He paused for a moment. 'He wanted to warn me: Harding has some damning accusations. Claims we know who set the fire and we're shielding them. It's running tomorrow.'

'But—' Raven began. That was ridiculous. If they knew who'd done it, he'd be in court by now. 'That's slander.'

Kennedy shook his head. 'He's saying it's what he *believes*. No mention of any evidence to back it up. But some people will take it as gospel. It queers the pitch, but that's what he wants. It puts us on the defensive.'

'We'd better find Miles's killer sharpish,' Mortimer said. 'The papers are going to lap this up. They've had it in for the police ever since that pay cut in '31. No order on the streets anymore, guff like that. And,' he added pointedly, 'we still don't have a clue as to who murdered Alwyn Davies. You know Harding's going to get that in there, too.'

'He wants to make us look like fools,' Raven said.

'Worse,' Kennedy told him. 'He wants to make it seem as if we're conspiring against the British Union.'

'About the only reason I can imagine for anyone killing Davies is that he was a fascist,' Mortimer said. 'But he was only small potatoes. Hardly worth the effort, poor sod. About as inoffensive as they came, according to everyone. Go over it tomorrow, Raven. Maybe a fresh pair of eyes would help.'

'Yes, sir.'

*

At six, he was in the Pointer. He'd started on his own pint. Another stood next to it. By five past Johnny Harris hadn't appeared. Raven waited another few minutes, then said to the barman, 'Mr Harris is always in here by now. Any idea what's happened?'

A man, resting his elbows on the wood and taking small sips to make the drink last, turned to look at him.

'You haven't heard?'

'What?' He felt the panic beginning to rise.

'Coppers hauled him in for questioning. Soon as he got back to work, the boot factory said he was an undesirable element and gave him his marching orders.'

He'd told them. He'd insisted the communists had nothing to do with the killings or the fire. And now it had cost his best friend his job. He pushed the glass along the bar.

'You might as well have this, then.'

He could go round and apologise. But what good would that do? It wouldn't bring back Johnny's job. He'd take it out on Raven, and who could blame him? Better to leave it another day or two.

He glanced at his wristwatch. He'd go over to the hospital early and pick up some fish and chips on the way.

*

Marjorie looked brighter, wearing a new nightgown he hadn't seen before.

'Gladys brought it this afternoon. Do you like it?' She pushed herself up the bed and winced. 'It's getting easier,' she said. 'Honest.'

Her sister had left magazines and fruit and a bottle of Lucozade that sat on the bedside table. He listened as she ran through the gossip in her family and on the ward, pointing out women and their different problems.

'Any idea when they'll let you out?' he asked finally.

'They're talking about keeping me in until the stitches come out.' She reached across and put her hand over his. He was surprised at how bony and thin her arm looked, as if weight had melted off her in the last couple of days. 'Are you coping all right? I'm afraid I'm not going to be much use for a while with this leg.'

'Don't you worry,' he said, feeling a rush of tenderness for her. 'I'll make up a bed in the front room so you won't need the stairs so much.'

This would put paid to seeing her fancy man for a while, he thought, then he felt a fresh rush of guilt. Maybe he'd just imagined it all; there might be a simple, innocent explanation.

'Gladys and the others said they'd come round and take care of everything.' Marjorie smiled. 'Like having my own nurses.'

A house full of her sisters. The last thing he wanted. But he had to be at work all day and they'd be gone by evening. Together, they'd manage. Maybe it would even bring them close again.

'I love you, you know,' he said.

'Good.' She smiled. 'I've never stopped loving you.'

The bell sounded for the end of visiting hours. At the door to the ward he turned, but she was already reading one of her magazines.

*

'Can I see that letter again, sir?'

'Letter?' Mortimer frowned.

'The one about Benson's killing.'

The inspector took it from his drawer, still in cellophane.

'I don't see why you need it. We have that one wrapped up.'

'I'm not so sure.' He looked at the writing again. *I kilt him*. 'Miles went on the run right after the march. He didn't want to be found. So why would he send this?'

'People do strange things, Raven. You know that.'

'I just don't buy this. I'm going to see his parents and get a sample of his writing.'

'We have Benson's murderer. For God's sake, we've told the papers.'

'For all the good it does.' He'd glanced at the *Post* and the interview with Harding. It was every bit as bad as Kennedy predicted and the reporter had lapped it up. Why let the truth get in the way of a good story?

Mortimer sighed. 'Go ahead if it makes you happy. And here—' he pushed a thick folder, '—that's everything on the Alwyn Davies shooting. Much good may it do you.'

*

Mrs Miles was in mourning black, of course. A simple dress that reached beyond her knees, with long, puffed sleeves. Her hair had been curled, plenty of grey showing through the black, and her eyes held years of sorrow.

'My husband's not here,' she said. 'He's at work.'

Of course. That was how men hid their grief. They carried on and pushed it down. It was exactly what he would have done.

'I'll only be a minute. I was wondering if you had anything your son had written. A letter, a list, anything?'

'I suppose so,' she answered grudgingly. 'Why do you need it?'

'Just rounding things off.' How could he even begin to tell her his suspicions? He could hardly even form them into something coherent.

'You'd better come in.'

A framed photograph of Joe Miles hung over the fireplace, wearing a garland of black crepe. He could hear the woman rummaging around upstairs, then the crop of her heels on the steps.

'There's this.' She held out a folded piece of paper. 'He didn't write much.' A sad smile. 'He didn't need to.'

It only took a second for him to know. The handwriting was nothing like the letter sent to the police.

'Thank you,' he told her.

'What's it all about?' She was wary now.

'Like I said, just rounding things off.'

'Do you know when they'll release his body? We'd like to bury him, you know.'

'I wish I could tell you. The coroner's office should be able to say.'

*

What now, he wondered as he drove back into the city centre. Everyone was happy to have the Benson murder wrapped up; they wouldn't appreciate this spanner in the works. But someone else was involved in all this. And he was the man who'd killed Miles and set fire to the building.

For now, though, he had other things on his plate. For the rest of the day he went through the Davies file, making notes of any inconsistencies and questions that came into his brain.

The heating had come on; the room was hot and close. Raven draped his jacket over the back of his chair and unbuttoned his waistcoat. His short collar rubbed uncomfortably against his neck and the braces felt tight against his back.

By five o'clock, he'd been through everything twice and made four pages of notes in his cramped writing. Plenty to go through in the morning. He was going to need Noble's help: things would go more quickly if they split the tasks.

*

He lit the gas in the grill, cut two slices of bread, and opened a tin of baked beans. Simple, reliable. Above all, it was a quick tea. A meal, a cuppa, wash the pots and he was on his way again, off for visiting hours at Jimmy's.

It was funny, he thought later on the tram back to Gipton, that they could get along so well when Marjorie was in the hospital. There was tenderness in the way she looked at him, the kind of real affection they'd had years before.

He still loved her. Perhaps this accident was a blessing in disguise. Maybe they could turn a corner and everything would be different when she came home. The way it used to be. He smiled. That would be good. Put all the bad behind them. There was no need to ever talk about it. Let it all sink and be forgotten. If she'd had someone on the side, well, no matter. It was only to be expected, given the way he looked.

But a new leaf. Yes. He was willing to try.

*

'Get yourself moving and talk to this lot,' he told Noble, handing him a sheet with five names.

'What are we looking for, Sarge?'

'There are things that don't quite tally in their statements.' He pushed papers held together by a clip across to the lad. 'Have a read and press them. You can ask if they have a pistol in the house, but I doubt the murderer's going to admit it.'

'Not unless he's stupid.' Noble grinned.

'I wish it was that bloody easy,' Raven said with a sigh. 'Report back at the end of the day. Any suspicions, let it lie and tell me later.'

He had people of his own to see. A few where he'd push hard for detail. Then he'd finish with a name he'd added, one that was going to make him very unpopular.

It wasn't difficult to reconcile the problems in the statements. A slip of memory and just fragments of life that didn't sit together easily. Nothing was ever exact, he'd learned that. With those out of the way, he sat in the Riley, wondering if he really wanted to make this visit.

Yes, he decided. He'd be hauled over the coals, but maybe it would stir things up a bit. God knew they needed it.

The traffic lights on Park Row turned red. He hated these things, he'd started driving well before they existed and he'd never had an accident. But these days, with all the vehicles around, maybe they were for the best. Better than coppers out on point duty, although there would be enough of those once the winter fogs arrived and visibility was no more than a few yards.

Out along York Road, past Crossgates, then into Barwick-in-Elmet, the area where the rich lived. Another world.

Eighteen

THE HOUSE LOOKED as if it had sat at the end of a long gravel driveway, across from an old church, for centuries. The lawn was neatly cut in cricket pitch strips of green. No weeds in the flower beds, everything cut back for winter. A gleaming Jaguar SS1 stood in front of the garage. Raven parked the Riley behind it and listened to the crunch of his soles as he walked to the door. Ten to one there would be a servant, maybe more.

He was right. A maid in her late forties answered the door, pinch-faced and doubtful until he showed his warrant card.

'I'd like to speak to Mr Gilbert.'

The woman crossed her arms over the white pinafore.

'He's not well.'

'I'd still like to talk to him.'

She stared into his face for a moment, showing nothing although he knew what she was probably thinking.

'You'd best not be hard,' she said. 'His bronchitis has come on early this year.'

The hall smelt of beeswax. A golf bag stood in the corner, club heads peering out like mushrooms. A coat rack with mackintoshes and hats. A woman's clothes, too, brighter: he'd never wondered if Gilbert was married.

But the man was nothing like he'd expected. Raven had anticipated someone older. Ian Gilbert couldn't have been over forty. He was wearing a sports jacket, mustard waistcoat, and a blue shirt with a pale yellow cravat. A pair of old, baggy cavalry twill trousers and brogues that had seen better days. The rich could afford to dress down-at-heel.

His face was pale, the features gaunt and sunken. There was nothing dangerous about this man, he thought, and then he saw the eyes. Very dark brown and full of calculation.

'Sergeant... Raven, is it?' A very cultured voice with barely a trace of Yorkshire. 'What can I do for you?'

'Just a few questions about the fire at the British Union office, sir. I understand you're involved with them.'

'Yes.' Gilbert began to cough, a deep, wet rasp that only ended when he put a handkerchief to his lips and spat out some phlegm. 'Forgive me,' he said. 'Bronchitis. I've had it since I was a boy.'

Perhaps that explained the thin physique. He hadn't spent his childhood running around the streets or the fields. Probably hadn't ever been within miles of the trenches, either.

'You're aware that we discovered a body after the blaze.'

'Of course.' Gilbert sat down, took a cigarette from a gold case and lit it. 'And I know that he was murdered, poor chap. Roland Harding told me. I'm not sure what it has to do with me.'

Raven turned the brim of his trilby in his hands. He was standing like a servant.

'What you might not know is that it seems as if the dead man was a killer himself. He strangled a fellow called Frank Benson on the day of Mosley's march.'

Gilbert tapped the newspaper sitting on the side table.

'I do read the papers, Sergeant.' A condescending smile. 'But let me ask again: what does this have to do with me?'

'What's your role in the party, sir?'

'I offer advice. Purely an ad hoc sort of thing. I've known Roland and Andrew for donkeys' years; they were friends of my father. And I know Sir Oswald, of course.' He smiled, showing a good set of teeth. Like a wolf, Raven thought. Gilbert began to cough again, a longer bout that made him double over. Blindly, he reached for a glass and took a drink of a brown liquid. 'That's better,' he said after a little while. 'We were all shocked by the fire. Even more by the murder.' A pause for a fraction of a second. 'It seems the police don't have any suspects yet, doesn't it?'

'We're following a number of leads, sir.' It was the standard response. 'I'm afraid I can't say more than that.'

'Which means you have nothing at all. I'm sorry, Sergeant, but I don't see the purpose behind your visit. You don't seem to have any real questions for me.'

'Were you at the Holbeck march?'

'Sir Oswald's rally? No, I was visiting friends in the dales. Why?'

Very handy, keeping his distance from the trouble and the danger. Clever.

'How much advice do you offer to the Union, sir?'

'Whenever they ask. I lunch with Andrew and Roland regularly and we discuss things, of course.'

Of course.

Gilbert stubbed out his cigarette in a glass ashtray then coughed again. The spell subsided quickly.

'I think I've answered all the questions I'm going to for now.' He cocked his head to one side. 'You were in the war, I take it, Sergeant?'

'I was. Were you?'

'The bad chest. They wouldn't have me.' There was no regret in his voice. 'Tell me, what do you think of Herr Hitler and Germany?'

'Wouldn't give you tuppence for him or any of the Huns. I'd trust them as far as I can throw them.'

'Hitler fought in the war too, you know. A corporal. He knows what it's like. Do you think he wants to go back to that?'

'I wouldn't put it past him. Met him, have you, sir?'

'I have, as a matter of fact. He wants peace with England. You might think about that. Good day, Sergeant.'

Standing like a servant, dismissed like a servant, and neatly put in his place. He didn't like Ian Gilbert one bit.

The drive back to headquarters seemed like returning to reality. None of the refinement of the big houses with their smells of self-satisfaction. In Harehills and Sheepscar, people knew the value of every farthing in their pockets and purses. Maybe they didn't live rich lives but they knew what was important.

Christ, he thought, he was turning into Johnny Harris. He turned the car onto Manor Street and bumped along the cobbles before stopping outside number thirty-four. Across the road, curtains twitched slightly. No other vehicles around. Washing lines strung up high over the street; every Monday they'd be filled with washing.

Maggie answered his knock. Johnny's wife was a small woman with gentle eyes and dark hair pulled back from her face in a severe bun.

'Urban,' she said in surprise and looked quickly over her shoulder. Her cheeks were flushed from working.

'I heard what happened. It's terrible. Is Johnny in?'

She shook her head. 'He's out looking for work.' She stared into his eyes and he could feel her judgment. 'Couldn't you have stopped them taking him in for questioning? Or at least had them wait until he'd left the factory instead of dragging him out of work?'

'I wish I could, Maggie. It was the brass's decision. I told them he didn't have anything to do with it.'

She gave the sigh of a woman who'd known disappointment all her life.

'Even if he was here, I'm not sure he'd want to talk to you. Not yet.'

'I understand.' This would be a terrible way to lose one of his oldest friends. 'Tell him I stopped by if you want.'

'I will.' She gave a faint smile. 'How's Marjorie?'

'In Jimmy's,' he began, and then he had to tell her the story.

'That's awful. Does she need anything?' That was Maggie: always ready to help everyone, never a person to hold grudges. Her communism was deeds, not talk. She was a good match for Johnny.

'Thank you, but her sisters are taking care of it all. I hope he finds something very soon.'

'So do I. But, you know, it'll be good to have him out of the place. It was killing his soul.'

*

Raven parked the Riley on Alexander Street, behind the library. Over on the Headrow the buses and lorries and cars passed, petrol fumes filling the air.

Inside, he climbed the stairs to the CID office. The only question was whether he'd be hauled over the coals today or tomorrow.

It was going to be today. He saw the figure sitting in Kennedy's office, then the superintendent's finger bent to beckon him.

'Sir?'

'This is Inspector Reid from Special Branch. He's made a very serious accusation against you.'

The man wore a tan mackintosh, an old blue suit and heavy coppers' boots. A bowler hat on his lap, a thick moustache over his top lip. Every inch a policeman. He was heavily built, with a dull look and big fists, fingers golden brown with nicotine. The Branch to the tips of his toes, Raven thought.

'What's that, sir?'

'He said you went to see Ian Gilbert this afternoon.' He glanced at Reid. 'Is that correct?'

'Yes, sir. We observed the sergeant park his car outside the residence at fourteen thirty-three hours. He remained inside for approximately twenty minutes, emerged alone, then drove away.'

'Is all that true, Raven?'

'It is, sir.'

'You'd been ordered to keep away from Gilbert.'

He knew Kennedy wouldn't let him off lightly. He couldn't; he'd issued the order himself. Now the Branch had complained, the super had no alternative but to tear a strip off him.

No raised voices. Kennedy kept puffing his pipe and speaking in his low, even voice. But by the time Raven was dismissed he felt as small as a blade of grass. He deserved it; the only thing that got his goat was to see the man from the Branch smirking.

Noble was waiting in the office, ready to report.

'Sarge—' he began, but Raven walked right past him and didn't halt until he reached the tram stop. He'd ruffled a few feathers today. He just needed to wait and see if it had been worthwhile.

*

The chip pan stood on the cooker, the dripping pale and solid. He didn't want to cook, he couldn't be bothered. Besides, there wasn't time if he was to reach the hospital by seven. Instead, it was fish and chips again, heavily doused in vinegar and salt.

Beckett Street. It was already dark, the first damp smell of fog in the air. As he walked through the hospital gate, a hand clamped on his arm.

Raven turned, already making his left hand into a fist. There was always someone, some chancer out for revenge. This was a bloody daft place for it, though; too many witnesses.

But this wasn't a thug looking to beat the living daylights out of him. It was Inspector Reid from Special Branch, even bigger and broader standing up.

'I don't like you stepping into my territory, son,' he said. 'You could have just buggered up a delicate operation.'

Raven shrugged and removed the hand from his arm.

'Is that all?' he asked.

'You speak to me, you'll say "sir". Got that?'

'I said is that all?'

'Think you're a clever devil, don't you? War hero with all that on your face.' Reid snorted. The man was trying to provoke him, to make him take a swing. There was probably another of the Branch boys around ready to step in if he tried.

'No, I think I'm a copper trying to do his job with my brains instead of my boots.'

'You'd better keep your nose clean, son, or I'll be all over you.' Reid spat on the ground and walked away.

Well, well, he thought as he walked down the corridor to the ward. If the man was going to all that trouble, the Branch must have something important going on. Interesting.

*

'The doctor said I'm making good progress. I can come home the day after tomorrow,' Marjorie said. She was smiling, happy. 'The district nurse can come round and take out my stitches.'

'That's wonderful news,' Raven told her. 'I'll make up a bed in the parlour for you.'

'Gladys said she'd take care of that. Everything'll be ready. She's going to pop in every afternoon and make tea, and Pearl will stop by in the morning to dust and do some lunch. They've got a rota worked out.'

It's my bloody house, he wanted to say. But he also knew the help would be welcome. He couldn't take any time off. And Gladys would be off looking after her own family by the time he came home.

'That sounds perfect.'

Nineteen

THE BRANCH WOULD be watching him now. Kennedy would be keeping a weather eye open. He needed to be careful. But he'd done what he intended. What was the phrase? Beard the lion in his lair, something like that. With all this fuss, he hoped something would happen.

Now he could get back to the job at hand.

'Right, what did those people have to tell you about Alwyn Davies yesterday?' he asked Noble as they sat in the detectives' room. No need to tell the lad what had happened. Everyone on the force would already know he'd had a dressing-down.

'Not much, Sarge. There's one I don't trust a bit. Peter Cave. Shifty as owt, but in a quiet way.'

'What about him?'

'Nothing specific. More the stuff he didn't say, if you know what I mean.' The young man pursed his lips, showing his thin moustache. 'You ask me, I reckon he knows more than he wants to tell. Scared, maybe.'

'Where does he work?'

'Pearl Assurance, just over the road.'

'Let's go and see him, then. You think he'll like my smile?'

*

Cave hadn't come into work that morning, the efficient receptionist told him. Raven looked at Noble.

'Is the head of his department available? We're with the police.' Raven produced his warrant card.

'Let me see, sir.' Very cool and professional. She played with the complicated switchboard for a few seconds then spoke into the phone. 'He'll be down in minute,' she said when she'd finished. Before they could turn away, she asked, 'I hope you won't think I'm rude, but where did you get that?'

No need to ask what she meant; it could only be one thing.

'France. Just before it was all over.'

The woman nodded. She had a stark, sober face and thick hair set in a wave. Thirty or so, he guessed. No ring on her finger.

'My brother caught it at the Somme. He spent the rest of the war in hospital. Missing a leg, a hand and half his face.'

Christ, Raven thought, and he felt sorry for himself sometimes. At least he had all his limbs.

'How does he manage?'

'I look after him,' she answered with a sad smile. 'He trained as an engineer after he came out of hospital. But there's not much call for them these days. Especially ones who aren't whole,' she added, and he heard the strain of bitterness.

'I wish him well.'

He'd barely completed the sentence when a man bustled through a heavy wooden door.

'These are the policemen, Mr Parker.'

A heavy man in a double-breasted suit with some sort of club tie. Bald, the little hair that remained glistening with Brylcreem, a sour expression plastered on his face.

'You're looking for Cave?' His voice had an officer's bark. A captain, Raven decided. Just enough rank to get a taste for authority.

'That's right, sir. But I gather he isn't here.'

'That's correct.' The man's back was ramrod straight. 'It's audit time, too. Everyone knows they have to be here unless it's an emergency. But he hasn't reported in today. No message.'

'I see, sir. He's normally a good employee?'

'Fair,' the man replied. 'Why?' He turned to Noble. 'You were here to talk to him yesterday. Is it to do with that?'

'Can we get his address, sir?' Raven ignored the question.

'I suppose so,' Parker agreed reluctantly. 'Miss Ellison will help you.' He turned on his heel, back through the door.

The receptionist was glancing through a heavy ledger. She began to write.

'Here you go. What's Peter done?'

'Nothing, we hope. Give your brother my regards.' He'd never met the man, never would, but he understood they shared a bond. Miss Ellison did, too.

*

'He packed a bag last night and said he had to go away on business.'

Noble had been right; the man did have something to hide. Cave's landlady was a cultured woman with a rich voice and hardly any money. Once well off and now left with nothing by the Depression, forced to rent out rooms in a house that was far too big for her.

'Did he say where or how long?' Raven asked. She wouldn't look at him, but as long as she answered his questions, he didn't care.

'It's not my business to ask.'

He was willing to bet that she'd love to know, though.

'Is he prompt with the rent? Does he have guests?'

She sniffed. 'I only accept good tenants, and Mr Cave knows full well that visitors are not tolerated.'

'We need to take a look in his room.'

'I'm not sure I—'

'We're the police,' he reminded her. 'Please, madam, the key.'

She struggled with herself for two seconds then handed it over.

'The second door to the left at the top of the stairs.'

*

Cave's window looked out over the street. Quiet, in the suburbs, all graceful houses fallen on hard times. In the distance, the bustle of Chapeltown Road.

'Go through everything,' he told Noble. 'He's skipped out quick, he's bound to have forgotten something.'

A single bed, wardrobe, chest of drawers, table and chair, easy chair. Cave had a wireless set close to an empty fireplace. Right, Raven thought as he looked around, if he wanted to hide something, where would he keep it?

He took off his jacket and rolled up his shirtsleeves before kneeling and feeling his way up the chimney. For a second he thought he had something, but it was no more than a lump of old soot. He washed in the bathroom on the landing. The place was clean to within an inch of its life.

'Sarge!' Noble called, and he dashed back, still wiping his hands. The lad had pulled away a loose section of the skirting board. Right behind it, in plain view now, was the butt of a Webley revolver.

Oh yes, he thought. His heart was racing and he could hardly catch his breath. Got you now, son. Bloody got you now. Meladdo must have been running scared to have left that behind.

'Easy now,' he said. 'Don't get your prints on it. Bring it out with a pencil and put it in a bag. That's the ticket.'

The cellophane crinkled and crackled around the gun. Very gently, as if he was scared of it, Noble placed it on the bed. But he'd never handled a weapon, no surprise it terrified him.

'Now let's tear this room apart.'

Cave had left in a rush; he hadn't even taken all his clothes. There was nothing else incriminating, but the Webley should be enough. Give it to the boffins and see if they could tie it to Davies' murder. It seemed like a very small jump – why else would the man be hiding it like that? Still, time would tell. He tipped a pen from the table into another bag. Cave's fingerprints should be on that.

As they were leaving, Raven spotted a small photo album on the shelf with Wills Cigarettes printed on the blue cover.

'Bring that, too.'

Downstairs he persuaded Mrs Ellison to glance through and pick out a good likeness of Cave; they'd need one to circulate to other forces. As she leafed through the snaps he noticed that the carpet in the hallway was threadbare in many spots and the walls badly needed distempering. Genteel poverty, indeed. At least she had four solid walls.

'Think it's him, Sarge?' Noble asked as they drove back to headquarters.

'Odds-on certainty.'

Two hours. That was what the lab boys promised for an answer. Raven filled out his report and went to find some dinner. Woolworth's on Briggate, following the signs up to the cafeteria on the third floor. It was a bright, airy place, modern as could be, filled with workers from the shops and offices. He ordered sausage and mash, dressed cabbage, damson tart with custard and a cup of tea. One and tuppence. The best meal he'd had since Marjorie's accident.

She'd be chafing today, ready to go home. And her bloody sister would be relishing the chance to be in charge. Let her; he could always duck out of the way.

His mind snapped back to Peter Cave. There was something going on with all this and he couldn't make head nor tail of it. Miles strangled Benson, then vanished, only to turn up dead. Noble questioned Cave about the Davies shooting and the man did a flit but left behind the most important piece of evidence. Not a scrap of sense in any of it. Were they going to find Cave's body in a few days?

*

Belly full, Raven strolled back to headquarters. Sometimes he wished he'd picked up the smoking habit, it was a good way to fill time. But he'd tried it when he was twelve and it had made him cough so hard he thought he was going to be sick. Never again, he decided there and then.

No report waiting for him. He rang the scientists. No reply; probably off at their dinner. But Mortimer was in the office and he wanted all the details about Cave.

'All I know is what we saw, sir. I told Noble to start finding out about him. We should have more soon.'

'I've put out a bulletin to all forces. Detain him but be careful – you know, the usual.' He lit a Capstan and leaned back in his chair. 'You were a fool, you know.'

'Sir?'

'Going to see Ian Gilbert. What did you think was going to happen?'

'I'm not sure. It might come to something.'

'You know better than that. With the Branch watching him, there was certain to be a complaint. The super had no choice but to give you a roasting.' He leaned forward, the elbows of his jacket resting on the desk blotter. 'Between you and me, Mr Kennedy was glad to see you trying to shake things up. We're just not sure that was the best tactic.'

Raven shrugged. It was done. Something might happen. If it did, the boys from the Branch would be all over it, happy to take the credit. Good luck to them. He was concerned with crime, not the murky world of politics.

His telephone was ringing, the bell sounding urgent.

'Detective Sergeant Raven.'

The lab. The casing they'd found where Davies died matched another shot from the Webley. And the fingerprints on the revolver matched those on the pen. Bingo!

'It's definitely Cave!' he called out and the inspector gave the thumbs up. Now they just had to find the bastard. And also whoever had bashed in Joe Miles's head and left him to burn. Bit by bit, they were getting there. He smiled to himself. Now where was the lad with his information so they could start hunting?

It was after four when Noble returned, looking weary and footsore.

'Well?' Raven asked.

'I've had a word with his mates. Turns out he has a lady friend of sorts, too.' He smirked. 'Thing is, she's married, so I had to talk to her on the QT.'

'Spit it out. What have you found?'

'It seems there's a bit more to chummy than we imagined. He's a member of the British Union, no doubt about that,' Noble said triumphantly.

'Go on.' Raven's mind was roaring, trying to work that one out. Why would one of their members kill another?

'He was in the war, rose to sergeant in the artillery.'

'What regiment?' Frank Benson had been a gunner.

'Don't know, Sarge. We'll have to talk to the War Ministry. He liked a drink on the weekends, nothing excessive. And he enjoyed camping and orienteering. You know, using maps to find your way around. A real nature boy, apparently.'

He recalled the Ordnance Survey maps and compass on a shelf in Cave's room. He had military training, he knew how to find his way around. He could be hiding out somewhere in the countryside. Dammit.

'What about this girlfriend?'

'Yes.' He cleared his throat. 'Mrs Naylor. Elsie. We had a natter. I told her I'd keep everything under my hat.'

'This is murder, son. You should never make promises like that. The lab boys say Cave's gun definitely killed Davies.'

'Yes, Sarge.' Noble was flustered now, his neck reddening a little. 'Anyway, she was seeing Cave, keeping it very discreet. She's a rambler, too. Seems they'd meet up to go walking and do their mischief out in the open air. Takes all sorts, I suppose.'

Raven was thinking.

'Any particular places they liked to go?'

'Nowhere that far. Ilkley Moor and up near Skipton, places like that. Otley Chevin.'

Miles and miles of land. Plenty of room to hide if you knew what you were doing, and Cave probably did. No point in trying to search. But the days were growing shorter and wetter, and the nights could soon be cold. No one was going to stay out there for weeks as winter arrived. Not even someone desperate.

'Did she know Davies at all?' A love rivalry could be a good motive for murder.

'Second question I asked,' Noble answered with a grin. 'She swears she's never heard of him. I believe her. She was terrified that her husband would find out and beat the tar out of her as it was.'

'All right,' he said. 'Keep looking around and see what else you can find on him.'

Noble nodded. 'How's your wife, Sarge?'

'Home tomorrow.' He'd better get himself back there and see what damage Marjorie's sister had done to his home.

*

The house was empty but he could smell her cigarette smoke in the air. The place was like a new pin, all the woodwork gleaming with polish, every plate, cup, and pan washed, dried and put away. She'd made up a bed on the settee in the front room, pillows plumped and ready.

He saw a note on the table: *Sandwiches for your tea in the larder.* He found them, thick roast beef with dripping. Nothing wrong with that, all they needed was a touch of horseradish sauce to add some bite.

She'd done a good job, he had to admit it. But Gladys Queen Victoria Clayton was thorough in everything. A hair over five feet tall, hardly weighing more than a sack of feathers, but a dynamo when she set her mind to anything.

He finished, drank his tea and washed the pots. He'd hear about it tomorrow if he didn't. Then it was back to the trams and St James's hospital.

Raven wanted to give Marjorie his attention, but Peter Cave wouldn't leave him be. Where was the bugger? With skills like his, the man could stay lost for a while…

'Have you heard a word I said, Urban?'

'I'm sorry. And yes, everything's ready for you.'

'The ambulance is supposed to collect me at eleven. Gladys will be waiting at home. She'll see I'm settled in and cook something before she leaves. Then you can look after me in the evening.'

'I will. I'll be happy to have you back,' he said and meant it. The place had seemed empty without her. Too quiet.

As soon as the bell finished visiting hours and he was back on Beckett Street, Cave jumped into his mind again. The street lamps gave their yellow glow as a vehicle rumbled along. The wheels had their rhythm in the steel tracks, and brakes grated hard enough to cause sparks to fly. He barely noticed. Walking back down the road, hands buried in the pockets of his overcoat, he hardly noticed the first dark spatterings of rain on the pavement.

Twenty

'HAVE YOU SEEN the headline?' Raven tossed the *Post* down on Mortimer's desk.

COMMUNISTS ACCUSED OF ARSON AND MURDER

'We've all seen it,' the inspector replied. 'It's rubbish.'

'Then why the hell are they printing it?' He banged his fist against the paper.

'Probably because Roland Harding is a friend of one of the directors and he slipped in a word. There's not a scrap of evidence in the article. We're not taking it seriously.'

'If you repeat something often enough, people will start believing it.'

Mortimer balanced his cigarette on the edge of the ashtray.

'Maybe some will,' he said. 'I can't help that. But we're not a bunch of bloody idiots, Urban. Even if the communists did set fire to the office, which I doubt, there's absolutely nothing to connect them to Joe Miles.'

Raven started to calm a little. He'd been raging as he stormed down the Headrow, taking the stairs to the CID office three at a time.

'Is it true what they say there about Ian Gilbert owning the building with the office?'

'That's probably the only shred of truth in there. His grandfather bought it fifty years ago. He let them have it at a peppercorn rent. Insured through Reynolds's agency. And not for any large amount. They'll be lucky to rebuild for the settlement. We've looked into all that. It certainly wasn't torched for the money.'

'Of course it wasn't. Someone wanted rid of Miles's body.'

'Yes.' He picked up his cigarette and tapped ash on the newspaper. 'And things like this don't help us find out who did it.'

*

'We're going to need God's own luck to find Cave,' Raven told Mortimer and Kennedy. The superintendent calmly puffed on his pipe. The inspector took nervous draws on his cigarette.

'That doesn't mean we stop trying,' Kennedy said. 'We've put a bulletin out to every force in the country. Keep an eye out for people walking and all that.'

'Yes, sir.' For all the bloody good it might do. People like Cave could make themselves invisible in a wood.

'But let's say that's on the back burner for now,' the super continued. 'Do we have any connection between him and Joe Miles?'

'Nothing we've come up with so far,' Mortimer muttered. 'Apart from the BUF.'

'And that doesn't make a blind scrap of sense,' Raven pointed out. 'Why leave the body in their office then set fire to it? It's asking for suspicion.'

'We've talked to that chap from the communists—'

'He lost his job after you hauled him in, sir.' Raven hadn't planned on mentioning it but he couldn't stop himself.

'I see.' He was silent for a few seconds. 'That's a pity. Well, gentlemen, let's get to work. We're making progress.' He gave a quick smile. 'Slow, but we're getting there.'

*

Progress? It came in fits and starts. And sometimes it hardly seemed like moving forward at all. Yes, they knew who'd shot Alwyn Davies in the middle of the night. But they didn't have the slightest inkling why and they certainly didn't have Peter Cave behind bars. There didn't seem to be any reason for it.

Then there was the killing of Joe Miles. Not even the smallest lead there. Not a hint or shadow of anything to show why he'd ended up with his skull caved in and burned to a crisp. No suspects at all.

'Raven?' The superintendent's voice called him back from his thoughts. 'A word, please.'

He closed the door behind himself and stood to attention.

'You might as well relax, Urban.' Kennedy relit his pipe and crossed one leg over the other, smoothing his suit trousers at the knee. 'What were you playing at the other day when you went to see Ian Gilbert?'

'Sir?'

'Don't play the bloody fool, man. I know you're brighter than that. What did you hope to achieve? I'm not going to give you another bollocking. I just want to know.'

'Well, sir.' He tried to gather his thoughts. 'He's obviously an important man to the Mosleyites; the Branch wouldn't bother with him otherwise, right?'

'Go on.'

'We've been told to keep our distance, no matter what.' He waited until the super nodded. 'I thought that if I went to see him it might make him do something.'

'Like what?'

'I haven't a clue, sir,' Raven admitted. 'But one way or another, the fascists have been involved in three murders. And if he's the power behind the throne...' He let the idea hang, simply because he'd been unable to take it any further.

'So far the only thing that's happened was what you saw,' Kennedy said mildly. 'The Branch came down on us like a ton of bricks. Strictly between us, I don't respect them any more than you do, but they've done a few good things in their time.'

'Yes, sir.'

'Do you feel you shook Gilbert at all?'

'Not really,' he answered after a second. 'I think he found me more of an annoyance than anything.'

'Then leave him be. I know this whole case is tangled, but my guess is that someone's trying to make the BUF look bad. Seems to me they can manage that without any help, but something's going on, and I doubt we've seen the end of it yet.'

'The question is who's behind it, sir.'

'I know. Don't worry, I'm sure it's not the communists. Quite honestly, I doubt they could plot their way out of a paper bag, let alone carry off something like this. I'm sorry about your friend, but we had to follow up. I'm sure you see that.'

'Yes, sir.'

'Look, you've solved two of the murders. That's a damn good job by any standards. I want you to work with Inspector Mortimer on the fire and the Miles killing.'

'Gladly, sir.'

'No more taking off and disobeying orders.'

'Understood, sir.' He smiled.

'How's your wife?'

'Coming home today. Going to have the sisters-in-law around all the time looking after her.'

Kennedy raised an eyebrow and grimaced.

'I hope they're more agreeable than mine.'

'Martinets, sir, the pair of them.'

'Women, eh, Sergeant?'

Kennedy was a good leader. During the war he'd probably been the type of officer men followed blindly, just because they liked him and believed in him. The talk had taken the sting out of the dressing-down he'd been forced to give.

*

'What you do want to do on Miles, sir?' he asked Inspector Mortimer. They'd gone to the Kardomah café for a cup of coffee, away from the pressure cooker that the CID office was becoming.

'I wish I knew. Any bright ideas?'

'No.'

'Let's go and look at the fire again. Maybe it'll give us some thoughts.'

There was an autumnal bite to the air and the smell of coal burning as they walked through town to Basinghall Street. In the windows of Schofield's department store, mannequins wore fashionable winter clothes that cost a week's wages.

At the crest of the Headrow they could feel the sharp wind from the west. Raven tapped the trilby more firmly onto his head, hunched into his overcoat and felt his turn-ups flapping around his ankles.

Browns and greys; those had been the colours of Leeds for the last few years. Muddy, dull, drab. Ten years before, everything had been bright and vivid. Reds, yellows, brilliant blues. Nowadays that seemed like another age altogether.

Workmen were already swarming around the building, removing all the debris from the shell. It was hard to spot where the body had been. All that remained was a cracked patch of concrete floor smeared with dirt and soot.

'Doesn't make sense for Gilbert to burn his own place down, does it, sir?'

The inspector shook his head. 'None at all. And you can leave a body anywhere. If you ask me, the fire was a message. We just don't know who sent it or what it's supposed to mean. Like that letter about Benson,' he added.

A man in a donkey jacket moved them aside; they were going to bring down a beam. But there was nothing to see here, anyway. Even the back door had been carted away and the alley at the back cleared.

'Who hates the Blackshirts?' Raven wondered.

'Apart from the communists? More people than you can shake a stick at, probably. But I can't think of any who'd resort to murder and arson. No, we're still on square one with this.' Mortimer lit a cigarette and glanced over his shoulder at the demolition. Plenty of noise and shouting. The workmen seemed to be enjoying the job. Why not? They were being paid.

'Have you had any luck tracing Miles's whereabouts before he died?' Raven asked.

'None. For all the reports we've had, he might have dropped off the face of the earth.'

Someone must have been sheltering him. Who? That was the missing piece of the puzzle. Find him – or her – and maybe everything might fall into place.

'That's where we should be looking, sir.'

'I do know that, Raven.' There was a bristling edge to his voice.

'Sorry.'

'I've talked to family, friends, every name I can find and they all swear blind they don't know what happened.' He paused for a fraction of a second. 'Before you ask, I think they're telling the truth.'

'He must have had another group of people.'

'Or person. My money's on a girl. Someone well out of the frame.'

That was possible. Miles had been a good-looking lad. But that meant *cherchez la femme*; tricky enough at the best of times. No sister who might help.

'Then let's dig into that, sir. Go back and talk to his friends again.'

Mortimer sighed.

'I'll leave that to you. They're probably sick of the sight of me. I have a list in the office.'

*

It didn't take long to go through it. The inspector was right: all he found was confusion and regret. Miles didn't have a steady girlfriend, barely even someone he saw once in a while. He came away with a couple of names and little hope.

But he had two people he wanted to question again, the friends who'd been at the march with Miles, the ones who'd been with him when Frank Benson tried to humiliate him.

*

'I told you before,' said Hardisty. He was wary of Raven after the experience he'd had before. 'Joe wasn't bothered. He played the field when he wanted company.'

But his companion was quiet. He sat in the interview room looking down at his lap, his expression hidden.

'What about you, lad? What do you have to say for yourself? Joe was your mate, wasn't he?'

Rafe Tollman raised his head slowly. Another chum of Miles and Hardisty. Shy, scared. Guiltily he glanced at his friend, then said, 'There was someone.'

That was better, Raven thought. He hadn't even needed to play the hard man this time. His notebook was on the table, open to a fresh page. He picked up the pencil.

'What's her name and where do I find her?'

'She's called Barbara.'

'Surname?'

The young man shook his head. 'Don't know. But she lives on South Accommodation Road. At that pub.'

'What else?'

'That's it.' As Raven stared at him, he reddened. 'Honest. I don't know any more than that.'

It was something, enough information to track her down.

*

'See what you can find out about her this evening,' he ordered Noble. 'Don't talk to her. We'll save that for tomorrow.'

Mortimer leaned against the edge of his desk.

'You and I will see her together,' he said.

'Yes, sir.'

The inspector's face creased into a tired smile.

'Get yourself home, Raven. Make sure your wife's fine. This can wait another day.'

'Thank you, sir.'

*

On the tram, then walking along the road, he felt strangely nervous. Don't be so daft, he told himself. You're not courting. She's your wife, for God's sake. You've shared a bloody house with her for years.

Marjorie was on the couch, her plastered leg up on the pouffe. The curtains were drawn, the light burning bright. A fire burned in the grate; the room felt warm. She had a pile of magazines at her side, a copy of *Photoplay* open on her lap. As he opened the door she looked up and smiled.

'Oh, Urban, you've no idea how good it feels to be home,' she told him. 'Come and give us a kiss.'

She was wearing perfume and face powder, dolled up for leaving hospital. A pair of crutches was angled beside her.

'I'm glad you're back,' he said. 'How do you feel?'

'Tired,' she admitted. She was dressed in a blouse and cardigan and her favourite tweed skirt. The cast on her leg was a clean, brilliant white. 'Tender and sore. Gladys left your dinner in the oven but you'll have to wash the pots.'

He balanced the plate on his lap as he sat on the chair across from her. They talked about her time in hospital, how the district nurse would arrive in a few days to remove her stitches. And then his case. There was no distraction from the wireless. It was like the old days, he thought. The good old days.

When he returned from the kitchen he brought two cups of tea. She smoked as she drank, the smile never leaving her lips. At bedtime he helped her upstairs to the bathroom, astonished at how nimble she was on the crutches.

Back in the front room he tucked her into the bed, kissed her lips and turned off the light. As he closed the door she said, 'I do love you, you know,' and for once it didn't sound as if she was trying to convince herself.

*

'I've found her,' Noble announced proudly as they sat around Superintendent Kennedy's desk. 'Barbara King. She's a barmaid at the Royal Oak on South Accommodation Road. Lives on the premises.'

That was handy, Raven thought. Everything in one place.

Mortimer checked his wristwatch. Just turned nine.

'We'll have plenty of chance to talk to her before they open.'

The inspector smiled as he drove nervously across Crown Point Bridge and into Hunslet. The man had every right to feel good; the case was starting to crack wide open. A couple of hunches and some solid police work. Cave was still out there somewhere, but hopefully it was only a matter of time before someone called in a tip.

Soon they'd discover who was really behind all this.

Rubbish littered the streets. Sheets from old newspapers, cigarette packets, dog dirt. The cobbles were cracked, some of them gone. All the buildings were filthy with generations of soot; rub against one and your clothes came away black.

The inspector hammered on the pub door and waited. No answer. He tried again, harder this time. From somewhere inside a muffled voice yelled, 'Hold your horses. We're not bloody open.'

Finally the bolts were drawn back by an unshaven man wearing a cardigan over a shirt with no collar.

'Well?' he asked. 'You're not from the brewery and I'm not expecting anyone else. If you're selling owt you might as well push off now.'

Mortimer didn't say a word, just produced his warrant card.

'Right.' The man was flustered. He had something going on the side, Raven decided. 'I suppose you'd better come in.'

A young woman was polishing the bar, hair pulled up and out of the way under a turban, an old apron covering her body. As they entered, she looked at the landlord and put down her cloth, ready to leave.

'Miss King?' Mortimer said.

'Yes.' Her eyes flickered around the men.

'You'd better stay. We've come to have a word with you.'

It was a simple sentence, but one to bring fear when a copper said it.

'Joe Miles.'

'He's dead,' she answered.

'It's where he was before he died that interests us, miss,' Raven said gently. She looked at him and the horror of his face registered as her mouth became a small, tidy O. 'Was he with you?'

'He wasn't in here,' the landlord said. 'She knows the rules. No lads. There's me and my wife and daughter. We're not having anyone set a bad example.'

Mortimer turned to the man.

'Is there a reason you're still here?'

'It's my bloody pub.'

'Tell me, sir, do you want to be taken in for obstructing a police officer?'

'I'm not doing anything.'

'No, you're not,' the inspector said. 'So perhaps you should go. Please.'

*

Barbara King looked terrified. Anyone would if the police came calling. She sat hunched in on herself, head gazing at her lap, fingers fidgeting with her apron. Raven sat to the side, away from her line of vision. No need for his face to keep scaring the girl.

'I believe you knew Joe Miles,' Mortimer began. He kept his voice quiet, easing her into the conversation.

'Yes, sir,' she answered without looking up. A timid voice that wanted to be anywhere but here.

'Good pals, were you?'

'Sometimes.' She glanced up for a second. 'When he wanted to be.'

'Were you sweet on him?' Raven asked and she nodded, quickly turning away from him to look at Mortimer again. 'But he didn't feel the same way?'

'When he wanted something.'

'Did he come to see you before he died?'

Tears were starting to trickle down her cheeks. She dabbed at them with the apron. It was a sad scene, he thought, among the smell of polish, stale cigarette smoke and old beer.

'What did he want?' Mortimer asked softly. He had the knack of sounding like a caring uncle, keeping his insistence hidden.

'He needed somewhere to stay.' She took a breath. 'I told him he couldn't have anywhere here. Then he asked about the shed at the back.'

'Go on.' She'd started now. The rest would arrive, piece by piece.

It sounded as if Miles knew he had her in his spell and took advantage whenever he wanted. This time, it was a place to hide for several nights and food she managed to smuggle out from the kitchen. She begged them not to tell the landlord; he'd sack her on the spot. During the day, Miles would vanish, coming back once it was dark, seeking shelter and a kiss and cuddle. He never said where he went or if he met anyone. He'd brought a bag with a few clothes, his razor and brush. Then one evening he hadn't returned at all. No word, no sign, no hint he wouldn't return. The next thing she knew was when she read about the fire.

'Is the bag still here?' Mortimer wondered.

'In the shed.'

'We'd like to take a look at it, Miss King.' She looked at him doubtfully. 'It might help us find out who killed him.'

'My job…' she said.

'Don't worry. Sergeant Raven will have a word with your boss.' He raised an eyebrow and Raven gave a short nod.

The man was just behind the door where he'd been listening. As the inspector and Miss King passed, Raven put a hand on the man's arm.

'What's your name?'

'Aldous Carthy.'

'Well, Mr Carthy, it would be a shame if a very helpful witness found herself out of a job. If that happened we might have to look at the licence of the man responsible, maybe put in an objection when it was due for renewal. And I daresay the brewery wouldn't be happy with someone who didn't help the police, either. Do you get my drift?'

The landlord pulled away.

'I do.'

Raven gave a dark smile. 'I'm glad we see eye to eye, then. Good day to you.'

The shed was tight and dry. There was a platform ten feet off the ground, a ladder leading up to it; a hayloft once, he guessed. This must have once been a stable. Now empty crates were stacked against the walls and bundles of papers littered the floor. Miles would have been dry here, even if it wasn't warm.

'Where did he sleep?' Mortimer asked and Barbara King pointed to the loft. The inspector climbed carefully, testing each old rung before putting his weight on it. 'There's a grip up here,' he called, 'and some sacking.'

He returned with the bag and opened it. Underwear, socks, a shirt and two collars. A sponge bag with soap, old shaving brush, safety razor, toothbrush and a tin of Calvert's tooth powder.

All that remained of Miles's life on the run. It would go with them and be entered as evidence.

'Tell me something, Miss King,' Mortimer said, sounding puzzled. 'Why didn't you come forward and tell us he'd been here after you learned he was dead? We've had a devil of a job finding out where he'd been. You could have saved us a lot of time.'

It came out as a question, but it was a reprimand. She looked down at her feet.

'I'm sorry. I thought you'd arrest me. You're not going to, are you?'

'No,' the inspector told her. 'But if there's anything else you know, or anything you think of, you need to tell us. You've no idea where he went during the day or who he met?'

'No.' She looked at them both, not flinching this time as she stared at Raven. 'Honest, he never said.'

At least they were leaving with something. The case was like one of those jigsaw puzzles Marjorie liked to do during the winter, making the table unusable for days on end. They had all the edges and slowly they were moving towards the centre. They already had all the pieces, he felt sure of that. They just had to know what they were and how to make them fit.

'Well?' Mortimer said as he started the Riley and lit a cigarette.

'I think we're still going to have one hell of a job getting to the bottom of this.'

'Yes.' The inspector sucked on his teeth. 'Can't exactly say we're making great strides, can we? More like shuffling along.' He gave a long, frustrated sigh, then smiled. 'Still, you solved two of the killings. That's something. It makes us look halfway decent.'

'We still don't have Peter Cave in custody, sir,' Raven reminded him.

'He can't stay out in the wilds forever. There's sleet and snow in the forecast for the dales. That should flush him out soon enough.'

He hoped the man was right.

Still, this was a fair morning's work. They had Joe Miles's bag in the boot and now they knew some of his movements before his death. That was good. But the important stuff remained elusive. Who did he see during the days? And how in God's name did he end up dead in a burning BUF office?

Twenty-One

'WE'RE GETTING THERE, aren't we, Sarge?' Noble asked with a smile.

He had to admire the lad's optimism. Short of sheer luck there was still a long road ahead and it was all uphill.

'A little,' he allowed. 'We still don't have the foggiest who's behind it all. That's the bugger we're after. The one who's pulling all the strings here.'

'You must have some idea, Sarge.'

'Don't you think we'd be banging on someone's door if I did? We need evidence, son.'

But the afternoon didn't bring them any. At five, Raven was back at headquarters, writing up his report on the day. Both Mortimer and Kennedy were out; the office seemed curiously silent. A deflating end to the day. But Noble was right, he had to admit: they were getting there.

*

Marjorie was hobbling around on her crutches. She wasn't about to start the hundred yard dash, but he was impressed. The chamber pot was still easier for her than going up and down stairs every time. He didn't mind emptying it; it wasn't so long ago that they'd shared an outside privy with two other families. In those days the pot had seemed like luxury on a cold winter's night.

They talked. Easy, pleasant conversation. Not about anything in particular, nothing he could even recall the next morning. Just the simple fabric of a couple that had spent many years together. He went to bed contented, and slept without dreams.

*

Another day, another chance to track this case back to the source. It was a foggy morning. Not one of the bad ones, at least not in Gipton as he walked to the tram. But he could taste it at the back of his throat, acrid and bitter. There'd be plenty more of this, all through the winter.

Already people were coughing, trying to get rid of the dark, sooty phlegm collecting in their lungs. Bloody weather. But what could anyone do?

He bought the *Sketch* at the newsagent's, then added a copy of the *Yorkshire Post* as he saw the headline, reading the story on the trip into town.

It was Ian Gilbert's turn to open his mouth to a reporter. He was trying to remain balanced, he said, and everyone wanted murderers caught and charged. But the way the police were hounding law-abiding members of the BUF, people who only desired a truly great Britain, was outrageous. It was as if the force believed that the Union had been killing their own supporters, and that was ridiculous. They were besmirching good names.

More assertions, more generalisations, one or two outright lies. Finally he tossed it aside in disgust. What was the bloody point of that, other than to bash the police? They were trying to do their job. If things led back to the fascists, that was where the clues lay.

Sod him, anyway.

*

Kennedy closed the door to his office. Mortimer sat and smoked. Raven stood by the window, staring out at the fog. It was thinning; just a taster, a warning of what was to come.

'The *Post* rang the chief constable yesterday for a comment,' the superintendent said. 'They decided not to print it.'

'Choice words, sir?' Raven asked.

'No.' Kennedy puffed angrily on his pipe. 'They wanted to present just one side of the argument and make us look bad again. If anyone from that paper wants anything from you, say no. Orders.'

Mortimer nodded. 'We're edging closer, sir.'

'That's fine. But it's reached the stage where we need it all wrapped up.'

'How?' Raven asked. They were good detectives but all they could do was follow leads. And those were as rare as a hot summer Sunday.

The super sat back. Today he was in his best suit, a sober, dark grey worsted three-piece that must have cost a fortune. A rounded collar on his shirt and a regimental tie with a four-in-hand knot. His moustache was neatly clipped, hair well brushed. He looked every inch the commanding officer.

'Beat the bushes,' he ordered quietly. 'Someone knows where Miles spent those daylight hours when he was sleeping at the pub. Someone saw him. Find that person.'

'There's the letter,' Raven said. 'The one that starts *I kilt him*. Two to one the person who wrote that saw Miles on those days and murdered him.'

'Then go out and find him.'

*

'You're on your own today,' Raven told Noble. 'Go back to anyone who's given us a scrap of good information and squeeze them until they squeak. Don't come back here until you have something new.'

'Yes Sarge.' The lad went off glumly. Nothing like an impossible task to grind down the spirit. But now he had to go and do the same thing himself.

It was a waste of a day, dodging between people coughing, spitting on the pavement or into their handkerchiefs. Talk after talk after talk. So desperate that he slipped into the General Elliott to seek out Flash Harry.

He was there, right enough, but even he didn't have any tips to sell. What little charm he possessed had been replaced by despondency.

'The missus chucked me out,' he said.

'Half the men in Leeds would be celebrating if their wives did that.'

'You don't understand, Mr Raven.' He raised a pair of sad eyes. 'I love that lass. Have done since I first clapped eyes on her. I don't want to lose her.'

'Maybe you should have taken better care, then.' Even as he spoke the words, he realised he could have been talking about himself. He'd never given Marjorie the attention she deserved. He'd always been too busy with the job. 'Maybe she'll change her mind.'

'Perhaps,' Harry agreed doubtfully. 'I'll tell you what, there's no pleasure living in a rooming house.' He paused for a long moment. 'Now I think about it, there was something someone said. Hold on a mo.' He rummaged through the pockets of his cheap suit until he found a scrap of paper. 'Here we go. Bloke named Bowman.'

Raven stared. 'Who is he and what's he supposed to have done?'

'Well,' he began, and leaned close enough for the sergeant to smell his sour breath. 'I was told he'd been saying something about a fire. That was what did for the fascists' office, wasn't it?'

He ignored the question.

'So who is this Bowman? It's a pretty common name. There must be hundreds of them in Leeds.'

'Don't know.' He shrugged. 'I just overheard it. Michael, Martin, something like that.'

'I see.'

'I know it's a long shot, but you never know, do you, Mr Raven? I won't even charge you for it.'

'Not asking for money? Either this is worthless or you're sickening for something.'

'Only my missus,' Harry replied with a sad smile.

*

'Someone called Bowman,' he said to the desk sergeant. 'Maybe Michael or Martin. Can you see if there's anything in Records?'

It took almost half an hour. Five of them, three Michaels and a pair of Martin Bowmans. Raven glanced through the cards. Two were over seventy. Unlikely candidates at that age. Another had been arrested for shoplifting a decade before, when he was just sixteen. Nothing since. Very doubtful. That left one Michael and one Martin. Symmetry there, he thought.

Michael Bowman had a few convictions for grievous bodily harm, several years in jail. Nothing since 1934, but that only meant he hadn't been caught. Martin Bowman shot to the top of the list when he started to run through his sheet. An old conviction for arson, back in '28. Well, well, well. Time to have a few words with him.

The address on his record was rubble now, part of the area knocked down to make way for the new Quarry Hill flats. He could have gone anywhere in Leeds. Raven thought for a second then walked over to the Civic Hall, white and ghostly in the lingering shreds of fog.

The housing department was on the second floor. He showed his warrant card and asked if they had anything on Bowman. He spent a few minutes kicking his heels before the clerk returned.

'We have someone who moved from the address you gave us.'

'Where is he now?'

'The Gipton estate.' He'd written down the address.

Well, he'd be damned. Just three streets away from Raven's house. As he walked back to the Riley, he chuckled. Maybe he'd even nip home for a few minutes to see Marjorie. He checked his watch. Perhaps not; Gladys would still be there.

*

The street was empty. On a patch of waste ground, kids had been building a bonfire. Branches and deadwood chumped from the woods not far away, planks and boards nicked from the building sites where they were still putting up houses. November the fifth and it would all go up in flames. Parkin, toffee, potatoes baked in the ashes. A bigger blaze than any he'd enjoyed as a child. But out here there was space for it.

He shook his head, marched up the path and banged on the door. Footsteps clumped through the hall and a fleshy woman appeared at the door. She couldn't have been more than five feet tall and almost as wide as the doorway. Her stockings sagged around heavy ankles and a faded floral print apron covered a weighty bosom.

'We already paid this week, luv,' she said.

Raven smiled. 'I'm not the tally man. I'm looking for Martin Bowman.'

She eyed him more carefully and he could spot the moment when she made him for a copper.

'Not here, is he.'

'Do you know where I can find him?'

'Down the pub if it's open.'

'Which one?' That was the problem with this new estate, there was no local.

'Try the Brown Cow in Whitkirk. He sometimes takes the tram out there.'

'Right. What does he look like?'

She snorted. 'Not up to much are you, if you don't even know who you're after. Watch out for the miserable-looking beggar trying to make a half last until closing time.'

Him and so many others. He accelerated out along York Road. With luck he'd arrive just before last orders.

There weren't many left in the Brown Cow, but Bowman could have been any of three. It was lucky dip, but he chose right the first time.

'What do you want?' the man asked. 'I'm just trying to get away from the wife and have a quiet drink and now you lot are nagging me, too.'

Raven signalled the barman for a pint and placed it in front of Bowman.

'Now you've got your ale,' he said. 'The only price is a few questions.'

'Don't have much choice, do I?'

He wasn't too much taller than his wife, but much, much thinner, little more than skin and bone. Jack Sprat and his missus. The veins stood out deep blue on the back of his hands.

'Looking forward to Bonfire Night?'

'You what?' Bowman looked up, confused.

'I thought you might, since you love a bit of a blaze.'

'That was years ago.'

'The urge never goes, though. You have matches in your pocket?'

'Course I do.' He tried to look like a hard man. 'What else am I going to light my bloody fags with?'

'A couple of matches and a little petrol and you could start a handsome fire. At the British Union headquarters in town, say.'

'I told you, I haven't done that in years.'

'Then why have you been telling people about a fire?' That stopped him, with the glass halfway to his mouth. 'You'd be surprised what little birds tell us. Now, we can either have it out here or you can come into town with me. Up to you.'

The barman shouted out time and began collecting empty glasses. As he approached, Raven held out his warrant card.

'Leave us alone for a while,' he said and the man scuttled away. 'Now, what's it going to be?'

'I didn't set no fire,' Bowman said and Raven began to stand. 'No, hear me out, all right? I didn't, but I heard about someone who did.'

'Now, how would you hear a thing like that?'

'Because I've got all day on my hands with no work out there.'

'Plenty of that around.'

'Too bloody much,' Bowman said.

'What sort of fire did you hear about?'

The man looked around before answering, leaning forward over the table.

'At a place in town. An office.'

'And did all this come with someone's name?'

'Bert.'

Raven sat back in the chair and rubbed his chin.

'Bert who? He must have a surname.'

'Don't know. I run into him sometimes. People like us, we sort of know each other.'

That was probably true enough. But it didn't help him find Bert.

'Tell me about him. What does he look like? Has he been in prison?'

'I suppose he's about my height. Just ordinary. Sandy hair, forty-five, maybe.'

'Thin? Fat?'

'Ordinary, like I said.'

That was no use at all.

'Has he been inside?'

'He never said. Sometimes, though, the way he looked at people, maybe he had.'

'Looked at people how?' Raven asked sharply. Someone who'd been a convict developed a particular stare that never went away, no matter how long they were free.

'Sizing them up. I've heard he can be a right bastard, but I've never seen it myself.'

'So what did this Bert say about the fire?'

'That he'd fooled them all, made it look like an amateur job.'

That fitted; amateur was exactly the word the arson investigator had used. And a bit of a bastard. Enough to kill a man in cold blood and leave his body to burn?

'Where would I find Bert?'

'I don't know.' Raven stared into his face; he was telling the truth, not looking away. 'I don't. I just run into him here and there. Last time was down the market, two days back. We went for a cup of tea and he told me. He was flush, pulled out a wad of notes.'

'Have you ever heard of Joe Miles?'

'No. Should I have?'

'He died in that fire. Someone killed him first. He was like a burnt Sunday roast when we found him.' He saw the man flinch. 'Have a think about that.'

He stood, looking down at Bowman as the man played with his pint glass.

*

'It's not much,' Mortimer said, 'but I'll have the Records people search. We might be able to dig up something.' He raised an eyebrow and put a fresh cigarette in his mouth. 'That's good work.'

'Thank you, sir. Anything more on Peter Cave?'

The inspector shook his head. 'He might as well have fallen off the earth for all we've heard. Even the ridiculous sightings have stopped. Honestly, Cornwall and Aberdeen on the same day? I ask you.'

*

As he walked home from the tram, he spotted Gladys striding along the street, shopping bag in her hand. A good winter coat in dark blue and a hat with a feather perched on her head.

'How is she today?' he asked.

'Better with her stitches out.' He'd forgotten that the district nurse was coming. 'I swear though, there was dirt on her uniform when she showed up at the door and she went through it all in two minutes flat. No consideration these days.'

He let her blether on, knowing she'd repeat it to her husband once she was home. Poor bugger. Maybe she meant well, but sweet bloody Jesus, the woman could find fault with heaven. She'd probably say the harps needed a good dusting.

Five minutes later he was home, feeling as if he'd been put through a mangle. Seeing Marjorie came as wonderful relief. She did look more relaxed and at ease, following him into the kitchen on her crutches as he dished up the tea.

'I don't even know that I need to sleep downstairs anymore,' she said with a teasing smile. 'I'm getting around well enough.'

'That would be wonderful,' he told her and meant it.

'Let's give it a try tonight, what do you say?'

'All right. Don't overdo things when you're healing, though. I want you well again.'

*

Her head lay on his shoulder in the bed, one of the rollers digging into his neck, but he didn't move. This was the closest they'd been for months. Almost how it had been in the early days of their marriage.

He felt her even breathing on his skin and his mind drifted away to the case. Everything rolled into one, he was sure of that. Frank Benson, Joe Miles, Alwyn Davies; they were all the kind of men who walked through their time here and hardly left a scratch on the surface. Expendable. Life's cannon fodder.

Was he anything more, though? Another fifty years and who'd remember his name? All the work they did on the force, was it anything more than running around and sticking Elastoplasts on all the problems? Things never changed much.

Too deep for this time of night, he decided. Especially without a few pints in him.

*

'I think we've found your Bert,' Mortimer said and handed over a Records card.

Albert Cross. Forty-eight – Bowman had been close enough. Convicted once for arson and once for assault. Very possible. An address in Hyde Park, just the other side of Woodhouse Moor.

'We'd better go and rouse him,' Raven said and called for Noble.

'I'll come with you,' Mortimer said. A half-smile flickered across his lips.

'Bring him back here and give him a proper grilling,' Kennedy ordered, then said, 'I might ask a few questions myself.'

They took two cars; Noble and the sergeant in one, Mortimer in the other, a hefty constable beside him. Raven could feel the rush in his blood, heart beating faster now things were moving again. Cross looked like a good suspect, and he didn't believe Bowman had been feeding him a yarn.

With cars parked at the end of the street of through terraced houses, they split up; Raven and the constable would go to the front door, with Mortimer and Noble at the back in case Cross tried to scarper.

A knock and the man answered with the door on the chain. It was Cross, no doubt about it, the image of the man in the photograph. He took one glance, slammed the door shut and they heard the slap of footsteps down the hall.

'What do you want to do, sir?' the constable asked. 'I can knock this down if you like.'

'May as well leave him. They'll have caught him at the back by now. We might as well go.'

Cross was already seated in the back of Mortimer's car, Noble beside him looking triumphant. The inspector had a happy smile as the ignition caught and he put the vehicle into gear.

'Short break,' Raven said as he started the Riley. 'Hardly seems worth the effort if he's caught that easily.'

'Gets me away from filing for a few minutes, Sarge. I'm not complaining.' He glanced out at the people bundled up in their overcoats. 'Mind you, be better if it was summer.'

'We'll have a long wait for that.'

*

Cross was already in the interview room with Superintendent Kennedy and Mortimer. Noble was reading the *Evening Post*.

Nothing to do except wait and see what the questioning of Bert Cross turned up. As the clock turned five, they were still in there. Must be getting something good. Stay or go home? Give it another half hour, he decided. If there was nothing he'd pop over to the Pointer and see if Johnny Harris was there.

*

Quarter past six and Johnny hadn't arrived. Raven had hoped, but... money would be tight when he was out of a job and luxuries like a pint would be the first thing to go.

They were keeping Cross in overnight, Mortimer had said. He hadn't broken yet but there was something there; they could sense it. A night in the cells might shake it loose.

He finished his glass of Tetley's bitter and left the pub, feeling the stares. They knew who he was and what had happened to Johnny; they'd all blame him for it.

Home felt bright and welcoming. Marjorie was brimming over with gossip and he let her talk as he ate. In one ear and out the other, but she sounded bright, smiling, eyes shining. It was funny how the accident seemed to have changed everything. They'd been on the brink of falling apart. Now it was as if all those bad times had never happened. He wondered what was going on in her head. But he wasn't about to ask – why risk upsetting things? If she ever decided she wanted to talk about it, he'd listen. For now he'd hold his breath and see if it lasted. Life, you could never predict what it was going to do.

*

He whistled on the way to the tram, steam from his breath clouding the air. The first time in years and the sound was startling. But all was right with the world. Things at home kept going from strength to strength, and once Cross started spilling what he knew, they should be able to clear up all the murders. He pushed his hands deeper into his overcoat. Cave was still out there but a few more mornings like this and he'd probably be happy to surrender just to find somewhere warm to sleep.

His mood was still good as he walked up the stairs at the library and into the CID office. Mortimer and Kennedy were talking, planning the morning's interrogation. Raven glanced through the notes on his desk. Thank God he'd never heard any more from Ava Benson. He'd had visions of her plaguing his life for the next few years, turning up every week with some new idea or clue.

One item caught his eye. He read it again then strode down to Kennedy's office and knocked on the door.

'Sorry to barge in, sir, but I've come across something interesting.' He read it out and saw the men look at each other.

'Why didn't someone pick up on this before?' the superintendent asked.

'No idea, sir.'

'Fine,' Kennedy said after a moment. 'You and Noble. But I want you both armed. For all we know, he has a gun. I don't want anyone else dead, especially one of my men.'

'Yes, sir.' The only times he'd handled a weapon since the war were the annual shooting practices. Each time he fired the revolver it brought back memories of the Front, of bullets and shells and a fuel dump going up in flames. He hated guns. Thank God they weren't like America, where every copper was armed. 'What about bringing in the marksmen?' The force had three of them, all highly skilled sharpshooters.

'We can't. They're on a course with the army.'

'Yes, sir.'

*

Noble handled the gun as if it might bite him.

'You've had your training. Just remember that. And we don't fire unless he shoots at us.'

'I still don't see why you think it's Cave, Sarge. From that report it could have been anyone.'

He was driving out along Harrogate Road, then past Moortown, he turned along the ring road towards Shadwell. It was all farmlands and woods here. The city hadn't reached this part yet, it was still fields and wilderness, and all the better for it.

The trees had lost most of their leaves. Another month and they'd all be bare.

'Someone's seen smoke from a fire for the last couple of nights. Who's going to be out camping at this time of year for the fun of it? Not this close to Leeds. It's even near his house. Makes sense it'd be him.'

He turned along a lane where the hedges were overgrown and saw the sign for Sunny Bay Farm. No sun today, though. All overcast. He pulled into a yard where a man was shovelling up a pile of cow dung.

*

Simple enough. The farmer directed them towards the woods up on the hill where he'd seen smoke. With the news about Cave on the loose he'd called the police instead of investigating himself.

'See that field over there, though?' he asked.

'Yes,' Raven answered.

'Don't go in that. There's a bull.' Noble took a sudden step back and the man laughed. 'I'm only pulling your leg. There's no bull. You're safe enough.'

If only that was true…

There was no point in trying to keep out of sight. They were amateurs at this lark.

'Do you think it's really him, Sarge?'

'I don't know. We'll find out, won't we?' He wasn't in the mood for stupid questions. He knew Noble was only trying to calm himself by filling the silence, but he'd prefer quiet, to have the chance to concentrate.

As soon as they were into the trees, he halted. Dressed in their suits and crunching around they'd look like walking advertisements to a man like Cave. They might as well have been wearing the flashing Bovril sign for all they'd be able to hide themselves.

'You go to the right,' he whispered, 'I'll take the left. Keep your gun in your pocket. We don't shoot unless he fires first, got it? And try to be quiet with those bloody size elevens.'

He took a deep breath and began to walk. Even now he could hear Noble, the crack of twigs under his soles as he moved deeper into the wood. It wasn't a large place, but heavily overgrown; you could hide a platoon in here without any problem.

A few quiet paces, then stop, look, listen. Again. Finding anyone here would be more good luck than anything. But he was due some of that.

It took him twenty minutes to discover the tent. Dun coloured and almost invisible among the fallen leaves, on the edge of a clearing. Close by, a small ring of stones and the blackness of ashes. This was the place, no doubt about it. But was Cave here?

A rucksack lay in the tent, on top of the groundsheet. Blankets had been rolled up to give space.

Raven started to search through the pack. For God's sake, why did the thing have so many bloody pockets? His fingers fumbled with buckles until he had everything on the floor.

A wallet, and inside a folded note addressed to Mr Cave. That was all he needed to know. Where was the man? He would never have run off and left all this.

Off somewhere foraging for food, most likely. What could anyone find at the shank end of October? He didn't have the foggiest idea. The only thing he could do was wait for Cave to return and arrest him. No sign of any weapon in the campsite. But the man would have a knife, at the very least; he'd need one out here. Maybe a shotgun.

Noble, he thought suddenly. The lad was blundering around out there somewhere. He couldn't call out to him; that would alert Cave. Leave him be and hope for the best? It was a toss-up. Finally he decided to settle in the bracken beyond the clearing, out of sight, and wait.

An hour passed. He kept glancing at his watch, then made himself stop. Time wouldn't go by more quickly if he looked. After a while, he found he could hear things he'd never noticed before: the quiet song of a bird up in the branches, the hesitant scurrying of some small animal in the undergrowth.

Raven was alert and ready. He had handcuffs in one pocket, the Webley revolver, a heavy, awkward bulge in the other and he prayed he wouldn't need to draw it. A weapon had only one purpose, the instructor in the army had taught him. It was there to kill.

Another thirty minutes. The sky was heavy, thick clouds and the promise of rain off in the distance. Where the hell was Noble, he wondered? He couldn't still be wandering around like a little lost lamb, could he?

The rustle of a bush made his head snap around. His body was tense, ready to move.

Bloody hell.

It was Cave. And right in front of him, pale-faced and stumbling with fear, was Noble. The revolver poking into his back kept prodding him along.

CHRIS NICKSON

They stopped by the tent, just ten yards away.

'I know you're round here somewhere,' Cave shouted and paused, as if he expected a reply. 'You can see for yourself. I'm sure you don't want your friend to die, now do you?'

He had an assured voice, very reasonable. No note of fear in it. Raven held his breath. He was close enough to make out every feature of Cave's face. Being on the run and living rough had toughened him, sharpened all the planes and the angles. The hand that held the revolver was steady. But really, he looked so *ordinary*, a man to walk past on the street and never look twice. Not a murderer, not an assassin.

'You might as well be a good chap and show yourself. I hold all the cards here, you know that.'

Gradually, inch by inch, Raven moved his hand, easing it under the flap on his jacket pocket and around the butt of his pistol. Trying not to move, not to make a sound, he began to tug it out. The hammer caught on the lining and he grimaced as his fingers silently tugged the material away. The gun was in his hand now, and he raised it very carefully until it was trained on the figures in front of him.

He didn't have a shot. Not yet; Noble was in the way. He needed to bide his time. Was there justification to shoot? Stupid thought; of course there was. Patience, he thought. Let Cave get frustrated and make a mistake.

'Well?' The man's voice was louder this time. His voice echoed around the trees, but no reply. Raven was sitting, hidden and waiting.

'I'll kill him.'

He pushed Noble and the constable fell to his knees as Cave raised his weapon.

This was the moment. There'd never be a better chance. Raven squeezed the trigger and heard the sound, feeling the hard recoil jar his shoulder and smelling the cordite.

Cave was on the ground. Where his right eye had been there was now just a dark, bloody hole. The gun had fallen away just beyond his fingertips.

It was over.

Noble was cowering on the ground, hands over his head.

'Oh Christ. No, Sarge, no.'

'It's fine now, lad. He can't hurt you.' He helped Noble to his feet. 'Come on, let's walk down to the farm and ring this in,' he said gently. 'You can do that, can't you?'

*

Kennedy had the report he'd made. Raven had also been questioned by the coppers who arrived at the farm after his telephone call and had written a record of it all in his notebook. An ambulance had taken Noble to the hospital; he was in no state yet to be interrogated.

'You had no choice?'

'No, sir. I honestly don't believe I had.' The gun had been taken for examination and a group of constables was out examining the scene. The photographers and the scientific bods had done their work and Cave's body carted away to the mortuary.

He hadn't lied or fudged the truth in anything he said. No need. Raven knew he'd done the right thing, the only thing. That didn't make it easier, but he could look at it all with a clear conscience.

'How did he get Noble's gun?' Mortimer asked.

'I don't know, sir. The first I saw was when they returned to his camp.'

They went through it all, time and again, until the superintendent was finally satisfied.

'I wish you'd just wounded him, though,' Kennedy finished with a sigh. 'He could have told us who's behind this.'

'I just wanted to stop him, sir.'

'I know.' He glanced at Mortimer. 'Between us, you did exactly the right thing. We'll see what Noble's statement brings, but you're completely clean as far as I'm concerned.'

'Thank you, sir.' He'd never doubted it. This time, at least, he could tell the entire truth and know he was in the right. Still, it was good to know there would be no comeback.

'Go home.' It had turned seven, the city dark outside the office window.

*

'I was worried about you.'

Marjorie had hobbled out of the front room as soon as she heard his key in the lock. He held her long enough for all the tension and the fear to start to melt.

'I heard about the shooting on the radio, but they didn't say much.'

'I was the one who fired,' he told her.

She looked into his face.

'Come on. Sit down, I'll put the kettle on.'

*

'I didn't want to do it. I just didn't have any choice.'

She'd listened to his bald account of it. But he was simply describing the film that kept playing in his head. A single scene, over and over that ended with him helping Noble to his feet then glancing back at the body as they walked slowly away.

'It sounds as if you did the only thing you could.' She put her hand over his and he nodded. 'Were you scared?'

'No.' Funny, he'd never given that a thought. He'd done what he knew he had to do. That had been the only thing in his mind. Now, as it all ebbed away from him, he felt drained. Exhausted. 'Do you mind if we just go to bed?'

'Of course not.' Her face was full of tenderness. She kissed him lightly. 'You lock up. No need to help me up the stairs. I'm starting to feel I could dance the foxtrot with these things.'

She smelt of cold cream and her flannel nightie itched against his skin.

He didn't care as he held her close, the rough plaster of her cast against his leg. Marjorie slept soundly; he wished he could. As soon as he closed his eyes he was back in the wood, waiting for Cave to approach with Noble in front of him. It wouldn't turn off and he couldn't look away.

He managed a few hours. He must have. The time passed and morning arrived. But he didn't feel rested as he drank his tea and looked in the mirror. An ugly face of stitched-together pieces. The skin was almost grey today.

*

Noble was already in the detectives' office, cradling a mug of tea between his hands. His cheeks looked as if they'd been hollowed out and he had deep, dark shadows under his eyes.

After a minute he walked over to Raven's desk.

'Sarge,' he began. 'About yesterday…'

'Just tell them the truth.'

'It's not that. I wanted to say thanks. I really thought it was all over.'

'I'm not going to let you be rid of us that easily.' He grinned. 'We survived. That's what matters.'

'Yes, but…' He winced. 'I let him get my gun. I told him you were around.'

'It doesn't matter.'

'Will they kick me off the force?'

That was his real worry. Losing the job.

'I think you'll be fine. It could have happened to any of us.'

'I know.' Noble frowned. 'But it happened to me, didn't it?'

'You've got the makings of a decent detective. They're not going to throw you to the wolves.'

'I hope you're right, Sarge.'

'I'm always right, you should know that by now.'

At least the lad smiled a little, then turned as the door at the end opened and Kennedy called his name.

Twenty-Two

'WHAT LUCK DID you have with Cross yesterday?' he asked Mortimer. The superintendent's door was firmly closed. Through the glass he could make out three figures, one of them in full uniform.

'Nothing. He wouldn't admit a thing and we don't have a scrap of evidence.'

'Do you think it was him?'

'Sure as eggs is eggs.' He pulled out a cigarette, lit it, then frowned. 'He knows we know and that we can't do a thing about it. He was smirking like the devil. We had to let him go in the end.'

'Did he write anything while he was here?'

'Write?' The inspector thought. 'I don't believe so. Why?'

'To compare his writing with that letter. The *I kilt him* one.'

Mortimer shook his head. 'I don't see him for that at all.'

'Someone wrote it.'

'And that's who we have to find. Back to square one.'

Raven inclined his head towards Kennedy's office.

'What about the lad?'

'He'll get a roasting for losing his gun but that's all.'

'He's scared he'll be kicked off the force.'

'Noble's safe enough. More than you can say for the super if we don't solve this case properly.'

'Oh?' Raven asked.

Mortimer's eyes narrowed and he lowered his voice.

'The price of failure. He'll be expected to fall on his sword and resign.'

Christ. They couldn't solve everything. But then this case had too many political overtones, and the people at the very top weren't likely to take responsibility.

'We'd better make sure that doesn't happen, sir.'

'Good man. Now let's get to work.'

*

He knew what he needed to do. Break Bert Cross and drag the truth out of him. Kennedy and Mortimer were both good at interrogation. But they had to play by the rules, to find answers in a way that would stand up in court.

Raven wasn't going to be that fussy.

Noble was still with the superintendent when he left; it was better to keep the lad out of this in case anything went wrong. He started the Riley and drove out to Hyde Park. It was a real autumn morning, pearl light and stark shadows. There were piles of dead leaves on the ground around the Victoria statue on Woodhouse Moor, and the air was cool enough to steam as he breathed.

He parked and rolled a pair of leather gloves onto his hands, then pulled the brim of the trilby down to shade his eyes. That was it. No truncheon, no cosh, no brass knuckles. Time to see just how hard Bert Cross really was.

He knocked and waited until he heard footsteps in the hall. As the door opened an inch he was ready, pushing hard enough to knock it back and send Cross sprawling to keep his balance. Raven was in, and he dropped the latch behind himself. No strangers interrupting.

'Someone hasn't been telling the truth,' Raven said. 'That's not a good thing to do.'

His face was his fortune this time. The web of scars and grafts from surgery was his advantage.

He didn't wait. Before the man could defend himself, Raven bunched his fist and hit him hard on the jaw. Cross went down, stunned for a moment. Raven grabbed him by the tie and dragged him along the floor to the kitchen. The man tried to protest, shouting and kicking, but Raven just let him fall to the linoleum floor.

'Stay there,' he ordered. 'Move and you'll wish you hadn't been born. I haven't even started yet.'

In his fifteen years on the force he'd only done this twice before. Once when he was still in uniform, working with a detective constable on a rape case where the suspect wouldn't confess, then when he needed to break the alibi of a gang who'd beaten a sailor so badly he'd never walk again.

Both times it had worked and he'd had no regrets. No guilt or bad dreams later. Raven filled the kettle and lit the stove as he kept an eye on Cross. Then he knelt, took the man's chin between his fingers and squeezed.

'Tough man in the interview room, aren't you, Bert? Well?' he asked when Cross didn't respond. 'Aren't you?' A terrified nod. 'But we're not there now. It's just you and me here. No rules. No law. You understand?'

'You can't do this,' Cross said as Raven increased the pressure on the bone.

'Can't I?' He looked around. 'We're right here. And we're going to stay until you give me some truth. I've got all day.' He slapped the man's cheek lightly. 'You want to start?'

'Fuck off.' He tried to spit but it just ran down his cheek.

'Not very nice, Bert.' Raven shook his head. 'You hear that kettle heating up? Well, do you?' Cross nodded. He looked ready to try something. Raven punched him in the gut. 'I told you, don't even think about it. Now, what do you want to tell me about that fire.'

'Nothing to say,' Cross gasped as he tried to catch his breath.

'You see my face, Bert?' He tilted his head back to show off the stitches and shiny skin. 'Well, do you?' He waited until the man nodded. There was real fear in Cross's eyes now. That was what Raven had been waiting to see. 'You could have a face like this, Bert. Three years of pain and surgery and you end up with something like this. You'd be surprised at the damage a kettle full of boiling water could do to your mug.'

Raven had used the same threat on those two previous occasions. He'd never had to carry it out; he didn't know whether he could, if push came to shove. But as they looked him in the eye it was very effective.

The sound of the kettle filled the room as the water began to bubble.

'What's it going to be, Bert. Some truth or an unfortunate accident with a full kettle? And don't even think of accusing me.' He smiled. 'I was never here.'

The men stared at each other. Softly at first, then louder, the kettle began to whistle. Raven wrapped a handkerchief around his hand and lifted it off the gas.

'Well, Bert? Last chance.' He tried not to sound nervous. Raven knew how it worked: once you make a threat, you'd better be prepared to go through with it. Otherwise it meant nothing at all.

They were right on the brink. A few more seconds and they'd either fall back on the ground or tumble over the cliff. He brought the kettle close enough to Cross's face for him to feel the heat and started to tilt it.

Steam rose from the spout and the first drops of water landed on the linoleum before Bert Cross turned his head away and said, 'I'll tell you,' in a defeated voice.

*

Raven didn't feel any satisfaction as he left the house. He didn't feel any pleasure and he didn't feel any pride. Cross had pissed himself as the first drops hit the floor. By then he'd believed the sergeant would go through with it.

But he'd given the information. They'd both gone as far as they could, a dangerous game of chicken, and Raven had won. He could never tell anyone. Kennedy would sack him if he knew what he'd done; he was a man for playing by the book. No pension, nothing. In disgrace.

But the book hadn't done them a damned bit of good so far. All it had brought was frustration. Ten minutes and a kettle had brought some answers. Cross would never grass him up. It would make him into a laughing stock.

Sitting in the Riley, he eased off the gloves then looked at himself in the mirror. Maybe he wasn't happy at the way he'd done it, but he'd found enough to push ahead. Cross had told him the truth, no doubt about that. A man who might lose half his face didn't lie. Not when they only had to open their eyes to see the result.

*

Back at headquarters they'd finished with Noble. He sat at his desk looking down at the paper in his hand without even seeing it.

'Come on,' Raven told him. 'You're on the payroll, you'd better do some work to earn your money.'

He followed like a child, not saying a word until they were in the car and travelling north.

'About yesterday,' he began in a low voice.

'Nothing to discuss.'

'But he got my gun. He was going to kill me.'

'He didn't, though, did he? You're still here.'

'Thanks to you.'

'I just did what I had to do.' He turned to face the younger man.

'You'd have done the same.'

The silence returned for five full minutes, until Noble asked, 'Where are we going, Sarge?'

'To see a man about a dead body and a fire.'

'Joe Miles?' the constable asked in surprise.

'Unless we have any arsons I don't know about.'

'I don't understand. I thought we didn't get anything from that bloke.'

'Don't you worry about what you don't understand.' Raven tapped the side of his nose. 'A little bird told me.'

'Who?' Suddenly he was interested.

'Never you mind. And keep yourself quiet while I talk to this man, understand?'

'Yes, Sarge.'

This time he'd play it kosher. Threats wouldn't work against a man like Terry Gordon, anyway. In his time he'd probably issued more of them than most people had eaten hot dinners, and followed through on them when he needed.

He was a fixer, a hard man, whatever he had to be. Well connected and virtually untouchable. Crime had made him wealthy, and that money, along with the people he'd cultivated, helped to keep him out of jail.

Gordon wasn't someone who'd break at a questioning; Raven didn't expect that. But Bert Cross – squealing, sweating Bert Cross – had sworn blind that it was Gordon who'd hired him to haul Joe Miles's dead body from the back of a van into the BUF office and start the fire that would destroy the building and turn the corpse to crisp meat.

'Why did you make it look like an amateur job?' Raven had asked. He was still holding the kettle at an angle, ready to pour.

'Because that's what he bloody ordered,' Cross shouted. 'Stop any suspicion, he said.'

Now he was on his way to talk to Terry Gordon. The news that his little secret was out should rattle him. And Bert Cross was packing a suitcase and leaving Leeds for safer pastures.

Gordon lived well. A house on the far reaches of Alwoodley, almost halfway to Harewood, down a long, hidden drive. The Riley bumped over the gravel and stopped in front of a Georgian brick building.

'Blimey,' Noble said softly.

'Remember, let me do the talking.'

There was a maid, then a butler. Of course; Gordon liked to flaunt his riches. The only thing it couldn't buy him was taste. He was in his forties, with an expensive haircut that flattered his rough face, a thin moustache, and clothes that hadn't come off the peg from Burton's; the suit probably cost more than Raven made in a month.

The man had taken elocution lessons and absorbed them so well that he sounded like a BBC newsreader. But Raven knew he'd started his life down near the bottom of Meanwood Road, a raggedy-arsed little boy with plenty of ambition and ruthlessness. Gordon might have made the surface as smooth as satin, but the Sheepscar boy still lurked underneath.

'Police?' Gordon said. He was standing by a roaring fireplace. A large, ugly dog slept in the corner. 'What brings you all the way out here, Sergeant... Raven?'

'A little matter of business.'

'Oh?' Gordon raised an eyebrow, took a cigarette from a gold case and lit it with a Dunhill Tallboy lighter. 'What sort of business?'

'Just the usual, really. Arson and murder.' He could feel Noble tense beside him. Don't do anything silly, he thought. Let this one play out.

'Really?' No shock on his face, just a lightly amused smile. 'What does that have to do with me?'

'Oh, just that you're behind it.'

'Am I now? Who's been telling you this?'

'Someone who knows.'

'You believe that rubbish?'

'I do. I just wonder what was in it for you.'

'Nothing,' Gordon answered with a smile, 'since I haven't the faintest idea what you're talking about.' He was a big man, over six feet tall and a good fourteen stone of muscle; using it was how he'd first made his mark and he still looked in good shape. He was menacing as he walked forward. 'If that's all you came to say, it's time for you to leave. If we ever talk again I'll have my solicitor present and I'll sue you for slander.'

*

'What good did that do, Sarge?' Noble asked as they drove back to Leeds.

'Just to let him know that his little secret is out, that's all. We'll see how he jumps now.'

'Put the frighteners on him, you mean?'

'No,' Raven answered with a chuckle. No one put the frighteners on Terry Gordon; it was the other way round. But it could give the man a spur to do something, anything that might lead them to whoever was really behind this fire.

Someone had hired Gordon for the job. It couldn't have been any other way. Money was the only thing that interested him. It was why he rose from his fancy pit every morning. But there was no profit in that fire or killing unless someone was paying him.

The letter they'd received could have been Gordon's touch, too, his way of rubbing their noses in it. He wouldn't put it past him.

Bert Cross, Terry Gordon. They were his big rolls of the dice. Now he had to wait and see if he'd scooped the jackpot.

He drove them back to Woodhouse, parked round the corner from Cross's house and gave Noble his instructions.

'You've got that straight? Keep out of sight, and if anyone comes knocking at his door, bring them in.'

'Yes, Sarge. How long do I stay?'

'I'll come along later to relieve you.'

*

'You really have to go?' Marjorie held him close, both arms around his neck, the crutches leaning against the wall. They were just inside the front door. He had the Riley parked outside, drawing plenty of admiration from the boys on the street when he pulled up.

Now his wife was amorous and he was reluctant to go. He'd wanted this for so long, dreamt about it. And he was going to have to leave her.

'I wouldn't if I didn't have to,' he said quietly into her ear. 'I'll be back as soon as I can, but it might be a while.'

Gordon would know the information had come from Cross. There was no one else. He'd send a man round to plug that leak permanently. They just had to catch him.

She kissed him hard on the lips. He wasn't complaining, but he'd never have thought an accident could have altered so much. Clouds and silver linings.

He glanced in the mirror as he drove away, seeing her standing in the doorway with the cast on her leg, waving.

*

Noble was still in position. With evening it had turned cold and he shivered in his raincoat.

'Not a sausage, Sarge. I'll be glad to go somewhere warm.'

'You do that and I'll see you in the morning.' He paused. 'Are you all right after yesterday?'

A shadow passed across the young man's face.

'I'll be fine, Sarge. No black marks on my record, either, Mr Kennedy said.'

'Good.'

*

It was a good place for staying out of the way, but Christ, it stank. Close to a set of outdoor privies, past a block of terraced houses. As people came and went from them he could slide back into the darkness and they never knew he was there.

It was impossible not to be reminded of Frank Benson. They'd found his body behind a place like this, the trigger that began it all. Maybe he was close to completing the circle.

With full darkness he walked a little, keeping the trilby pulled down to hide his face. It was going to be a bloody cold night, probably a frost. Maybe he could dig over the garden on Sunday. The exercise would do him good.

Nothing stirred around Cross's house. No lights on. Hopefully Bert had done what he said and scarpered. Raven returned to the spot, sliding into the blackness and wishing he'd put on an extra layer of clothes when he'd popped home.

He was just thinking about Marjorie when something caught him on the back of the neck. The next he knew he was pinned against the brick wall with the stench of piss in his nostrils and a heavy hand against his throat.

A red, ugly face under a bowler hat was close to him, eyes bulging and breath foetid. Inspector Reid of Special Branch.

'I told you once to keep your nose out of Branch business. Seems like you didn't hear me properly. It's time to teach you a lesson you won't forget.'

He didn't understand. Why would the Branch be interested in Bert Cross? He was nothing. Then it clicked. Terry Gordon. Couldn't be anyone else. But he was damned if he'd take a beating from someone like this for doing his bloody job.

During his brief army training, Raven had excelled at unarmed combat. A natural, the corporal instructing them had said, and shown him a few moves that weren't part of the course. He hadn't been a scrapper when he was young, and he'd never had the chance to try it all out in action.

But it had served him well on the force, especially when he was on the beat. He knew the first rule: surprise.

Reid never had a chance. He lumbered, he moved slowly and telegraphed his moves. The whole thing took less than ten seconds. By then, Reid was crumpled on the ground, barely conscious, and Raven was breathing hard as he walked away.

The inspector would never report the incident. It would be too humiliating. But he'd want his revenge sometime, and he wouldn't come alone. Never mind; he'd think about that when it happened. For the moment he had to wonder why the Branch should be so interested in Terry Gordon.

There was no sense in hanging around here any longer. If Gordon sent anyone for Bert Cross, the officers from the Branch would snatch him. Raven wouldn't even get the crumbs.

Twenty-Three

'I'M SORRY, SARGE, I had to tell them about going to see Gordon,' Noble apologised.

'Doesn't matter,' Raven told him. He wasn't surprised. Right now the lad would want to keep his nose so clean that it shone. 'I was going to tell them myself.'

He did, once Kennedy called him into the office. He simply edited out his encounter with Bert Cross. An informant had mentioned Terry Gordon, he said, and in its own way it was true enough; he'd just been a reluctant informant. He also erased the Branch from his tale; no need to complicate things.

He finished and Kennedy puffed quietly on his pipe, then asked, 'What do we gain by Gordon knowing we're onto him?'

'He's going to have to do something, sir. At least that's how I see it.'

'You didn't get in a fight with him, did you?' Mortimer nodded at the scrapes on his knuckles, a souvenir from his meeting with Reid.

'No, sir. I had to break up a bit of a barney, that's all. Nothing to do with this.' Again, he was shading the truth.

'What next?' the superintendent asked.

'We wait and see.'

'Who's watching Gordon?'

This was where it grew tricky.

'No one at the moment, sir.'

'So he could have slipped out and we'd be none the wiser.'

'Hard to keep an eye on his place, sir. There's nothing out there.'

'Then what are you going to do?' Mortimer looked at him curiously.

'Wing it, sir.'

*

'Sarge, do you keep thinking about shooting Cave?'

'Not that much.' It was true enough. The thing had run through his head, it still did, but that was all. Less now than right after it had happened, and it would fade away. No regrets, no what if. He'd done what he had to do. He'd had worse things on his mind. Things that would never go away, like the explosion of that fuel dump in France.

'I can't get it out of my head. It's like sitting in the cinema and the film just keeps repeating.'

'It'll go gradually. Put it away if you can. We have a job to do.' He shifted down a gear and floored the accelerator so they overtook the lorry lumbering up Harehills Lane. They passed Potternewton Park and turned onto a small road that wound by the artificial limb hospital.

The Canadian estate was new; fresh streets of semi-detached houses all named after places in Canada. Close enough to Chapel Allerton for the wives to walk home easily with their shopping, a cinema at the top of the road. No council housing here; these places went for more than any police sergeant could afford.

Regina Drive. That was it. The road circled a large green space with a young tree struggling to grow in the centre. And there was number seventy-five tucked away in the corner by a ginnel.

'Who are we here to see?' Noble asked.

'Him.' Raven pointed as the door of the house opened and a tidy man appeared with a mongrel on a lead.

'Who is he? He looks old.' They watched as the man shuffled away down the ginnel, pausing often as the dog sniffed at the ground.

'That, my lad, is someone who's forgotten more about the politics in Leeds than we'll ever know.'

Raven had met David Gott not long after he became a constable. He'd been assigned to guard a Labour Party meeting. Gott had been a councillor in those days, a powerful figure in Leeds. As things broke up, a man with a broken bottle took a run at Gott. Raven had been quicker. Five seconds and the man was disarmed and in handcuffs, ready for a spell in jail.

Gott had retired in '29, a few months before the big Crash. Now he lived quietly. His wife had died the year before; Raven had attended the funeral. No one would look at the old man and guess at the influence he'd once wielded in Leeds. Still did, if he chose to use it.

'Morning, Mr Gott.' The old man turned and smiled as he recognised the face.

'Good morning, Urban. A pleasant surprise. And—' he squinted, '— young man?'

'This is Detective Constable Noble.'

'Happy to meet you, young fellow.' His gaze returned to Raven. 'You've been in the newspapers.'

'I know.' The Cave shooting. He hadn't bothered to read the articles, he didn't want to know how they judged him. 'That's partly why I'm here.'

'The BUF? That chap was a member, wasn't he?'

'Yes.' They stopped as the dog sniffed around a spot on the verge until

Gott finally tugged on the lead and said, 'Come on, Daisy. What do you want to know about them?'

'About two of them. Roland Harding and Ian Gilbert.'

'Nasty pieces of work.' Gott shook his head in dismay. His white hair was so thin that his scalp shone through, freckled and pink. He'd shrunk in the fifteen years Raven had known him. Lost a little height and plenty of weight, until he looked as if a heavy gust of wind might send him soaring into the skies. 'You can't believe a word they say.'

His accent was broad Leeds. He'd grown up in one of the yards off Briggate, working from the time he was a child. Then he'd heard Tom Maguire address a crowd of striking builders and the political fire had been lit. He'd read and learned. He'd become involved and very slowly climbed the local political ladder.

'How bad do you think they'd be?' Raven asked.

'What have they done?' He hesitated and corrected himself. 'What do you think they've done?'

'I'm not sure. It's so bloody tangled that it's hard to know. And it doesn't make a lot of sense.'

'Have you ever heard of Machiavelli?' Gott said.

'No.' This was the man's way, taking the longest route to an answer.

'He was an Italian, lived hundreds of years ago. Wrote a book called *The Prince*. If you want to see devious, it's in there. Wheels within wheels within wheels. I'd bet that Gilbert and Harding both live by it.'

'What's in it?'

'Some very sly ways to power,' Gott said. 'Ruthless ways.' He thought for a moment. 'It's a book of tactics, if you like. Most politicians have a copy. All of them, probably. I did.'

'And did you learn from it?' Raven asked.

'Of course. Know your enemy, that's why I read it.'

'I don't think I follow.'

'Why don't you tell me what's happened. This is all to do with the bodies and the fire, I take it?'

'Yes, and the shooting at Golden Acres.' He told Gott what he knew. Not just the stuff in the papers but all of it. Raven could see Noble looking on doubtfully, but he continued. He needed someone to try and untangle this ball of yarn. He certainly hadn't managed it by himself.

They'd reached the old St Matthew's graveyard. All the grass around the headstones was neatly trimmed, the last cut before winter. The dog sniffed and snuffled around. Gott brought a small bag of sweets from his pocket and offered them. Mint imperials, sharp and sweet.

'It looks to me as if there are two possibilities,' the man began. 'First, you have someone or some group attacking the fascists. That's quite possible, I might be tempted myself if I were younger.'

'That's one,' Raven said. 'Who would you make for it?'

'The communists are the obvious candidates. Too obvious, that's the problem. And they'd never operate like that. Not the British ones, they're far too polite. So I don't really know, but I'm out of touch these days.'

'Then what's your other possibility?'

'The British Union are doing it themselves.'

'Why, though? That's the bit I don't understand.'

'Machiavelli,' Gott told him. 'It makes them look under attack. Suddenly they're the underdogs, and the people doing this are a threat to Britain and democracy. A good way to gain sympathy. Maybe even a few members. Their people have been attacking you in the papers, haven't they?'

'Us and the communists,' Raven said. 'Lying.'

'Of course. But a lie's a funny thing, Urban. It changes. Repeat it often enough for people to get it into their skulls and it grows into the truth.'

'So you're saying they could have killed their own members and set the fire themselves?'

'Could,' Gott replied carefully. 'I don't know enough to be certain.

But it's possible.'

It made a twisted kind of sense. He'd thought about it, but it wasn't something he'd wanted to believe, because it was so awful. But the steps moved logically, one, two, three. He came back to the conversation. The old man was still talking.

'—and there's going to be a war. Three years, four perhaps. Half the people in Whitehall are pushing their heads in the sand, but some are preparing. We're rearming.' He looked at Noble. 'You'll be in uniform.'

'If it happens, I'll go.' There was a shine to his eyes and eagerness in his voice.

'Don't sound too happy, son,' Gott said sharply. 'There's very little glory out there. Just ask your sergeant here if you don't believe me.'

*

'Do you think he's right, Sarge?'

They were in the Riley, heading back to town. Noble had been silent for two minutes, fingers fidgeting in his lap.

'About what?'

'The war. Will there be one?'

'Probably.' In his experience Gott was usually correct.

More silence. Hardly surprising. It all sounded so good at first, the burst of patriotism. That was how it had been for him, so proud to put on the uniform. But these younger ones, they'd had the chance to see all the men who came home broken from the last war. Maybe they'd be a little more hesitant.

While the lad was stewing, Raven thought about the other things Gott had said. The BUF behind it all? He'd considered that and dismissed it. Now he dragged the idea out again and examined it.

Look at the whole thing a certain way and it was there. He could imagine Ian Gilbert or Roland Harding writing the *I kilt him* letter. But if they were behind it all… how did they find Joe Miles? How did they persuade Peter Cave to shoot someone? He could accept the rest; those were the parts that he found difficult to believe.

There was one person who could connect the BUF to the fire. Terry Gordon. He'd done what he could, but perhaps the man wasn't naïve enough to fall for any copper's trick. Anyway, if the Branch was watching him, he'd be hard to follow.

Where could he go from here? He was blowed if he knew.

*

Kennedy and Mortimer listened. He didn't mention Gott; no names, no pack drill.

'It's interesting,' the superintendent said. 'How do we connect the dots and prove it?'

'I don't know, sir. I'm stumped.' He looked at their faces. 'I was hoping one of you might have an idea.'

'Handwriting samples,' Mortimer said. 'One each from Harding and Gilbert and see if they match the letter we received.'

'Wouldn't they twig it if we just asked them straight out?'

'Question them again,' Kennedy suggested. 'The usual checking a couple of facts, and ask if they could note something down for you. That might work.'

'What about Terry Gordon, sir?'

'We're not likely to break him down. But if we can get something on the top BUF men, they'll happily give him away.' He puffed on his pipe. 'Well, gentlemen?'

It could work.

'Which one do you want, sir?' Raven asked Mortimer.

'I'll take Gilbert. What about Special Branch?' he asked Kennedy. 'They warned us off him before.'

'I'll deal with them,' the super said with relish. 'Don't worry about it.'

*

Harding wasn't at home. Out for the day was as much as the maid would reveal, and she only gave that out after Raven had produced his warrant card. A scrawled note stood on the hall table.

'Who else lives here?'

'Him and his missus,' the maid said. 'What's it to you?' She grimaced as she looked at him. Good; he could use that.

'Just a copper's curiosity, that's all.' He grinned. 'Can I use the facilities since I'm here?'

'Go on,' she agreed after a moment. 'Top of the stairs, second door on the left. And don't make a mess, I've just cleaned that.'

It was easy enough. She didn't see him palm the scrap of paper as he passed. By the time he returned it was safely tucked inside his waistcoat pocket. He'd glanced at it, it was Harding's handwriting; a reminder about something to his wife. They had their sample, and it would never really be missed.

Raven returned, buttoning his overcoat. As they walked back down the drive, he began to smile.

'That was clever work, Sarge,' Noble said.

'If they're devious, we need to be trickier. Now let's see if the writing is the same.'

*

He unfolded the note and smoothed it with the edge of his hand. Then he placed the original letter, in its cellophane, beside it.

No match. Not even close.

Dammit. Raven brought his fist down hard on the desk. Now they had to hope that Mortimer returned with something Gilbert had written and that it matched, and something that Reynolds had written. If not... well, no ladder to take them closer to the end, just a quick slither down a snake, back to the beginning.

His belly rumbled. He needed some food. He'd woken late and dashed to catch the tram, not even time for a cup of tea.

The café in the market sat just inside the entrance, up a short flight of iron stairs. Inside, it smelt of grease and stale smoke. Raven settled by the window and wiped away the condensation to stare down at the shoppers and the stalls. Friday and it was busy, housewives with their bags, stocking up for the weekend.

They were close to finding the real solution to this case. He could feel it. But every road to the finish was blocked. There had to be a way. Bloody had to be.

He ate his egg and chips in silence, dipping everything into a large puddle of brown sauce, and washed it down with dark, strong tea. A dinner fit for the gods. Coming out into the clamour and movement of Vicar Lane, he spotted a figure on the other side of the road. No point in shouting: with all the traffic, he'd never hear.

Raven dodged between a tram and a lorry, then dashed in front of a bus. He had to be desperate if he was risking his life to catch up with Flash Harry, he thought. He tapped the man on the shoulder, a few yards shy of the General Elliott. A quick nod and they went around the corner into the shadows of Fish Street.

Raven took a pair of pound notes from his wallet.

'What's this for?' Harry asked suspiciously as the money vanished into his trouser pocket. He was wearing a brown suit today, with a broad chalk pinstripe. Double breasted, with a red tie and a trilby pulled down over his forehead.

'Services rendered.'

'You promised me—'

'If your tip was right.' The look on his face brooked no argument. 'It pushed us in the right direction. I'm paying you for that, and well over the odds. Now, do you have anything else for me? Anything solid?'

Harry looked down and shuffled his feet a little.

'There might be something I heard.' He hesitated. 'I can't guarantee it, like.'

If he could it would have been a first.

'Go on.'

'What's it worth?'

'Let's call it goodwill. Something if it pans out.'

Harry considered that, then nodded.

'I've heard Terry Gordon's involved somehow.'

'Old news, Harry. I want something I don't know.'

'Well… someone delivered something to that British Union place the night of the fire. Not heard what, mind. Just that they did it.'

'Who?'

'A man told me it was Charlie Gregg, but I'm not saying that's right. I thought he was on the straight and narrow now.'

'It only takes one little slip. You know that. If you're right, there'll be a couple more quid.'

'Make it a fiver, Mr Raven.' The man's long face stared hopefully. 'I could use it. The missus has taken me back. It would keep her sweet.'

'No guarantees, Harry. Just like you.'

Charlie Gregg. He thought the man had given up his old ways, too. His name hadn't come up in a few years, not since that last stretch for grievous bodily harm. Before that, he'd been a hard man for hire; he'd done work for most of the crime bosses in town. It could fit. He strode out quickly for the Headrow and the CIF office.

*

Mortimer was sitting back in his chair and grinning. He waved a piece of paper in the air.

'Got him.'

Raven looked at the note, then at the letter. The same loop on the 'l', the dash that crossed the 't'.

'Are we going to pick him up, sir?'

'I want to talk to the super first.' He nodded at the empty office. 'Did you come up with anything?'

'Something from Flash Harry.' He passed on the information.

'Sounds as if we need a word with Gregg, too.'

'Shall I bring him in?'

'Let's have a chat with the superintendent. It's all waited this long; an hour or two more won't change anything.' Raven walked back to his desk. 'By the way, do you remember Inspector Reid from Special Branch?'

'Of course, sir.'

'Someone said he received a battering the other night.'

'Did he?' Raven kept his face impassive. 'That's a shame.'

A smile flickered across Mortimer's face.

'I thought you'd be concerned.'

*

'Let's wait a bit before we get Gilbert in for questioning. He'll have his solicitor down here like a whirlwind. I want enough facts to keep him here a while.'

'Yes sir,' Mortimer agreed with a frown.

'Charlie Gregg, though, that's a different matter. If we can find something on him, he'll be looking at a long stretch.'

'He's been out for a few years,' Raven said. 'He won't be keen to go back. That might give us some leverage.'

'Would he crack if we questioned him?'

'If we threaten him enough.'

'We'd better find out.' He took the pipe from his mouth and stared at it for a second. 'I know how you're both feeling, believe me. But just a little patience. We're close to the end now.'

'Not close enough until we're putting the cuffs on them,' Raven said.

'We will,' Kennedy assured him. 'That's our job. Without fear or favour.'

'And without Special Branch lumbering around.'

'I'll talk to them.'

*

Charlie Gregg had a file that was half an inch thick. His last conviction had been in 1928, the six years for GBH. He'd come out in 1932; sentence shortened for good behaviour. A model prisoner who'd reformed, according to a scribble from the prison governor. But if he had, it ran against the decade that preceded it. Assault, battery, an aggravated assault charge that evaporated when the victim refused to testify. The same with another GBH.

He'd been connected to a number of bosses, but never part of any gang. Strictly freelance. Not a whisper about him in the last four years, though. Almost as if he really had turned his life around. Some people managed it.

Raven knew he was staking a great deal on one of Flash Harry's tips. But half the moves on this case had felt like rolling the dice. Sooner or later he had to come up with a double six.

*

'Oh, bloody hell,' Gregg said as soon as he saw them. 'Coppers. What do you want?'

Raven stood in front of him at the door, Noble off to the side. The young man had his fists bunched and ready. A waste of time. Gregg might give them some grief, but he wouldn't do it here on the doorstep with every curtain on the street twitching.

'We'd like you to come down to headquarters with us.'

'Why?'

'We'll discuss that there.' Raven smiled.

'What am I supposed to have done?' Gregg protested. 'I've gone straight since I came out the last time.' But the light in his eyes said that was a lie.

'We'll discuss it at the station. If you'd get your coat.'

Gregg gave a reluctant nod and started to reach for a jacket hanging on the wall. With a quick movement, he tried to slam the front door.

But Raven was ready. His foot was already braced in the gap and he leaned forward, pressing his weight on the wood. The door swung back open and crashed against the wall.

Gregg was already in the kitchen, disappearing into the yard behind the house. But he just wasn't fast enough. As he tried to scramble over the brick wall that led to the ginnel, Raven grabbed him by the legs and pulled.

The man came crashing down on his back. The sergeant's knee pressed down on his chest before he could move.

'Not very bright, are you? Now we'll put the bracelets on.'

Noble escorted Gregg out to the Riley. Raven noticed that he had hung back from the action. Probably still wary after the shooting. But he'd need to snap out of that.

He dusted himself off and followed them.

*

'Joe Miles,' Raven began. 'And don't say who, because you bloody well know.'

'Never heard of him.' They were in the interview room, sitting across a scarred table.

'And you've never heard of United losing on a Saturday, either.'

'I don't know Joe Miles.' A face like stone. But he'd had plenty of practice at this.

'Nobody does now. Not since you delivered his body for Bert Cross to burn.'

'Who says?'

'I do.' He paused and took a breath. 'So does the witness who picked out your photograph. Why do you think we came calling today?'

Gregg's eyes widened slightly. Got him. It was a lie, of course, but the man didn't know that. He'd be going over every second of the night in his mind, hoping and praying that no one had seen him.

'I don't believe you.'

'You should, Charlie. They're going to hang you for this. Bert Cross might get life, since Miles was already dead when he started that fire. And Terry Gordon will get himself a good enough lawyer to escape the noose because he only hired you. When we arrest him do you really think he'll protect you? Don't be so bloody daft.'

Gregg started to reach into his pocket for a cigarette.

'No smoking,' Raven ordered. Keep him off balance, keep him on edge. 'What did you use on Miles? Iron bar, was it?'

'I don't know what you're talking about.'

'Or maybe he was already dead when you collected him. That might stop them hanging you. Terrible way to die, they say.'

It was a small lifeline, a chance to sell out the others and stay alive. Now he had to see if Gregg reached for it.

'You don't want to go back to prison, do you?'

'Why would you send me there? I haven't done anything.' He smirked.

'You have, Charlie. And we can prove it. Now do you want to start again and this time tell the truth?'

Round and round for another hour. There were chinks in Gregg's armour. Now Raven had to prise them apart. And he had to do it properly, legally. This had to stand up in court. The man was guilty. He'd suspected it as soon as he saw Gregg and knew beyond any doubt as soon as he tried to run.

Finally, silence. Raven let it build. After all the denials it was comforting. Gregg shifted on his chair and said, 'If he was already dead when I collected him, what happens?'

'Then you don't go down for murder. As long as you tell me who killed him and we can make it stick.'

'You know who.'

'Humour me. Tell me anyway.'

'Terry Gordon.'

Twenty-Four

'I'VE GOT HIS statement, sir.' Raven waved the typewritten sheets, 'and he's signed it. He names Terry Gordon. Smack in the middle of things.'

Kennedy read it through quickly.

'Enough for an arrest.'

Raven and Mortimer stood, waiting for the word. The superintendent looked at the statement again.

'Go and get him.'

*

Raven drove, his foot hard on the accelerator once they passed Moortown. Mortimer stared out of the window and smoked quietly. Finally, after the turning for the Golf Club he said, 'How many times do you think Gordon's been arrested?'

'I'm not sure I can count that high, sir,' the sergeant answered with a laugh.

'And how often has he been convicted?'

'Never.'

'Let's see if we can change that, shall we?'

*

In his tweeds and plus fours, Gordon looked every inch the country gentleman. The only thing missing was a shotgun cradled in his arm. He looked amused as Mortimer told him that he was under arrest.

'I'll be out in an hour.' He nodded at the man standing by the door. 'Call the brief. He knows what to do.'

On the journey into Leeds he was silent in the back seat, observing the changes as country became suburb and then city. In the office he was fingerprinted and photographed, then led to the interview room.

'My solicitor will be here shortly,' Gordon announced. 'I'm not saying a word until he arrives.' He pulled out a cigar case, selected one, clipped the end and lit it.

Mr Crabtree was a senior partner in the firm. He clung to the old ways with his black frock coat and high wing collar, a knowing smile to inspire confidence. A quarter of an hour later, Raven followed Mortimer into the room.

'My client is aware of the charges against him,' Crabtree said. 'He has a short statement: "I have had no part in the murder of Joseph Miles or the transportation of his body." That's all, gentlemen.'

'No,' the inspector told them, 'it's very far from all.'

They hammered at the man for two hours but didn't make a dent. Charlie Gregg's accusation was thin stuff, his word against Gordon's. He gave dates and times, but Terry Gordon could easily conjure up a dozen men to give him an alibi.

Finally Mortimer had enough.

'Take him down to the cells. He can cool his heels there for a while.'

Crabtree objected, but the inspector didn't care. Neither did Gordon. He simply sat, expressionless, until a constable led him away.

'Any ideas?' Mortimer asked when they were back in the office with its dirty walls and stained ceiling. Sometimes he thought it was only the layers of nicotine that held the bloody thing up.

'Not a single one, sir.' How did you break down a brick wall without a sledgehammer?

'There has to be some way through.' He lit another cigarette. 'He did it. I'm sure of it. Did you see him smirking while Crabtree read out that statement?'

'All we have is Gregg.'

Suddenly Mortimer was on his feet and running for the door. Raven followed. Across the road to the Town Hall and then down again to the cells.

'Open the door,' he ordered the constable, then marched ahead.

They'd put the pair in adjoining cells. Why not? There had been no orders, the men down here didn't know what was going on upstairs. Gordon sat on his bunk, a blank expression on his face. Next door, Gregg lay crumpled on the floor.

'I want an ambulance and a doctor here now,' Mortimer shouted. Raven took the keys from the stunned jailer and unlocked the cell. He held a fingertip against Gregg's neck, feeling for a pulse, for any sign of life.

He looked up and shook his head.

'Looks like he was strangled, sir. Windpipe crushed.'

It was easy enough to picture. No walls between the cells. A hand through the bars dragging Gregg close and then the force of Gordon's big, powerful hands. There would have been hardly any noise.

Raven walked back along the corridor. In the end maybe there'd been some skewed kind of justice. Gregg had squirmed and grassed his way out of a murder charge. He'd avoided the hangman, and now he'd paid for all that. And Terry Gordon... what had happened to make him lose his self-control? Maybe it didn't matter. They had him and he'd die for it.

Before the heavy door closed behind him he heard Mortimer's voice: 'Terence Gordon, I'm charging you with the murder of Charles Gregg.'

*

'You look all in,' Marjorie said.

She was on the settee, her plastered leg up on the pouffe.

'I'm exhausted. It's been an interesting day,' he said with a sad chuckle. A day he was glad to leave behind. He leaned back and closed his eyes.

'They said on the news that you've arrested someone.'

'More than one. It's reached the point where you can't tell the players without a scorecard.' Raven ran his palms down his cheeks. Even after all these years he could never get used to the plastic feel of his skin. 'I hope Gladys left something good for tea. I'm starving.'

She kissed his ear.

'She made a meat and potato pie. It should be done by now.' Marjorie started to reach for her crutches. 'I'll help you.'

'It's all right. I'll dish up.'

It felt strange to have the plate balanced on his lap. All his life he'd taken his meals at the table. That was how you did things. This was easier for Marjorie, but he couldn't feel comfortable, as if he was about to tip his food onto the rug.

He cleared away the plates and brought cups of tea. She lit a cigarette and stared at him.

'There's something I've been wanting to say.' She paused for a moment. 'Well, not *wanting* to say. But I have to if everything's going to be right.'

She couldn't just let it drift away and be forgotten, could she? He'd have been willing to let it lie. Bygones could be bygones. No, she had to drag it out and air it.

'Go on,' he told her softly.

Marjorie took another draw on her cigarette and watched the smoke rise. She looked scared.

'I've got to tell you because it was wrong,' she began. 'I met someone.'

'I thought you had,' he said into the long silence and her face fell. 'But—'

'It doesn't matter.' Christ, he could put a criminal through the wringer for hour after hour but even a minute of talking about his own marriage made him squirm and want to run. 'I suspected, that's all.'

'I never… It was just a man I met a few times. For a drink. To talk.'

'Was it because of me?' He didn't want to ask the question, but part of him had to know if he was the cause of it all.

'No. Yes.' She stubbed the cigarette out angrily and reached for another. The packet slipped off the arm of the settee, out of reach, and she began to cry. 'I don't know,' she said. He moved, picked it up and placed it in her lap with a gentle smile.

'We don't have to talk about it,' Raven said. 'Is it over?'

She nodded as she looked away.

'It never really started. Honestly, it didn't. I started feeling that I couldn't say things to you anymore. How I was feeling. I was on my own and just getting smaller and smaller every day.'

'Your sisters…' he began.

'They're all older than me,' Marjorie replied. 'They didn't want to hear it. Not something like that.' He waited. She needed to let it all spill out. Listen to her, he told himself. It was like a cut: you needed to cleanse it before it could heal.

'I was sitting next to a man on the tram. He couldn't find his matches.' She glanced down at her cigarette. 'We started to talk. A week later he was there again.' Marjorie looked at him, eyes wide. 'It just happened. We started to talk. I don't know why, but he just made me feel comfortable. We started meeting for a coffee. I felt bigger with him, like I was a proper size again. Like I mattered. He listened to me, Urban. Not just the words, but what I meant.'

'What happened?' He had to force himself to ask the question.

'Nothing. Honestly. We kept meeting but it was just talk. That's what I wanted, you see. Someone who'd listen to me. We went out for a drink and to the pictures once. That's when I decided it was all wrong. I needed to sort things out here, with you, not someone else. I was on my way to tell him I couldn't see him anymore when the van hit me.'

He reached out to stroke her hair and she flinched. Did she think he was going to hit her? He'd never done that. Not to her, not to any woman. How could Marjorie ever believe he was that bad?

'It's all right,' he told her. 'We're here now, aren't we?'

'But…' she began. 'I thought you'd be angry.' A piece of coke shifted and the fire in the hearth sizzled for a second. 'You should be. You've every right.'

'I was.' If she wanted the truth, he'd give it to her. 'I'm a detective. It's my job; you know that. I'd be pretty poor if I couldn't see something in front of my eyes, wouldn't I?' He couldn't tell her he'd gone through her purse.

Marjorie dabbed at her eyes with a handkerchief.

'I'm sorry, Urban. I am, really. I know I was wrong.'

'Sounds to me like there was no harm done.' He sat next to her and put his arm around her shoulders. She sank into him and the tears began to flow. He held her until they became no more than little shudders. 'It's all fine now. And maybe I've been wrong, too.' No maybe about it. Guilty as charged.

'Do you mean it?' Her voice was thin and shaky, muffled against his shirt. 'Is it fine?'

'Yes. I'll try to do better.'

'That's all I want, Urban. Just listen to me sometimes, please.'

'I will.'

'You promise you won't bring all this up when we're arguing?'

She was serious, but it made him chuckle anyway. 'I promise.' It broke the tension.

It was done, over more easily than he'd expected. He didn't need the details, didn't even want them. Let the dead bury the dead. She'd cleared the air and they were back on track. That was the only thing that mattered.

*

He was up bright and early, humming to himself as he shaved in the bathroom. He turned the tap and hot water flowed. It still seemed like a wonder to him. Growing up, everywhere he'd lived until here, the only way to have hot water was a pan on the stove. Now he only had to flick the switch for the immersion. People could complain about progress all they liked. It was bloody wonderful.

Will He Or Won't He? That was the headline in the newspaper, whether the king would really abdicate to be able to marry Wallis Simpson. What the hell did it matter, anyway? On the throne or not, he'd never want for a bob or two.

Raven smiled and stared out of the window. Everything was right with the world at home. Whatever had been going on was done, dusted and put away. Not quite forgotten yet, but forgiven. Seemed to him they'd proved that in bed the night before. It had been awkward with Marjorie's leg in the cast, but they'd managed.

The weather was filthy, a chilling drizzle and a sharp breeze that cut through to the bone. People were coughing into their handkerchiefs on the tram. Bronchitis season had arrived.

'You look happy,' Mortimer said. He raised an eyebrow but Raven simply smiled.

'How's Terry Gordon?' he asked.

It was the inspector's turn to grin.

'Couldn't be singing louder if he was a trained canary. He was hired by Harding and Gilbert to take care of Joe Miles.'

'We've got them, then. And we can prove Harding sent that letter. All over bar the shouting.' He felt a wave of relief flow through him. 'Reynolds. How does he connect in all this, do you think, sir?'

'We're going to bring them all in this morning. Honestly, Raven, I wonder if Reynolds wasn't more used by the others than at the heart of it all. Just a true believer in the cause. We'll let the courts decide. Anyway, as soon as the press finds out, the BUF will be finished around here.' He sounded satisfied as he lit a fresh cigarette. 'What about you? You look content.'

'Just… life.' He shrugged; that was as much as he was going to give away.

'I thought you and I could pick up Gilbert. Give you some revenge for the roasting you got from the Branch last time you saw him.'

'Has the Branch been informed, sir?'

'No. They'd only balls it up for us.' A small hesitation. 'By the way, did you know they were keeping an eye on Terry Gordon?'

'Is that right?' Raven kept his voice bland.

'That man Reid was in here last night trying to read the Riot Act. His face is still a mess.'

'Pity, sir. What with him being so handsome and all. Is Noble going with the super?'

'Yes. He deserves to be in at the end, don't you think?'

A gun pointed at him, thinking he was going to die? Yes, he'd earned it, right enough.

*

Barwick was just as sleepy as the last time he'd been here. A row of shops along the main street, a couple of pubs, a pair of churches. And set back from the road, Ian Gilbert's little mansion. The Jaguar stood in the drive, raindrops on the shining coachwork. Raven pulled up behind it. Gilbert wouldn't be making any quick escapes in his fancy car.

As they walked to the door he half expected to hear the heavy footsteps of Special Branch officers. But the only sounds were the rain and the birds. Country life. Too bloody quiet by half. Upstairs, a curtain twitched for a moment then fell closed again.

It was the same hawk-faced maid who'd answered the door the last time they'd come. But she still insisted on looking at the warrant cards.

'Where is he?' Raven asked.

She frowned.

'In his room. He's been there since he received a message last night.'

The sergeant glanced at Mortimer.

'Who delivered it?'

'Just a man. I've never seen him before.'

'Which door is it?' Mortimer asked.

The woman looked up the stairs.

'At the end of the corridor. But he said he didn't want to be disturbed.'

'I'm afraid he's going to be,' the inspector told her.

A thick rug ran the full length of the hall, from the top of the stairs all the way to Gilbert's bedroom. It muffled their footsteps to nothing. The door in front of them was dark, rich wood, tightly closed.

Raven let the inspector go ahead. He'd broken Terry Gordon and got the information that brought them here. He deserved the collar.

Mortimer brought his fist down hard on the wood.

'Mr Gilbert, this is—'

The blast stopped the words. Shotgun pellets ripped through the wood and into Mortimer's chest. He staggered backwards, crashing into Raven. The sergeant lowered him gently to the rug. Blood was soaking his coat.

Time seemed to stop. Somewhere downstairs the maid was screaming, but he hardly noticed. The sound of the gun had filled the world, so loud he could barely hear his own thoughts. Stay alive. Stay alive, you bugger.

Raven opened his mouth to shout, to have the woman ring for help, but the words were drowned by a second shot inside the room.

He put a finger against the inspector's neck. The pulse was there. Slow but strong. He squeezed the man's hand.

He didn't care about Gilbert. With any luck, the bastard would have blown his brains out.

'You hold on, sir,' he said, then dashed down to the telephone. Police, ambulance. The maid was screaming and crying. He tried to ignore her as he rang and identified himself.

Someone was knocking on the door. He turned the knob and two men ran in wearing heavy overcoats and bowler hats. The Branch. One shouldered Raven out of the way as he made for the stairs.

By the time he returned, Gilbert's bedroom door had been forced open and the men were inside. Raven knelt by the inspector. Christ, it looked bad. Plenty of shot in his chest. But he was breathing and his pulse was still there.

'They're on their way, sir. Don't try and speak. The hospital will fix you up good as new.' He smiled. 'And only a couple of tiny grazes on your face. You won't end up looking like me.'

The Branch officers were trampling around inside the room. Gilbert's body was sprawled on the floor, the shotgun close by. Blood and brains spattered the walls and the ceiling.

It took half an hour for the ambulance to arrive, followed by two police squad cars. Mortimer was still awake, that was something. Weak, not speaking, only half there, but alive. Raven watched as they took him away on the stretcher. A CID officer he didn't know was badgering him for a statement. He gave it in three short sentences, then looked at the Branch men.

'You'd better talk to them, too.' They turned, looked at him with contempt and returned to work. Law that thought it was above the law; he had no time for them.

A man was waiting outside, leaning against the Riley. Inspector Reid of Special Branch, the bruises on his face just beginning to fade.

'It was our job,' he said. 'You should have left it to us.'

'It was police business,' Raven told him. 'Murder. Or aren't we all on the same side anymore?'

'We'd have had him,' Reid said. 'Alive. We told you lot to stay out of it.'

'We don't stay out of murder.' He moved forward but Reid shifted to block his way. Then, with a grunt, he was falling and clutching his belly. Raven rubbed his fist.

'I have better things to do than talk to you. Sir.'

*

Kennedy had gone to the hospital. He'd spent an hour questioning Harding.

'He couldn't hardly spill it fast enough,' said a uniformed sergeant who'd been listening at the door. 'The bastard's scared for his life. Reynolds is talking, too. Not that he seems to have much to say.'

At his desk, Raven wrote up his report on the morning. Hard to believe it was only the middle of the afternoon; it seemed as if he'd lived through entire days since he got out of bed. He left the sheet on the superintendent's desk, walked out to the Riley and drove to the infirmary.

The warrant card got him past clerks and nurses, to the waiting room outside the operating theatres. Kennedy was still there, smoking his pipe.

'Any news yet, sir?'

'They're still working on him.' He glanced up at the clock. 'It's been two hours.'

'I left the report on your desk.'

The superintendent nodded. 'And now you can tell me while we wait.'

He went through it, seeing it all like a series of photographs in his mind.

'I saw Inspector Reid on the way out of there, sir,' he finished. 'He wasn't happy. He might make another complaint about me.'

Kennedy raised an eyebrow.

'I think he'll find he hits a brick wall if he tries.' He smiled. 'Mind you, I hear it looks as if one hit him.'

'Yes, sir. Thank you.'

'Go home, Raven. Between your wife, the Cave shooting and this, you've had a lot on your plate lately.'

'Sir?' It was the job. He did it, he stayed with it.

'I said, get a good night's sleep and come into the station tomorrow morning. Take a look at yourself, you're like a ghost.'

'But the inspector—'

'Is in very good hands,' Kennedy overrode him. 'As soon as I know something I'll telephone you. That's an order.'

'Yes, sir.'

Twenty-Five

HE HAD TOO much to think about on the tram. A relentless flurry of soundless images, like watching one of the old silent newsreels. Lights were already on all over Leeds, the afternoon cold and brilliant. Half the bulbs on the Bovril sign across from the Corn Exchange had burned out. No one had bothered to replace them, as if nobody cared any longer.

He saw a boy sitting by a stuffed guy outside a shop, asking for pennies to buy fireworks and toffee. Then a pile of wood on empty ground, waiting for the lighting of a bonfire on the fifth.

Too many years since he'd had the innocence to enjoy that. Maybe if Marjorie had been able to have children and he'd been able to see it through their eyes... but that wasn't to be. He listened to the chorus of wet coughs along the top deck.

At the usual stop he stepped down onto the pavement, then crossed the road. It was hard to resist the smell of frying fish, and he strolled home with a newspaper parcel warm under his arm.

*

'I've been scared witless.' She was up and hobbling into the hall as soon as she heard his key in the lock. 'They said on the radio that a policeman had been shot. I kept expecting the phone to ring.'

'It's Inspector Mortimer. I was there.'

She stared at him for a moment, then threw down the crutches and put her arms around his neck.

'You're sure you're all right?'

'Not a scratch. You know me, luck of the devil. Let's eat these while they're hot.'

He told her most of it, missing out the details of Gilbert's body and the panic he felt as he held the inspector and lowered him onto the rug. She didn't need any of that.

'When will you know about your boss?' she asked when he'd finished.

'Mr Kennedy said he'd ring.'

He was in the kitchen, washing the plates and the mugs, when the bell began to jangle. He picked up the receiver, gave the number and listened.

Mortimer would be fine. A full recovery, although he'd be on the sick list until the New Year at least.

'As soon as he came round from the anaesthetic, the doctor told him he needed to stop smoking for a while,' Kennedy said. 'There's some damage to his lungs.'

'I bet that went over like a lead balloon, sir.'

'The air was blue.' He could hear the super's relieved chuckle. 'It means we'll be short-handed for a while, but we'll get by.'

'Yes, sir.'

'What about you? Are you all right?'

'Yes, sir.' And he was. He had his marriage back, and they'd cracked the strangest case he could remember. Everything was fine.

'Very good. I'll see you in the morning.'

Marjorie raised her eyebrows in a question as he came back into the sitting room.

'He'll be back on the job next year.'

As he sat, relief and exhaustion rose through him in a wave. Raven leant his head back and closed his eyes. He opened them again as something shook him.

'You've been asleep for an hour, Urban.' Balanced on her crutches, Marjorie smiled down at him. 'Let's go to bed.'

He rubbed his cheeks. She was right. He'd just dropped off, and now he felt as if he could sleep for a week. All the excitement and the horror of the day had drained away. He was empty.

*

If he dreamt, he didn't remember it. Maybe that was just as well. Methodically, he shaved, washed and dressed, then helped Marjorie out of bed. Raven knew what today would bring: hour after hour of questions. He'd relive it all so many times that it would be impossible ever to forget.

The papers were full of it, turning it into a cheap, grisly sensation. Mortimer was a *hero policeman who risked his life*. That would make him laugh. Gilbert and Harding were cowards, afraid of justice. Reynolds barely received a mention. And the local BUF was shown to be a sham, killing their own people as they plotted to show they were being persecuted. A national spokesman for the British Union claimed to have no knowledge of what had happened and condemned it. Of course.

Kennedy was in his office, wearing his pale grey suit and regimental tie.

'They're going to give you a grilling,' he warned. 'Just be honest. There's nothing to hide.'

'Yes, sir.'

'Although you might want to miss out the part about meeting Inspector Reid outside the house.' He gave a wry grin.

'How's Mr Mortimer this morning?'

'Complaining about not being able to smoke, according to the ward sister. Have you seen the papers?'

'I read the *Post* on the tram.'

'It's mostly right. The fascists are finished here now. That's something from all of this, I suppose.'

'I've been thinking, sir. There's something else we can do.'

'Oh?'

*

Two senior officers, one plain clothes, one in uniform, ran him through it all, over and over and over until the words blurred into each other. By one o'clock they'd had their fill and his head was swimming.

Noble sat in the office, fingers pecking at the typewriter keys as he typed his report.

'Sounds like you took Harding apart well when you questioned him yesterday.'

'All I had to do was listen and take it all down.'

'Still, it looks good on your record.'

The young man shrugged. 'I suppose so, Sarge. How was it in there?'

'I'm sick of hearing my own voice.' He put on his overcoat and hat. 'I'm off for some dinner.'

A sandwich and tea at the Kardomah on Briggate, then he walked over to the infirmary. There was a nip in the air, a wind slicing along the Headrow. Never mind autumn, it felt as if winter was coming around the corner. Women had red, chapped cheeks, men held onto their hats. Just a hint of what was to come.

*

'Turns out you're a hero, sir. That's what the papers say.' He winked. 'So it must be true.'

Mortimer was sitting up in bed. He was still pale, a couple of wounds on his face where shotgun pellets had hit him. Under the pyjamas, his chest was heavily bandaged.

'Me?' He tried to laugh and ended up coughing. 'Ruddy ridiculous. If I'm a hero, why won't they let me smoke?'

'I'm sure they have their reasons, sir. You know everything that's happened?'

Mortimer nodded. 'Mr Kennedy dropped by earlier.'

'Have they said how long you'll be in?'

'I should be out next week. That's what the doctor told me. Evidently I was lucky that bedroom door was closed. Didn't feel like it when those pellets hit.'

'Didn't look it, either, if you don't mind me saying.'

The inspector snorted. 'I'll be back on my feet soon enough. And some time off.' He tried to shrug. 'At least I can catch up on my reading.'

'Is there anything you'd like me to bring you, sir?' He looked at the bedside table with its bowl of grapes and bottle of Lucozade.

'Only if you can arrange it so I can smoke.'

'I'll do what I can,' Raven answered, already knowing he had no chance against a ward sister. 'I'll stop in again.'

'Thank you.' He started to cough, holding up a hand until it passed. 'I just wanted to say, you've done very well through all this. You've kept going.'

He didn't know what to say. He'd done his job, nothing more than that. Praise embarrassed him. It seemed unnecessary.

'Thank you, sir.' He picked his hat off the bed. 'I'd better be on my way.'

Epilogue

Christmas Eve, 1936

The house was full of food. A turkey took up one whole shelf in the larder, waiting for the oven in the morning. Bowls of this and that, a tin of fancy biscuits.

The women would cook. Marjorie had been serious about inviting both families, although Raven still hadn't a clue where they'd put everyone; he'd borrowed a small table and more chairs from the neighbours but it still didn't seem like enough; at this rate, half of them would be eating in the back garden.

He stirred the coals with the poker and settled back in his chair, watching the flames jump. Edward's abdication was still making the front pages of the newspapers, two weeks after it happened. The man had given a good speech, he'd made his decision, and more power to him. But it was time to put that behind them.

He was off until the twenty-seventh. That morning he'd been in court to see Gilbert Harding sent down for seven years on a conspiracy to murder charge. A not guilty verdict on Reynolds. Terry Gordon was already in jail, awaiting execution in January.

All in all, they'd wrapped things up well. It had taken too long, but who could have imagined anything would be so twisted?

On his way home he'd stopped in at the Pointer. On the corner of Roundhay Road a Sally Army band was playing carols. Six o'clock and Johnny Harris was there, propping up the bar, his brother Paul beside him. Raven slapped them both on the back and ordered a round.

Harris was back at work. He didn't know that Superintendent Kennedy had rung the manager at the boot factory and dropped a heavy hint that taking the man back would be a good idea. And he'd certainly never learn that the original suggestion had come from Raven.

Paul had his treatment coming up at the beginning of the new year, scared but hopeful. If it worked, it could make a huge difference in his life.

The three of them spent a comfortable hour setting the world to rights. Raven left with a promise to meet Paul for a drink when he was out of hospital, the pair of them knowing it would probably come to nothing.

He finished the cup of tea. In the kitchen, Marjorie was peeling potatoes for the morning, dropping them into a bowl of water. The cast was off. She still moved stiffly, but it was improving.

He was a lucky man; Raven knew that. A job he enjoyed, a good house, a marriage that was steady and loving again. Better than many. He wondered what Christmas was going to be like for Ava Benson and her mother, or Joe Miles's parents. And there were plenty far worse, lucky if they had enough coal for a fire or something decent to eat. The phrase Mortimer had used once came into his mind again: *the dead on leave*. He glanced at the headline of the paper again. So many bloody awful things and they worried about a king.

Maybe things would change.

ENDEAVOUR QUILL

Endeavour Quill is an imprint of Endeavour Media.

If you enjoyed *The Dead on Leave* check out
Endeavour Media's eBooks here:
WWW.ENDEAVOURMEDIA.CO.UK

For weekly updates on our free and discounted eBooks
sign up to our newsletter:
WWW.ENDEAVOURMEDIA.CO.UK/SIGN-UP

Follow us on Twitter:
@EndeavourQuill
And Instagram:
endeavour_media